T0146476

MISSION TO MURDER

A Tourist Trap Mystery

Books by Lynn Cahoon

Mission to Murder

Guidebook to Murder

MISSION TO MURDER

A Tourist Trap Mystery

LYNN CAHOON

KENSINGTON BOOKS
KENSINGTON PUBLISHING CORP.
www.kensingtonbooks.com

KENSINGTON BOOKS are published by

Kensington Publishing Corp.
119 West 40th Street
New York, NY 10018

All Kensington titles, imprints, and distributed lines are available at special quantity discounts for bulk purchases for sales promotion, premi-
ums, fund-raising, educational, or institutional use.

Special book excerpts or customized printings can also be created to fit
specific needs. For details, write or phone the office of the Kensington
Special Sales Manager: Kensington Publishing Corp., 119 West 40th
Street, New York, NY 10018. Attn. Special Sales Department. Phone:
1-800-221-2647.

Kensington and the K logo Reg. U.S. Pat. & TM Off.

First Electronic Edition: July 2014
eISBN-13: 978-1-60183-239-9
eISBN-10: 1-60183-239-7

First Print Edition: July 2014
ISBN-13: 978-1-60183-305-1
ISBN-10: 1-60183-305-9

Printed in the United States of America

To Alex—for always believing his mother could rule the world.

Acknowledgments

How do you judge how good a book is in your family? For my son, it was the "Mom" rule—how many times he had to call my name and at what volume before I'd acknowledge him. Raising a child teaches you a lot about yourself and the child you've brought into your life. Husbands may come and go, but children are there, forever. His faith in me makes me stronger.

Of course, good books are made better by great editors. Thanks, Esi Sogah, for pushing me out of my comfort level.

CHAPTER 1

Some people like to hear their own voice. That jewel of wisdom hit me as I filled the coffee carafes for the third time. As chamber liaison, I'd volunteered my shop, Coffee, Books, and More, to serve as semi-permanent host site for South Cove's Business to Business meeting. The early morning meeting was scheduled to run from seven to nine but the clock over the coffee bar showed it was already twenty minutes past. With more items to cover on the agenda, we'd be ordering lunch, maybe dinner, before the end.

All because the newest committee member, Josh Thomas, owner of the new antiques store down the street, had issues. He didn't like the agenda, the city's promotion plan, and he especially didn't like the fact the city didn't have a formal animal control office. These subjects were not part of the regular list of discussion topics for the eclectic mix of owners of gift shops, art galleries, inns, and restaurants. I usually loved feeling the creative energy and listening to wacky ideas members brought to the table. Today, the meeting droned on and I couldn't wait for it to end.

"I wonder why he even moved here," Aunt Jackie fake-whispered to me as she sliced a second cheesecake. "He hates everything."

"Hush." I elbowed my aunt, trying to quiet her.

"Jill Gardner, don't tell me you weren't thinking the same thing." She started plating out the cheesecake.

A couple of the council members snickered, and Josh's face turned a deeper red than normal. His wide girth barely fit into the black suit he wore. From what I could tell, he wore the same threadbare suit every day. Watching the buttons on his off-white shirt, I worried one would pop off each time he took a labored breath.

"As I was saying, we must press the police department to deal with felonious teenagers running the streets." Josh didn't acknowledge he'd heard Jackie, a tactic I've often used with my aunt. She's overbearing, opinionated, speaks her mind, and I love her to death.

"There's no problem." Sadie Michaels replied, the words harsh and clipped. "There's not a lot for kids to do around here, so they hang out at the park. They don't cause problems for local businesses. We've raised them better than that."

"I beg to differ. Craig Morgan, the manager over at The Castle, has caught kids breaking in after-hours. They've been having drinking parties, swimming in the pools, and he's even caught a few couples in the mansion's bedrooms, doing heavens knows what." Snickers from the rest of the members floated around the room as Josh wheezed in another breath. "We must stop these criminals before there's real trouble. The antiques housed at The Castle are priceless."

"My son, Nick, is one of these hooligans you want arrested. I've never heard him or any of his friends talk about breaking into The Castle. They know better." The red on Sadie's face rivaled Josh's. She stood and pointed her finger at Josh sitting across from her. "You like causing trouble."

After setting the full carafes on the table, I put my hand on Sadie's shoulder, easing her back into her chair. "This topic needs to be tabled until next meeting. We'll invite Detective King to attend to address Mr. Thomas's concerns about property safety. Bill, do you want to get us back on track with the agenda?" I threw a lifeline to Bill Simmons, our council chair and owner of South Cove Bed and Breakfast on Main Street.

Bill shot me a grateful smile. "I'm sure Jill is anxious to get the meeting over and get back to business. As a side note, the mayor has reappointed Ms. Gardner as the chamber's liaison for next year. Mr. Thomas, if you have questions about our procedures, she will be happy to work with you."

Okay, now I officially hated Bill Simmons. Taking a deep breath, I pasted on a flight attendant smile and nodded. "Of course, I'll stop by and visit with Josh this week."

Josh didn't seem pleased with the idea of spending quality time with me, either. Cool, I could plan on the visit being quick.

Bill's relief at regaining control swept across the room, calming everyone, except me and Josh. "Let's move on. The Annual Summer Festival starts up next month. Can we get a report from the committee on how the preparations are going? Darla?"

As the owner of the local winery explained the committee's goals, I took a seat next to Sadie. "Thanks," she whispered.

"Not a problem." I liked Sadie. She and I had become friends in the last year, mostly over coffee after the business-to-business meetings. In her forties, the woman was a single mom, led the women's group at her church, and ran a small business. She got more done in two hours than I accomplished in eight. She'd been a rock for me when I'd been put in charge of Miss Emily's funeral earlier this year. Without Sadie's help, my friend would have been sent to the afterlife without a proper good-bye.

My coffee shop/bookstore was the best customer for her business, Pies on the Fly. She was easygoing and would give you her left arm if you needed it. But no one messed with her kid.

Nick Michaels chaired the school debate team, served as youth leader for his church's Boy Scout troop, and led the high school football team as an all-star quarterback. Calling him a hooligan was like saying the pope ran around throwing rocks through windows. Trouble wasn't in the boy's DNA.

Somehow Bill pushed the last two items off until the next meeting, and before I knew it, the meeting adjourned. Sadie stayed around to help clean up after the others refilled their cups with a last free coffee and said their good-byes. I started wiping down the hodge-podge of tables we'd shoved together for the meeting. Sadie shoved paper plates and used napkins into a sack with a gale wind force.

"I can't believe that man." Sadie crumpled a leftover paper cup and shoved it into a trash sack. "He doesn't like kids. That's all. He's so used to working with the past, he can't see the future right in front of him."

"He's a character, I'll agree with you on that point." I wiped a table clean and returned it to a spot near the window. Pulling chairs around the table, I watched my friend's face as I said the words she didn't want to hear. "Listen, Craig's been complaining to everyone the town kids are sneaking in after-hours. Greg's been out on calls there three times this month."

Detective Greg King had returned to town after his divorce to serve as the town's lead police officer. Greg also was my boyfriend. The word still rankled when I thought it, let alone said, *boyfriend*. Seriously, wasn't there a grown-up word a thirty-two-year-old could call the hunk of boy toy she dated?

"You don't think my Nick would be part of anything like that, do you? He knows better." Sadie's eyes filled with tears. She'd raised Nick alone after her husband was killed on an off-shore oil rig when their son was five. His mom's eagle eye kept the boy in line, but sometimes I wondered if he wasn't too controlled. Boys needed a wild side and breaking in to swim in the most expensive pool in town could be Nick's way of getting his freak on. So to speak.

"Wouldn't be the worst thing for the boy," Aunt Jackie called from behind the counter, where she stood making a pot of coffee and eavesdropping. "Maybe he's getting lucky with some girl."

"Aunt Jackie!" I glanced over at Sadie, whose face had turned whiter than the wash towel in her hand. I tried to console her. "I'm sure it's not Nick."

"Now, Jill Gardner, you know as well as I do boys will be boys." My aunt huffed and left for the back of the store.

After making sure Jackie had left, I glanced at my friend. Her face now appeared mottled gray. "Sorry, you know how she is. Talk first. Think later."

"That's the thing. I'm not sure Nick's innocent." Sadie slumped down into a chair.

"Problems?" I sat at the table with her.

"There's a new girl at church. Her folks moved the family here from LA. The girl got kicked out of the last prep school she attended." Sadie scanned the room to see if anyone had remained and paused from wiping the same spot on the table for the tenth time. She whispered, "Drugs."

"I'm sure that's a rumor." I gently took the rag from her hand. There'd be no varnish left on the tabletop if I didn't intervene.

She shook her head. "It's not a rumor. Cindy told me and she heard it from Gladys, the church secretary. She'd overheard the girl's folks telling Pastor Bill." Sadie reached out for my hand. "She works at The Castle giving tours." She uttered the words she must have thought hammered the nails into Nick's prison cell.

I watched Sadie leave the coffee shop a few minutes later, a pie order for next week in her hand and her heart on her sleeve. Sighing, I sat down with the book catalogue and made a list for Jackie to order later that night.

Nearly two hours later, glancing around the still-empty dining room, I picked up the phone and called Amy, South Cove's city planner, secretary to Mayor Baylor, and my best friend—roles that got her kidnapped and stranded on a remote Mexican island a few months ago. But true to Amy's character, she'd been too excited by the mondo waves she'd ridden to worry about rescue.

"South Cove City Hall." Amy's perky voice came over the speakerphone.

"Lunch today?" I nodded at Toby Killian, who'd entered the shop for his afternoon shift. Toby worked for me during the day and for Greg most evenings as one of South Cove's finest. I pulled off my apron and glanced into the mirror behind the coffee bar. My makeup had disappeared, leaving my face pale and blotchy, and the curl in my black hair rivaled Little Orphan Annie without the flame-red. I finger-combed my curls into a controlled chaos, the phone still cradled between my shoulder and my ear.

"Eleven-thirty. I'm finishing last night's council notes." Amy disconnected the call. No good-bye, and since we only had one restaurant in town, no need to plan any further.

"Hey, boss." Toby came around the counter and put on an apron with *Wired Up?* printed on the front. Aunt Jackie's newest promotion for the coffee shop focused on the free Wi-Fi we offered our customers. From what I saw, after adding the service we gained a lot of the hooligan teenage crowd Josh had been complaining about. Our sales had doubled in the late afternoon hours, so I wasn't complaining.

"Do we have problems with the after-school crowd? Anything I should know about?" I leaned against the counter, watching Toby start a fresh pot of decaf.

"Like what?" Toby pushed the button to brew and flipped a clean rag over his shoulder. He rocked the indie-barista look and knew it.

"With the teenagers. Josh Thomas said he'd had some run-ins." I was pretty sure Josh had overreacted.

"Kids are kids. They don't give me any guff. Probably afraid I'll arrest them if I see them later." Toby straightened the flyers for the next Mystery Book Club meeting on Friday. "I can talk to a few of them if you'd like. But as long as he keeps yelling because they walk by his shop, he's going to get crap back."

"Keep your ears open. Josh said some have been sneaking into The Castle grounds for after-closing swim parties." I glanced at the clock, my shift was done. I'd been hesitant to hire anyone before Aunt Jackie had started working with me; now I had two employees and a lot of spare time.

South Cove sat inland on the central California coastline. Summer weather meant highs in the seventies, a lot like the weather forecast in spring, fall, and, thankfully, winter. Fog tended to disappear by noon and the day turned to shirtsleeve weather. Today was glorious. The flower boxes lining the sidewalks bloomed with bright colors, the flowers' sweet smell filling the morning air.

Walking past Antiques by Thomas, I noticed Josh moving a walnut side table into his store display window. I waved, but he glared back. My lack of support during the meeting hadn't gone unnoticed. I'd stop by the shop later this week with a box of cookies in an attempt to mend fences.

Cookies could fix anything and good fences make good neighbors. Or at least I hoped the old wisdom held true. Maybe I'd send Aunt Jackie over. She could charm a cobra, which she'd actually done on one of her senior hostel trips to India.

Having Aunt Jackie helping with the business had been hard to accept at times. But I had to admit, her ideas paid off. The local author readings she'd started tripled business in both the book side and the coffee shop on what used to be Dead Wednesday. Lille's diner traffic increased, as well, with customers migrating there for a meal after the readings ended.

Next month, a famous mystery author was scheduled to speak at the bookstore. Partnering with Bill at South Cove Bed and Breakfast, our only cost so far amounted to half the author's plane fare. Though I signed the checks, my aunt still kept the mystery author's identity a secret.

This marketing tactic might be her first big failure. Who would come to hear someone they didn't know? When I complained, she shooed me off.

"That's part of the fun. It's a mystery."

"We do have an author scheduled, right?" My stomach turned at the thought.

"Of course. He or she's already agreed to come and read. Their new book is arriving that week and we are hosting the book's home-coming."

"You mean launch." Sometimes she scared me how much she didn't know about the bookselling business.

"Yeah, that's the word. I knew he said it had something to do with a cruise."

"But what if no one comes?" I tried one more time. The author was a man. She'd let that slip. My mind raced through the upcoming new releases I'd ordered last week. Had I overstocked one book?

"Pish. You worry too much." She'd walked away, the conversation over. The shadowed flyers told people the date, the time, and that they would love this author, but the rest remained as the sign said, "Cloaked in Mystery."

Diamond Lille's was a block down on Main Street and I was in front of it before I realized I'd arrived. I shook my head clear of the book launch worries and put on a receptionist smile before I entered the diner. Believe me, gossip travels fast in South Cove. If I'd walked in with a frown, people would be betting on hearing some bit of bad news within a day. I'd either be dying of cancer, had found Greg cheating with a stripper from Bakerstown, or my business was on the ropes. And even though none of those things were going to happen anytime soon, truth didn't stop tongues from wagging.

Amy sat in our favorite booth. She'd already ordered our drinks, and a large glass of iced tea waited for me while she sipped on a soda.

"What, no ice cream shake?" I slipped into the bench seat across from her. Today, the lunch special featured potato soup. Adding a dinner salad to go with the bowl of creamy goodness topped with shredded cheddar cheese and a generous dollop of sour cream, made the meal appear somewhat healthy and part of my ongoing diet.

Amy's face turned red. "Am I that predictable?"

"If it's Tuesday, it's strawberry shake day. If we meet on Friday, you order a fish sandwich and chocolate shake."

Grinning, Amy nodded. "Why mess with routine? Actually, they were backed up in the kitchen, somebody bailed on their shift. Carrie got me this while I waited."

"Who didn't show?"

"Sadie's kid, Nick." Amy's voice came from behind the menu she studied. Not like she hadn't read the same list of items three times a week for the last year. "I think I'll get the grilled pastrami on rye today."

"No club on wheat with a side of chicken noodle soup?" I recited Amy's usual Tuesday lunch order.

She swatted at me with the menu. "Hank and I found the best New York–style deli when we were in the city last weekend. I've been craving pastrami since Sunday."

Carrie showed up to take our orders. "I'm sure I could let the kitchen know you're both here. But let's go through the motions. What can I get for you?" She regarded me first.

"I'm having a house salad, bleu cheese dressing on the side, and a bowl of loaded potato soup. But Amy's going to surprise you."

"God, you'd think I shaved my head and become a Buddhist." Amy kicked me under the table. "I'll have the grilled pastrami on rye with a side salad. And a strawberry milkshake."

"Crap, I forgot about the shake. No problem. But no club?" Carrie reached out to touch Amy's forehead to see if she felt hot.

"Did I say I wanted a club? Jeez, people change their minds." Amy pulled her head back out of Carrie's reach.

Carrie yanked the menus off the table. "Don't get huffy. I have enough to do with Nick out."

"Did Nick call in sick?" After the talk I'd had with Sadie, I didn't want to hear the answer, but like looking at a car wreck on the side of the road, I couldn't stop from asking.

"Nope. The kid didn't show. Lille's hopping mad. She got called in on her day off to wash dishes. He's going to get an earful tomorrow." Carrie turned and headed back to the kitchen, picking up plates and taking refill drink orders on the way.

"Looks like it's going to be a leisurely lunch hour." Amy leaned back. "So you probably want to know about Hank and the weekend."

"Actually, I wanted to know if anyone at The Castle complained to the council about teenagers."

I knew Amy wanted to talk about Hank. The four of us drove to the city for dinner as a double date two weeks ago. Hank dominated the conversation from the time we got in the car to the time Greg dropped the couple off at Amy's apartment. Hank was a disaster. I avoided the subject at all costs, but one day, the Hank discussion would happen. Then Amy would be crushed I didn't see his warm and loving side. But that conversation wasn't happening today.

"The Castle?" Amy tapped her fingers on the table, thinking. "Actually, Craig had an appointment with the mayor last week. I figured he was arguing for more advertising funding from the city. You know he thinks the only reason anyone comes to South Cove is to visit The Castle."

I knew. All the business owners knew Craig Morgan's opinion of them. In fact, Craig wasn't shy about calling us bloodsucking parasites to our faces. Sure, visitors to The Castle brought in shoppers. But sometimes, the traffic happened to flow from the town to The Castle. God knows, I'd sent my share of tourists to his door. And still he wanted the entire allotment of the chamber's marketing money? He even refused to come to the Business to Business meetings because he was busy, running a "real company." Like I wasn't?

Well, I guess with Aunt Jackie and Toby working the floor, I wasn't quite as busy as I'd been. But the shop was hopping. I'd filled my empty time finishing renovating the house I'd inherited from Miss Emily. Not to mention hours working with the historical commission on certifying the stone wall in the back of the property as the "real" South Cove Mission site. If the certification ever came through, South Cove would have a second historic site to promote. Craig wasn't happy about sharing the marketing money now. His reaction to sharing the budget with the mission site wouldn't be pretty.

"You don't think he's working the historical commission against certifying the site, do you?" Fear gripped my stomach. If the commission even smelled a whiff of community discordance around the project, they'd back off the process.

"I wouldn't put it past him. Ever since you shut down Eric's development plans, the mayor hasn't been too happy with you." Amy scanned the packed diner. Most tables were still without food.

"I didn't shut down Eric Ammond's development. His lying, stealing, murdering girlfriend handled that on her own!" I couldn't believe Amy was blaming me for the development shutting down. If I hadn't found her, she'd still be surfing on a reclusive island off the coast of Mexico. Okay, well, she could blame me a little. Surfing would be more calming than trying to manage all the jobs she had going here in town. But still, you'd think she'd be a little grateful.

"Everyone knows the crazy ex-schoolteacher bombed the project. Except His Honor The Mayor. Marvin still can't say your name without spitting." Amy nodded to Carrie on her way over with a tray. "Maybe we're getting lucky."

We were. Carrie dropped off food for us and the next table over. She stopped at the booth for a quick second. "Nick finally showed. He claimed his girlfriend needed a ride into the city and he thought they'd be back long before his shift started." Carrie leaned down and whispered, "You can bet what she wanted. She's going to ruin his reputation. Mark my words."

Amy watched Carrie walk away, then brightened as if she remembered something. "Oh, Esmeralda says to tell you hello. She wants you to come in for a reading." Amy laughed. "She said she threw your cards or whatever mumbo jumbo."

Esmeralda was South Cove's fortune-teller and police dispatcher. If my house won the prize for being the oldest building in town, Esmeralda's came in a quick second. The mayor loved her. As long as she kept foreseeing a great future for the man, he left her housing code issues alone. She'd done a quick read on me once in the mayor's lobby. Now, the fortune-teller and I were best friends—not. "What did the cards say this time?"

Amy grinned. She pointed her French fry at me and said in a lowered imitation of Esmeralda's voice so good, the words gave me goose bumps, "Death surrounds you again."

CHAPTER 2

I'd decided to head Craig Morgan's attack off at the pass. I would drive to The Castle and confront Craig on campaigning against the mission wall certification. It wasn't like I wanted a historical site in my backyard. I'd been planning on putting up a hammock in the trees back by the creek. Now that I knew the mission site existed, I felt responsible for taking care of the wall and the history it represented. And that meant protecting the stone blocks from money-grubbing walruses like Morgan.

I grabbed one of the day-old pastries I'd pulled from the back room of the shop yesterday and headed out to my Jeep. After winning the inheritance lottery last year when my friend Miss Emily passed on her worldly possessions (and problems) to me, I could afford to replace my falling-apart POS. I hadn't had the time. Or the heart. I loved the car, even if it did break down consistently. Greg warned me he would drive me to the car lot himself the next time the Jeep broke down.

Emma whined when I picked up my purse.

"Let me get your leash," I chided the golden retriever, a house-warming gift from Greg and the love of my life—at least my pet life. She was protective, fun, and loved to cuddle on the couch. She adored riding in the Jeep almost as much as I did.

Twenty minutes later, Emma and I parked at The Castle. I rolled down the windows partway, knowing she'd be fine in the car in the cool morning for the few minutes I planned to be in Morgan's office. And if I unloaded what I wanted to say, I'd be out lickety-split.

"Wish me luck." I rubbed the top of Emma's head. "We'll stop on the beach for a run on the way home."

That garnered me a short bark, making me wonder, not for the first time, how much my dog understood what I said to her. She definitely knew her name. And "ball." And "dinner."

Even Emma knew I was stalling. Time to march into Morgan's office with the righteous indignation I'd had when Amy told me he was poaching the historical funding right out from under my nose.

I hesitated. Scenes weren't my style. Heck, I'd stayed in way too many bad relationships for way too long to start fighting now.

Emma barked and I followed her gaze. Craig Morgan walked toward the parking lot and the Jeep.

Now or never.

"Craig," I called, fumbling out of the Jeep, slamming the door to keep Emma from jumping and attacking.

The man kept walking toward his BMW, ebony-black and recently washed, buffed, and shined.

"Craig Morgan. I came here to talk to you." Jogging, I got between him and his car, blocking his exit.

"Miss Gardner, I don't have time for any silly town stuff. My membership in the Business Basics group is as an advisory position, not an active member." He stepped to his right.

I bobbed left and kept him blocked. "This isn't about the group. Although you could be more supportive and participatory. We only win if we work together."

His sarcastic glare almost made me back down. "Miss Gardner, I don't have time for winsome platitudes. Please excuse me." He tried again to step around me.

I put my hand on his black suit coat. "Seriously, I want to talk to you. Are you trying to block funding for the mission wall project?"

His eyes flashed and for the first time, he eyed me. "Who told you such a tale? Your friend in the mayor's office, perhaps?"

"Does it matter how I found out?" My stomach lurched. I could tell the man had been caught no matter what answer he gave me. He was trying to block my funding.

The message I'd received from Frank Gleason, the local historical society inspector, confirmed Amy's leak. Someone claimed the wall in my backyard wasn't part of the old Spanish mission. And they said they had proof. Frank ended the conversation explaining he would talk to me after he'd examined the so-called evidence.

I could tell Frank was annoyed. My wall was a major find for him. He'd already been published in a local periodical, and he planned on speaking about the wall at a professional conference in New York this winter. Having his project proved false now would blemish his career, a blip that could get him fired.

"Miss Newman needs to keep her nose out of things that don't concern her. Look what happened last time she butted into a business development. I'm sure she doesn't want to be kidnapped again." Craig sneered and regarded my hand on his arm. He lifted the offending appendage off as if I were a bug on his five-hundred-dollar suit. "Now, if you'll excuse me."

"I will not. You aren't going to bully me, Craig Morgan. Not by threatening my friend or me. I won't stand for it. I'll, I'll . . ." Furious, I couldn't believe he even tried to threaten Amy. The girl had gone through enough when Miss Emily died. I glanced around the parking lot. We'd gathered quite a crowd for my public tantrum. I paused.

"You'll what? Stop promoting my business? Kick me out of the club? Stab me for ruining your cash cow—I mean, your 'Spanish mission' project." He made air quotes with his hands. "Honestly, Miss Gardner, you're about as worrisome as an insect on my windshield."

This time he did walk around me and get into his car. As I stood there in shock, he rolled down his window and added, "And yes, I'm blocking your funding. You might as well tear your garden wall down because if I have anything to do with it, you'll never receive a dime for your charade."

"I'll stop you. No matter what I have to do, you're not getting away with this!" I screamed as the overpriced sedan backed out of the parking spot. The gardener watering the plants lining the parking lot took two steps back as he watched me. I must have looked like a lunatic.

I took a deep breath, then plastered on the fake smile I'd become more and more familiar with using. Walking past the man with the hose, I called out, "Sorry, but talking to Craig drives me insane."

I heard him mumble something in Spanish, and the only word I caught was *loco*. Emma sat on the driver's seat, watching me. She barked as I came closer, obviously excited at my altercation with Craig. I pushed her back into the passenger seat and started up the car.

"I should have let you bite him." I absently petted Emma's soft coat as I drove the winding road down the hill toward the ocean. The sky exploded with a rare shade of blue that normally made my insides happy, especially on my days off. Today, I barely noticed it. I reached the main highway and considered turning back into town, abandoning my run.

A short bark reminded me of my promise.

"Okay, girl, hold on, we'll be on the beach in a second." I turned onto the empty highway, slamming on my brakes when a black pickup truck appeared in front of me. The truck barely made the turn onto the Castle road. As I listened to the squeal of the tires, I closed my eyes for the impact.

Nothing happened. I opened my eyes, glancing into the rearview mirror. The truck barely missed taking out the Jeep, my dog, and me with the turn. But he had missed.

I kept my foot hard on the brakes and watched the truck speed up the road. I tried to see the plate, but some type of cover made the numbers unreadable.

Should I confront the driver? I glanced at Emma. We hadn't been hurt. They didn't hit the Jeep. And I'd already made a fool of myself once. I decided one altercation a day was my limit. Time for a run. I turned the Jeep to the right and headed to the public access beach.

Two hours later, curled up on the wicker couch on my front porch, deep into a romance novel, a sound from the driveway dragged me out of the Earl of Perryville's rich garden lifestyle. Emma, who'd been asleep under the couch with today's chew toy, jumped to meet the visitor.

She ran out to the truck and waited patiently for the driver to notice her. When she wasn't greeted in the time Emma deemed appropriate, she placed her paws on the door and stuck her nose into the open window at Greg.

"Emma, get down." Greg wouldn't be happy if my fifty-pound puppy dragged her nails down the black paint job on his work truck. Walking toward the driveway, I couldn't help but grin as Emma totally ignored my command, and leaned in to give Greg a sloppy dog kiss.

"Get down." Greg's voice showed signs of stress as he repeated my command. He glared at me, still holding the phone at his ear. "Yes, Mayor, I'm here now. And I'll talk to her."

Crap. Morgan had called his friend the mayor and complained about my visit. But I hadn't been out of line. I tried to remember the conversation I'd been trying to forget since the fight happened. I'd been harsh. I'd apologize, he'd act like a double jerk, and I'd still hate him. I shook my head. The things I'd do for love.

Greg climbed out of the truck. His long legs, sexy in Wrangler jeans and cowboy boots. If he would wear western shirts rather than the standard-issue police uniform shirt, or his favorite casual rocker tee, people would swear he'd look like a young George Strait.

He stared down at me, his six-five frame shading my five-foot-six body from the heat of the afternoon sun. Yes, he was a tall drink of water, as my mother would say.

"Sir, I'll talk to you later."

I could hear Mayor Baylor yelling on the other end. I smirked. "Sorry, I guess my conversation with Craig got back to City Hall."

"Conversation? The way the mayor tells the story, you all but threatened the guy with a knife, gun, and your mad martial-arts skills." Greg pulled me into a hug. "You okay, tough guy?"

That was why I loved Greg. Even upset at me for the latest stupid thing I'd done, he always saw my side of things. I leaned into his chest, the smell of cologne overwhelming my senses. "That man can make me madder than a can full of ants."

"I think you mean a nest full of hornets." Greg chuckled.

"Whatever. The guy pushes buttons I didn't even know I had."

Emma pushed between us, forcing Greg to release me so he could pet her.

"How's my best girl?" Greg squatted down to the dog's level and she went wild. "You already take her on a run?"

"An hour on the beach after my fight with Morgan. She should be worn out." I leaned on the truck watching the two wrestle. Apparently the hour nap she'd taken under my feet while I read rejuvenated her energy level. "You done for the day? Or do you have to go report back to the mayor how you read me the riot act for being mean to his favorite business owner?"

Greg glanced up from his lovefest with Emma. "This isn't a joke, Jill. Craig Morgan's threatening to file a restraining order against you. You actually threatened him?"

"He's trying to stop certification of the mission wall." I kicked a dirt clod off the driveway. "Besides, he started it. Maybe I should file something."

"Instead, you should stay away from The Castle for a while, let the guy cool down. You know he can't stop certification by complaining. Let the system work." Greg stood and walked back to the truck. Kissing me on the top of the forehead, he climbed in the truck. "I'll see you at dinner. Get out some steaks and we'll grill."

I leaned into the driver's side window, not wanting to let him go. "Okay, cowboy, I'll throw together a salad and I think I've got a pie in the fridge."

"One of Sadie's?" Greg's eyes gleamed.

"You think I made pie this morning before I went on my rampage of the good citizens of South Cove?"

"Nut." Greg kissed me, this time a proper kiss, one making my toes curl. He smiled at me. "Don't worry about the wall. Only one thing could stop its certification—proof it's not the mission."

"But what if . . ."

"There you go again. I swear, you read too many murder mysteries. Not everything or everyone is a criminal." He patted the name tag hanging on his chest. "I'm the local expert, remember? And most days, unless my girlfriend is causing trouble, are deadly boring."

His cell rang. "Yeah, Esmeralda?"

I stood next to the truck, waiting to see if he would be grilling steaks tonight or if the dispatcher's call would keep him working past dinner.

He sat up and glanced over at me, his expression unreadable. "I'll head out there now."

Frowning, I waited for him to disconnect. "No dinner?"

"I'm not sure. Craig Morgan called in a complaint."

"Seriously?" I yelled at him. "What on earth can he charge me with?" This was getting out of hand. The man needed to get a life. But if I had to, I'd ride up with Greg to apologize. Not a bad idea. "Hold on a second, you can drive me up there and I'll say I'm sorry. And even sound like I mean it."

I'd expected a chuckle. Or at least a smile. Instead, he shook his head.

"Honey, not everything is about you." Greg started up the truck, patting my hand. "One of his back buildings where he stores antiques got broken into last night. They found the lock busted and several items missing."

"So no dinner." Craig Morgan had succeeded in ruining my entire day.

Greg glanced at the clock on the dashboard. "I'm sure I can get this cleared up before seven. Can you wait until then?"

"I can, but I can't promise there will be any of Sadie's pie left."

"Evil woman." Greg pulled me in for a final quick kiss, then released me, positioning his arm on the back of the seat and backing out of my driveway.

I pushed away from the truck, holding on to Emma's collar as I walked her back inside the fenced front yard. When I'd built the front fence, I'd been considering getting a dog and wanted the pooch to have free range of the entire property. I hadn't considered a large dog. The cute four-foot-high fence had kept Emma in so far, but I feared she hadn't realized she was big enough to jump now.

I waved to Greg and walked back into the house, bypassing the book and the comfortable chair on the porch. I needed to call the fence guy and get him to give me some options before Greg started showing up with complaints about my dog, as well.

I grabbed Emma's food dish and filled the bowl before I sat at the kitchen table to find the number and schedule an appointment.

"Face it, girl, we're public enemy number one in this town."

CHAPTER 3

Unexpected visitors will brighten your day. My online horoscope had been less than forthcoming. Greg stopped into the shop to give me one final lecture on blowing up on the mayor's favorite business owner. A raccoon turned over my garbage cans during the night, a sight that most definitely hadn't brightened my day. Especially since I didn't find the mess until noon after I got home from work when all I wanted to do was relax on the porch and read. Now, being superstitious, I waited for the third shoe to drop.

The fates didn't disappoint me.

A knock sounded on my front door as I rinsed the lunch dishes. Turkey sandwich and a slice of Sadie's pie eased the frustration I felt every time I remembered my run-in with Mr. Holier Than Thou Morgan. I still wanted to strangle the man. Since my run and the pie had only taken a dent out of my anger, my next step was a long hot bath, yoga, or killing the man.

Drying my hands on a dishcloth, I made my way to the front door, where Emma already sat at attention, staring through the wooden door like she had X-ray vision. Her tail wagged quietly. Frowning, watching my dog, I realized she never did that, except when one person visited.

Aunt Jackie had come to call.

Opening the door, a box was shoved into my chest.

"Take this, it's heavy." Aunt Jackie bristled past me into the living room, ignoring Emma, who followed the woman quietly into the house. Emma loved my aunt. Unfortunately, the feeling wasn't mutual, although often when Aunt Jackie thought I wasn't looking, I saw her pat the top of the golden retriever's head or sneak her a bit of meat off the table.

"Come on in," I said. The box she'd handed me wasn't heavy, but the contents smelled divine. Lifting the lid, the aroma of deep dark chocolate of our best-selling dessert, Brownies to Die For, wafted out. Six perfectly cut brownies, waiting to take the edge off the day. Now, this was a pleasurable unexpected visitor. The brownies, I meant, not my aunt.

"No coffee made?" Aunt Jackie called from the kitchen, where she and Emma had already landed.

"It's three in the afternoon." I shut the door and headed back to grab some plates to serve the brownies. I would have sat on the couch and eaten them straight out of the box with a glass of milk as a chaser. Add in a romantic movie on the women's network, I'd be in heaven. I glanced longingly at the couch as I walked by. Today was supposed to be my day off.

"No excuse not to have a pot brewing. What if company comes?" Aunt Jackie chided me, already running water into the pot.

"Then they make the coffee."

Aunt Jackie didn't respond until the coffeemaker started its brewing cycle and she'd settled into her favorite spot at the kitchen table. For the work I'd done to make the living room warm and inviting, my visitors seemed to congregate in the kitchen. Although Greg and I did like to cuddle on the couch after dinner. I smiled at the memory of last week's movie and wine marathon. The man did know how to cuddle.

My memory dried up with Aunt Jackie's next question. The one I supposed she'd been dying to ask ever since she'd boxed up the brownies.

"So, what went on out at The Castle today? I heard you decked Craig Morgan." She leaned forward, anxious for details.

"I didn't hit him. I wanted to hit him, but I restrained myself." I wasn't waiting for the coffee; I bit into a brownie, hoping the chocolate would calm my nerves. The moist, chewy cake tasted like sawdust. Another result I could blame on Morgan. I swallowed the brownie and got up to get a glass of water to wash my treat down.

"Well, at least one part's not true. Honey, the rumors are flying so fast, they run from you killing the man to you and him running off to Vegas to get married." Aunt Jackie glanced at the coffeepot. "You run vinegar through the machine routinely? The brewing seems to be kind of slow."

"I know how to take care of my appliances." Of course I wasn't admitting I'd never run vinegar through my coffeepot. When the drip slowed down to a crawl, I'd buy a new one.

Unsure which of the two subjects would provide fewer minefields, I chose to find out what the rumors were. "I didn't kill him. Last time I saw the smug jerk, he drove off in his expensive car. You wouldn't think he'd make enough off Castle tours to afford a car like that."

Aunt Jackie waved the idea away. "I hear he's a trust-fund baby. No other way he could pay the heat and cooling costs on that monstrosity and keep buying antiques to fill the rooms. Rumor around town is he has a shipping crate from China down at the pier with the items he bought this spring on his trip."

The woman sounded wistful. Before she'd lost her apartment and the money she'd carefully invested into a local and not-as-famous Ponzi scheme, my aunt had been spending her retirement traveling from one over-fifty cruise to another. She loved seeing new sights and bringing me home cheap souvenirs from faraway lands. Now she lived in the apartment over the coffee shop, establishing herself as my general manager and freeing me to remodel my house.

Honestly, I'd been feeling lost without my day-to-day work, so I'd taken on a more active role in the chamber's business section for the town. I'd been the go-between from the city council to the local businesses since I'd moved here. Even if the council never took my advice on anything. Being new in a town made your every action and motive suspect. I don't think they would have even hired me if Amy hadn't insisted. It helped that no one else in town wanted the job.

Although, after my outburst today, my days as liaison between the business and the city council were probably numbered. Crap, I hadn't considered that.

Open mouth, insert entire leg.

"Honey, are you listening to me?" Aunt Jackie interrupted my pity party. The coffee had finished brewing and a cup sat in front of me, courtesy of my aunt.

"It's been a long day." I glanced at the clock. Greg would be here around seven, hopefully. I could probably sneak in reading a few more chapters and a long, hot bath before my guy arrived. If I could get Aunt Jackie out the door in less than thirty minutes.

"Did you hear anything I said about the mystery signing? We have twenty people signed up already."

"For an author whose name you haven't even released? That's crazy." A drawing from the attendees would have one lucky winner getting a signed copy of the book and a free night at the B&B. Aunt Jackie scored council funding to help subsidize the advertising to the local papers in the towns surrounding South Cove.

I had to admit, for a crazy idea, she was going full-force promotion. And, since she'd come to manage the store six months ago, my profits had soared. The woman breathed business. And I breathed books. The council could hire her for the chamber liaison after they fired me.

"Not knowing is part of the fun. Besides, I'm layering hints into the promotions. If someone e-mails me a correct guess before the unwrapping, they win a fifty-dollar gift certificate."

She must have noticed the pained look on my face because then she quickly added, "Believe me; the increase in traffic now has paid for the gift certificates three times or more."

"What do you mean, increased traffic?" My morning shifts hadn't changed in volume or customers. I got the same rushed commuters stopping in before heading off to the city for their daily grind. I loved having them take a taste of home with them. In fact, I'd been thinking about opening an audio library to sell new and used audio books for the harried commuter.

Aunt Jackie frowned. "You're not seeing an increase during your shift?"

I worked the first shift—5 A.M. to noon. Then Toby came in and took over. "Nothing I could measure. I mean, there could be a few more sales since you started promoting, but not much."

"I believed the increase was divided between your shift and Toby's. I sure haven't seen more traffic in the close."

Aunt Jackie's words were clear, but the implication troubling. "You're telling me Toby's afternoon shift has increased traffic? How much, ten percent? Twenty?"

My aunt shook her head. "Our gross take is up one hundred and fifty percent since last month."

I leaned back in my chair and whistled. "What is he doing? Threatening to arrest people if they don't buy a second or third cup?"

"Now, Jill, Toby wouldn't do that." Aunt Jackie paused. "Would he?"

I stood and put my plate and cup into the sink. "One way to find out. It's time for a surprise visit to our newest barista."

We took Aunt Jackie's car, I'd walk back. I couldn't believe she'd fired up her car for the four-block trip. Miss Emily's house—my house, I corrected myself—sat at the end of town, an easy walk to everywhere in the small village, except maybe the winery. Everyone in town walked. Aunt Jackie drove.

I slipped into the passenger seat. Something shiny caught my gaze. A heart-shaped crystal hung from her rearview mirror. "This is new. Where'd you find it?"

South Cove's business section was filled with artisan craft houses. Glass-blowing and metal-bending artists loved the quiet community as a great place to work. With the tourist trade on the weekend, they could make a living selling their designs. A really good living, from what I saw of the cars tucked behind several combined shop, apartment, and studio buildings. We didn't get a lot of the craft house businesses at the chamber meetings, but they usually sent a token representative. I'd always imagined the group getting together and figuring out who drew the short straw. But most of the artists were at least civil when they attended, if not bored out of their mind. On the other hand, they didn't mind accessing the marketing funding we provided.

Aunt Jackie frowned at the rock, reflecting prisms of light throughout the car. "I didn't. The darn thing was hanging in my car this morning. I knew I should be locking my car doors. But no, South Cove's a safe little town, weren't those your exact words?"

I suppressed a grin. "You weren't vandalized. Someone left you a present."

"My car was broken into. That's a crime." Aunt Jackie started the car and headed back to Coffee, Books, and More.

"Maybe you have a secret admirer?" I teased as I spun the heart-shaped crystal. The way the stone spun, mixing the sunlight into a burst of rainbow lights, was beautiful.

"That's what I need, a man in my life." Aunt Jackie shook her head. "I loved your uncle and now he's gone. This is my time to live without worrying about making someone else happy."

I hadn't known Uncle Ted except for the birthday cards and Christmas gifts they'd sent while I was growing up. My mom, Aunt Jackie's sister, hadn't been the social type. In fact, if she'd been alive now, she'd probably be diagnosed with agoraphobia. She couldn't even bring herself to attend my school functions. She'd come to a Mother's Day tea once and I thought she would faint before my fifth-grade class finished singing the song we'd practiced for months.

"You don't have to marry someone to have fun." I snuck a look at my aunt, who turned her car into the alley that ran behind the building housing the coffee shop and the apartment. The woman's face was beet-red.

"We're not talking about this." She parked the car and headed to the back entrance of the shop.

Grinning, I followed her into the building. When we came into the sales floor, I stopped and laughed. Every table, couch, and stool were filled. With women. Blondes, brunettes, redheads, they ran the gamut of looks and styles. And Toby stood behind the counter, grinning and making drinks.

"Terri? Your large cinnamon tea is ready." Toby called over to a woman sitting on the couch and talking animatedly with a couple of others, already with drinks in their hands.

She popped up, sprinted to the bar, and gave him a cover shoot–worthy smile. "Thanks, Toby, you're the best."

Toby tilted his head and turned to see me and Aunt Jackie standing watching. "Hey, guys, I didn't know you were coming in today."

"Obviously." I glanced around the room. "Are you always this busy?"

Toby started on the next drink order while he talked. "I wasn't at first. Then a couple of the girls from the cosmetology school stopped in for a study date, and before I knew it, I got this."

The cosmetology school was a half hour down the road. "They drive all this way for a latte?"

A woman stepped close to me, waving at Toby. "And the treats. We love Toby's pastries. Be a doll and get me one of those brownies? I've got to head back for my afternoon classes and I need a pick-me-up for the road."

"No problem, Misha." Toby boxed up a brownie while waiting for the espresso to finish for the drink he was making. He handed her the brownie in a Coffee, Books, and More sack. "Three bucks."

"Here's five. The rest is yours." The blonde waved a perfectly manicured hand at Toby. "See you tomorrow."

I glanced at Aunt Jackie. I could see the wheels moving as she tried to figure out a way to capitalize on Toby's popularity. I could see the advertising copy now, Toby dressed in an apron and a police cap, holding a pot of coffee and a tray of brownies. A romance cover waiting to be made.

"Well, I guess we've got our answer." I grinned at my aunt. Toby, not her mystery night, was the cause of the increase in business. *Sex sells,* I thought. My aunt's hiring of the town's part-time deputy had been a spot of brilliance, but I don't think she really considered his draw as one of the few hotties around the area.

When she didn't answer, I slid behind the counter and boxed up a mixture of baked goods. "Toby, charge these off to marketing. I'm going to City Hall to mend some fences with the mayor."

"Thank God he has a sweet tooth. The mayor and you are like oil and water." Toby grinned.

"Yeah, what's up with that?" I headed to the front door and waved at my aunt. "I thought everyone liked me."

Toby laughed. "Face it, boss, you're like deep, dark coffee. An acquired taste."

I left Toby and my aunt to man the shop and headed out into the warm day. I'd stop by City Hall, deliver my peace offering, and then head back home in time to read a few more chapters, my energy cleansed and my mind free from worry. I hadn't moved two steps before I heard loud, angry voices.

Looking through the plate-glass window, I saw Josh and Craig in the antique shop yelling. Even though the shop door was closed, I could hear the vibrating tenor of the voices. I glanced down the street. I needed to pass right by the shop to get to City Hall. Crossing the street wasn't an option since the city's road department was replacing a section of sidewalk. I gritted my teeth and started a dignified strut past the windows, hoping the men would be too involved in their conversation to notice me.

"Hey, beautiful," a man called out.

I turned toward the voice and groaned. Ray Stewart, Lille's on-again, off-again boyfriend, sat on the hood of his pride and joy, a 1968 Chevrolet pickup, step sides and all. As far as project cars went, Ray's truck took the prize. The engine roared when he gunned the gas down Main. But Ray hadn't made any improvements on the outside. The fog that rolled in nightly from the ocean had been busy, rusting out the wheel wells and bed. It was a wonder the body didn't fall apart on the street the way Ray drove.

Ray's trailer outside of town sat on ten acres his grandfather had left him. A man rumored to have been as mean as Ray. Ten acres used as a junkyard, supplementing Ray's income from towing and auto repair. Greg was pretty sure Ray used the auto shop more for a chop shop from time to time for a gang located in San Francisco, but hadn't been able to gather enough evidence to land him a warrant.

"Kind of busy, Ray." My gaze returned to the shop window, where Craig and Josh were still yelling at each other. Ray followed my glance.

"They've been going at each other for a few minutes now. I saw Craig's car and thought I'd collect some money he owes me. Instead, I'm watching the festivities." Ray grinned, a gold tooth shining.

"It's not nice to—" I stopped. What was Ray doing? Eavesdropping? Watching? It felt like an intrusion into a private conversation. I changed my tactic. "You should go see Lille instead. I'm sure she'd be glad to see you."

"Lille's ticked at me again. Something about cows and free milk." Ray leered at me, scanning up and down. "You still dating cop boy?"

"He's not a boy, and yes." Even knowing I dated Greg hadn't stopped Ray from hitting on me. Often in front of Lille. The man had no class.

"Such a waste. I know you have a wild side. We'd be good together." Ray stopped talking. "Looks like my payday is arriving. We'll talk later."

"In your dreams." I walked away from him, heading back down the street to City Hall.

With my gaze focused forward, I didn't see the door opening and Craig Morgan barreling down on me. The box of treats fell to the ground and I turned to face the man I'd verbally accosted, according to the mayor, that morning.

"I guess you didn't see me walking." I picked up the box, lifting the lid gently to see the cookies weren't totally destroyed.

"Miss Gardner, you realize you aren't the only person in the world, right?" Craig Morgan growled at me.

"Hey buddy, you ran into me." I heard my voice rise along with my blood pressure as another, more rational part of me whispered to myself, *This is not a good idea.*

The man smiled at me. A truly evil smile. "Oh, Miss Gardner, you haven't seen anything yet. You and your wall are going to be the laughingstock of South Cove before I'm through with you."

I half-expected him to add, "And your little dog, too." The image made me giggle.

Craig Morgan appeared incredulous. "You truly don't know what's happening here, do you?"

"Look. I'm sorry I yelled at you this morning. I believe we, as business owners, should put aside this incident and work together for a better South Cove." I put on my best liaison smile. With any luck, I'd be able to report to the mayor I'd already fixed the problem when I delivered the treats.

"I am going to destroy you." Craig slipped into his BMW and gunned the engine, leaving me standing slack-jawed in the middle of the sidewalk.

"You made a bad enemy." Josh stood in the doorway of his shop.

"But I didn't—" Josh didn't let me finish my thought. He shut the door, leaving me alone on the street, my crumpled box sitting in my hands.

Once I arrived at City Hall, I breezed through the air-conditioned front hall, back to Amy's desk in front of the mayor's office. It was empty. I glanced at her computer and saw it was shut down. A note sat in her outbox—*See you tomorrow* was written in Amy's favorite purple pen.

I glanced at the mayor's door. If I got lucky, he was out for the rest of the day and I could leave the box and a note on Amy's desk. A crashing noise came from the office. Not so lucky today. I squared my shoulders, pasted a smile on my face, and walked over to the door. As I reached up to knock, the door inched forward.

I hesitated, my hand curled into a fist, but something kept me from knocking. "I don't care what you want," the mayor yelled into his phone. "You have to realize until this is finalized, I can't get involved. I have to look like an impartial party, at least in the eyes of the commission."

My stomach dropped. I'd lay odds Craig was on the other side of that phone call. I wanted to burst through the door and tell the man his cover was blown, but what would that get me? Nothing.

"Look." The mayor's voice dropped an octave, appeasing. "If we just hold on, we'll both get what we want out of this."

I heard him pause and then laughter echoed from the office. "You and me both, buddy."

I'd had enough. I set the box of cookies on Amy's desk, scribbled a note, and then almost ran out of the office. Forewarned was forearmed. As I walked back to the house, my mind kept returning to Craig's threat. I tried to find a positive spin on what I'd learned, but the man had money, power, and the mayor's ear. I was toast.

Still in a blue funk when Greg showed up for dinner, I told him about running into Craig. I left out my conversation with Ray and my eavesdropping at the mayor's office. Whenever Ray's name came up, Greg's temperature went up ten degrees. I wanted his opinion on

Craig's declaration, not a lecture on how Ray was dangerous and I should stay away from him. I sat on the deck, drinking a beer, watching Greg grill the steaks. I'd made up a green salad earlier, seeing Craig's face with every rip of the salad greens.

"Honey, you can't make everyone like you." Greg slipped next to me on the stairs as I stared out toward the place where the old Spanish mission had been located and where we'd found a fortune in old coins.

"I wish him not liking me was the only problem. He's made me his enemy, and I don't think there's anything I can do about it."

Greg pulled me closer. Before he could speak, his cell rang. He frowned. "Sorry. I'm still on call until ten when Toby takes over."

He flipped open the phone. "Hey, Esmeralda. What's happening?"

I felt his body stiffen and he stood. "I'll be right there."

He nodded to the grill. "You think you can finish these? I've got to leave."

I nodded. Of course he'd get called out tonight. My entire day had been crap, why not our dinner date? "I can handle grilling a couple of steaks. When will you be back?"

"I won't, not tonight." Greg pulled me to my feet and kissed me hard. Then he gently pushed me back, sweeping a lock of hair out of my eyes. "It's bad, Jill."

Fear gripped my stomach. Amy hadn't been at work. Last time she'd disappeared, she'd been kidnapped. *Please, let her be okay,* I silently prayed. I took a breath. "Tell me."

"Craig Morgan was found outside The Castle. He's dead."

CHAPTER 4

Eating dinner alone wasn't my favorite activity. But when you date someone in law enforcement, especially in a small town, you have to expect plans to be changed at the drop of a hat. Or in this case, a drop of a body.

I'd held off eating until daylight left the porch. Greg wouldn't be coming back, not when there'd been a murder. Maybe Craig died of a heart attack? Something natural? Slipping and falling into one of the three pools on site? The pools were beautiful, surrounded with buildings mimicking a classic Grecian bath, the clear blue of the water highlighting the extensive tile work on the bottom of the pool. Too pretty to imagine Craig floating in the water.

I couldn't be so lucky, I mused, as I cut a bite off of the steak. The man could grill. I had to give him that.

Craig Morgan couldn't have died from a heart attack because he had no heart. And if he'd slipped and fallen, the eel part of his nature would have saved him from drowning, even unconscious. No, I had to face the truth. The man had been murdered. And who'd been seen arguing with the deceased not once, but twice in the last two days?

Yours truly.

Even with the town's detective as my boyfriend, this didn't look good, even to me. And I knew I didn't kill the jerk. I had motive and opportunity. The temperament to take a human life? Not so much. My only hope was I'd have an ironclad alibi for the time of death. Like grilling steaks with the town's detective.

My thoughts went to the fight Josh and Craig had been having earlier. Could it have continued after I'd walked away? I didn't want to think that the portly antique dealer could be a cold-blooded murderer, but I knew I hadn't done the deed. I'd told Greg about the fight; that should be enough for him to check into Josh.

I pushed my plate away, and Emma whined at my feet. Leaning down to pet her, I noticed her hair standing on end, and then she uttered a low growl aimed at the kitchen door.

I stood and peeked out the window to the porch. Nothing. Checking the lock on the door, I reached down and petted Emma. "No one out there, girl."

She growled louder this time, sniffing under the door frame.

I turned off the kitchen light and stood in the darkness, watching the backyard. Sometimes wildlife would make their way over, under, or sometimes through the fence surrounding my property. I'd often seen deer grazing through what was supposed to be my garden.

Letting my eyes adjust to the darkness, I stared out the window. A white glow hovered at the back of the property. I squinted, trying to bring the light into focus. The glow went behind a tree, floating into the woods at the back of the property. Disappearing right at the edge of the stone wall.

Local legend claimed the mission was haunted by the souls of the dead Catholic fathers who'd founded the mission as a way to bring the local natives to salvation. The natives later blamed them for the cholera that almost wiped out their tribe. The mission had been burned and the residents killed.

All that remained of the mission was the gold coins in my safe deposit box and five feet of stone wall, less than three feet tall at the highest spot. The mission Craig called a garden wall and me a fraud for trying to verify the historical site.

Or had. Before someone killed him.

I leaned down and stroked Emma's head. "No one is out there, girl. No chasing rabbits, not tonight." I grabbed my plate and left it in the sink. I'd clean up tomorrow. Tonight, I was taking a glass of wine and a book to my room to enjoy what might be my last night of freedom.

I grabbed a bottle of white zin out of the refrigerator. Greg and I had picked up a case when we visited the Napa Valley last month. The trip had been our first overnight weekend just the two of us. I smiled, thinking of the small bed-and-breakfast where we'd stayed. Amy had watched Emma. That had been a good weekend.

I tried to convince myself there would be more weekends like that. I didn't kill Craig Morgan and at least I knew it. Innocent people didn't go to jail.

Grabbing my notebook and a glass, I headed upstairs to get into my pajamas and cuddle into bed. I needed to figure out who did kill Morgan before the spotlight landed on me. The mayor would love seeing me in jail for something I didn't do. The man hated me.

Two hours later, I finished my third glass of wine as I added the mayor's name to the bottom of my three-page list. Closing the notebook, I felt better. I might have been seen arguing with Craig in the last few days, but in less than an hour, I'd listed off pages of people who hated the man for a variety of reasons. I put a star next to one name. Ray Stewart. Craig owed him money. But for what? Towing an abandoned vehicle from Castle grounds? Ray didn't seem like a *do the work now, pay me later* kind of guy. What job had Ray done for Craig? And had Craig paid up?

Now I wished I'd mentioned Ray being outside Josh's shop when I was complaining to Greg about Craig being a jerk.

And Josh. I circled his name. Something had happened between Josh and Craig, and I was going to find out what.

Slipping under the quilt, I closed my eyes. I'd worry about this tomorrow.

The next morning, regretting the third glass of wine, I slipped on my running clothes and headed downstairs to start a pot of coffee. I had the day off from the coffee shop. Jackie opened and closed on Fridays. She liked having a weekend, so I handled her shift on Tuesdays, giving her two days off in a row.

Emma and I started on Main, heading toward the highway, where we'd cross and then head down the trail to the beach. I let Emma off her leash once we got to the beach, allowing her to chase the gulls out of the surf. Music flowed through my earbuds as I ran, and for a few moments, my world felt perfect.

The morning light was still gloomy, but the fog had burned off. The waves crashed on the sand, whitecaps rippling the ocean's surface. Lots of people thought the Pacific was always smooth and warm. They were right, it was, farther south down the coast, but here, the ocean turned cool; the waves, turbulent. I loved sitting on the rocky beach watching.

Glancing toward the parking lot, I saw Greg's truck. I turned around to find him, but didn't see him down the beach. I ran toward the bend, a cove inhabited by sea lions most of the time. Emma ran closer. Somehow the dog knew not to engage these large mammals. What amazed me even more was the sea lions seemed to ignore her presence, too.

Turning the corner, I saw Greg. And Toby. And another man. I started toward Greg, and he put up his hand. "Leash Emma. And stay back."

I clipped Emma's collar on her leash and then stood waiting while Greg walked over toward me.

When he came close enough to hear me, I said, "Emma never bothers the sea lions. I know I'm not supposed to let her loose, but Greg, she loves this part of the run."

"I'm not upset she was loose," Greg said, bending down to greet Emma, who pulled at her leash to get to him. "Sometimes it's not about you. Sorry I didn't get back to the house last night. It's been crazy."

"What's going on out here?" I turned back to glance at Toby and Tim still standing around something in the cove. "Something happen to one of the sea lions?"

"We found Craig's dog." Greg took my arm and started walking me back to the parking area on other side of the beach.

"What's Fifi doing out here?" Craig's wife, Brenda, had named the black puppy Fifi as a joke, even though the dog would eventually weigh over a hundred pounds. When they divorced, she'd left Fifi with Craig at The Castle rather than confine her to an eight-hundred-square-foot apartment in the city. The woman still came to visit the dog, five years later.

"Someone tied her to a stake they'd hammered into the ground. If Tim hadn't found her on his morning pass-through, she'd have drowned when the tide came in."

"Craig wouldn't have left her here." There was no question to my statement. The man loved his dog.

"I know. I'm thinking whoever killed Craig dropped Fifi off this morning as a way to get rid of her, too."

"You didn't notice she was missing last night when you went to The Castle?"

"Honestly, the dog never even crossed my mind. I guess I thought maybe Brenda had her." Greg stopped at the steps to the upper-level parking, leaning on the rusting metal railing circling the lot. "I should have realized she was missing."

"You had other things on your mind." I watched Greg reach for his pocket where he used to keep his cigarettes before he stopped smoking last year. Now he pulled out a pack of gum he kept on him at all times. I hoped the gum would ease his craving. Greg told me the cravings increased when he was on a big case. When he couldn't figure out the puzzle. And probably, when his girlfriend was the suspect with the best motive in a murder.

"Yeah. About that, can you tell me where you went yesterday after the run-in with Craig?" He kept his eyes cast down, not wanting to meet mine.

"Seriously? You need my alibi?" Anger surged through me. "I was the one who told you I got into it with Craig. Both times. You think I'd tell you about the fights if I'd killed him?"

"Now, honey, you know how this works. I have to rule you out, just like any other person with motive to kill the victim. If I didn't ask, people would think I wasn't doing my job."

"And by people, you mean the mayor." Man, that guy got my goat. No matter what the issue was in South Cove, Mayor Baylor always wanted me to be the cause of the problem. Ever since I'd squashed his plans for the new upscale senior development by refusing to sell Miss Emily's house and finding the evidence to throw the developer's girlfriend in prison for murder, he'd been grumpy.

Greg unwrapped the stick of gum and put the wrapper back in his pocket. "Yes, I mean the mayor. And the city council. And the citizens of South Cove. It's my job. You knew when we started dating."

"Yeah, but I didn't think I'd be suspect number one in every murder happening in South Cove."

Greg mumbled something, and with the wind kicking up on the beach, I didn't hear him. I was sure it wasn't an affirmation of love by the look on his face.

"What?" I pressed on. I knew better. I was egging on a fight I couldn't win. The guy took his job and his responsibilities seriously even when he knew there was no way I could have killed anyone.

"I said, if you wouldn't keep getting yourself in the middle of things that don't concern you, maybe you wouldn't be suspect number one every time." Greg's voice was low and his jaw clenched when he spoke.

"You can't even think . . ."

He stopped me in mid-sentence. "Do I think you killed Craig Morgan and then tied his dog up to be eaten by sea lions or drowned in the tide waters? No. So throw me a bone here. Where were you after the argument with Craig?"

I took a breath, trying to punch down my anger. Greg was right. This wasn't his fault and he had to ask. I didn't have to like it. I thought about yesterday afternoon.

"I went to City Hall to drop a box of cookies off to the mayor to apologize for whatever problems the fight with Craig had caused."

"You mean find out what Craig and the mayor were planning," Greg translated.

"Okay, you could see it that way." Emma bumped me with her nose, a doggie reminder we were supposed to be running. I reached down and patted her head.

"So you talked to Amy?" Greg pushed.

"No one was in the front office. I don't know where Amy was, so I dropped the box off on her desk with a note, and headed home."

"What time was that?"

"It must have been around four. Aunt Jackie had stopped by at three, then we went to the shop to check on Toby." I glanced over at the midday barista/part-time police officer who was walking toward us, leading a limping Fifi. "Do you know he has a harem of women who visit the coffee shop every day he works? Isn't he still dating someone?"

Greg watched as Toby walked up the beach. "A few someones, last I heard."

"The kid will never learn." I continued to watch Toby lead the dog. "Hey, what happened to Fifi's leg?

"I'm thinking one of the sea lions must have attacked her when she was tied up. Maybe she was too close to their usual sunning spot." Greg sighed. "I'm going to have to have the vet look at her. He's not scheduled to be here until next week, so he'll charge the city a premium, especially on a Friday."

"The mayor's going to love you when he gets the bill." I smiled.

"Back to you?" Greg pressed me.

"When I got home, I made a salad for dinner, then took Emma for a run down here." I frowned. "Fifi wasn't here when we ran through either way. Even if I hadn't seen her, Emma would have."

"Then what?"

"I took a shower, read a book, and waited for you. You showed up right at eight. And left at nine."

"So from four-thirty to when I showed up, you didn't see anyone, talk to anyone?"

This wasn't good. I could feel it. "No one except Emma." I watched Greg's face tighten. "I'm screwed, huh?"

"You never make things easy." Greg pulled me into a hug. "Now go finish your run. I've got to get Fifi over to the animal shelter until we can get a hold of Brenda to come get her."

"You going to stop over tonight?" I loved the feel of my face up against his chest as he held me. The man could make me feel safe in a hurricane. I could feel my body relaxing. "Maybe we could watch a movie?"

"As long as the invite includes pizza and a few beers, I'm game. And no chick flicks. It's my turn to pick the movie." Greg spoke softly into my ear. "It's time you were introduced to the wonder that is Jet Li."

"Great." I pasted on a smile and peered into his blue eyes. Last month we'd watched a string of Chuck Norris movies. Greg had even offered to pay for couple's tai chi classes. I was still holding off, wanting to bargain with the ballroom dance class starting next month. If we were sharing our interests, by God, we were really going to share.

"I'll be over at six. Toby's running the evening and night shift." Greg leaned in and kissed me quickly. "Stay out of trouble today. I don't want to ruin our dinner tonight, too."

"I promise, no fights, no arguments. I won't even call Aunt Jackie." I turned and headed back down the beach toward the end of town.

"And no sleuthing. I can handle this investigation on my own," Greg called after me.

I waved back, trying to look innocent.

Both Greg and Toby laughed. I guess innocent wasn't one of my best looks.

When I got home, the red light was blinking on my answering machine. Filling up Emma's water dish, I pulled the pitcher of filtered water out of my fridge and poured a glass before I pushed the button.

"Miss Gardner, this is Frank Gleason from the Historical Society. When you get a chance, will you give me a call? There's been some developments on the mission site certification."

The line went dead and my heart sank. Even dead, Craig Morgan was making my life miserable. If that jerk messed up the certification, I'd kill him again. Visions of my breaking into Flannigan's Funeral Home and beating up Craig's lifeless body filled my mind. I definitely was going off the deep end. I didn't even know if Frank had good or bad news. I should have trusted my hunch.

Frank hemmed and hawed over the problem when I finally reached him after being placed on hold twice, then having the line disconnected. Frustrated, I finally interrupted his lecture about needing community support and verifying historical accuracy for certified sites.

"Just tell me, Frank, what's going on?"

The line went silent for a second and I worried I'd been disconnected once again. Either the historical society had a crappy phone service, or Frank didn't want to talk to me.

As I was about to hang up and drive down to San Luis Obispo to camp outside Frank's office, he answered.

"There's been a challenge to the location of the mission site."

"We knew there might be, but doesn't the physical proof we found bolster our claim? It's not like there's a map showing the location." I shouldn't have worried. Challenges happened all the time.

"Actually, that's exactly what they said they have. A map showing the mission was actually located on the other side of town."

Now I was speechless. The wall and the gold coins matched the local legends perfectly. Heck, Bambi, the murderous history teacher, had tried to kill me and my aunt because she believed the mission wall was on my property. Had we been wrong?

"Miss Gardner? Are you there?"

"Sorry, just surprised. Who filed the challenge?"

"Hold on, I have the paper right here. It was a Josh Thomas and a Craig Morgan."

Craig, I'd expected, but Josh? *"Et tu, Brute?"*

"Excuse me?" Frank Gleason sounded concerned. "Do you know these men?"

Sighing, I knew Craig's challenge would be one more strike against me in trying to prove I didn't kill the weasel. "Actually, yes. And the one who's still alive owns the antique shop next to my coffee shop. Maybe I'll have a talk with him."

"Miss Gardner, I find it's better if you let the professionals handle these discussions. Sometimes emotions are involved." The man stopped talking for a second, then added, "Wait, you said the man who was still alive? Is one of these men dead?"

"Craig Morgan was killed last night at his home."

"Oh my. That complicates the challenge, then."

You don't know the half of it, buddy. I said my good-byes, then pulled out my notebook with the list of suspects. Next to Josh's name I wrote down the wall challenge. Looking at the list, I realized I'd forgotten to tell Greg about Ray again. Tonight. Before the pizza arrived, I'd show him my list and tell him about the challenge to the wall and the run-in with Ray. Before someone else did.

I was too late.

CHAPTER 5

Even a large meat lover's pizza and a two-hour karate movie had no effect on Greg's bad mood. Every attempt I made at conversation got either ignored or answered with one word. Finally, he grabbed the remote and turned off the television. Sighing, he leaned back against the couch and focused on me.

"What?" I knew I didn't want to hear the answer, but even being yelled at would be better than his silent recriminations. Emma sat up from her place under the coffee table, reacting to my tone.

"Why didn't you tell me about the run-in with Ray?" Greg shook his head. "Do you think this is some kind of game? You're seen hanging out with the town bad boy and all of a sudden the guy whom you want out of your hair winds up dead. Do you know how many people called the station with the news, claiming you hired Ray to kill Craig?"

I frowned, not wanting to believe his words. "Seriously? People think I'd hire out the deed? With Ray? The man can't finish a job, any job, to save his life. Ask Lille. She'll tell you he hasn't worked a full day in years."

"Because he's part of the California Mafia. He's connected. What, you think he lives off Lille?" Greg's voice raised.

"Yeah, I kind of did." I leaned back on the couch. "Wow. I didn't even know California had a Mafia."

Greg shook his head. "You're missing the point. Ray's bad news. Always has been. And now, the mayor wants to know why you aren't sitting in my jail cell calling for a lawyer."

"That's not fair. Mayor Baylor hates me." My back tightened. "You know that."

Greg ran his hand through his hair. "Jill, it may not matter. You have to stop getting involved in things like this. How come every time there's a murder, you're the main suspect?"

"Maybe because I'm the new kid in town? Hell, I don't know. Ask your friendly townsperson who ratted me out today. I didn't want to talk to Ray. Besides, I thought I did tell you. Honestly, I was trying to listen in and hear what Craig and Josh were fighting about." I felt the heat run to my face. "There, are you happy? I'm a nosy neighbor."

"Wait, you didn't tell me about Craig and Josh fighting. When was this?" Greg leaned forward, his cop face on.

I went through the encounter from the time I left the coffee shop with the box of cookies to the time Craig knocked them out of my hand. At least that one action would be the last time Craig messed with me and my store. Unless my boyfriend arrested me for Craig's murder, then the jerk would be laughing from whatever place in the afterlife he'd landed in.

Greg seemed thoughtful when I stopped. "You don't know what they were fighting about?"

"I've got a good guess." I outlined my conversation with Frank Gleason today, as well. "So you see, if they faked the evidence against the wall, maybe Josh wanted out of the arrangement, but Craig wouldn't let him?"

"Kind of a long shot. You think Josh could get the drop on Craig? He can't walk five feet without wheezing. Craig would have heard him coming a mile away. Besides, no way could the man drag Fifi away from The Castle and chain her up as sea lion bait. He's half-dead himself."

I hadn't thought about that. Of course, blaming Josh was the same thing as everyone else was doing to me, pointing their finger at the newcomer. Only one way to find out. "I'll go talk to Josh tomorrow."

Greg shook his finger at me like I was Emma. "No. You'll stay out of the investigation. If I catch you snooping around, this time, I swear, Jill, I'll lock you up for impeding an investigation."

"With handcuffs?" I tilted my head, trying to put on a sexy smile.

"Not joking here."

"Look, I'm not going to sit here while people talk about me. What if they stop coming to the coffee shop because they think I'm a murderer?" I raised my hands. "What do I do then?"

A smile teased the ends of Greg's mouth. "Most of the town would rather give you a medal. And a little notoriety will probably help business, not hurt it." Greg shook his head. "Everyone loves a car crash."

I swatted his arm. "Now I'm a car crash?"

He chuckled. "Honey, you're an accident waiting to happen. I've never seen anyone with the bad luck you have." He pulled me over to him, leaning my back against his chest, and put his arms around me. "Except for when you met me."

He couldn't see my smile so I let it stay on my face. "You think you're all that, mister."

His breath ran the length of my neck. "I know it." And then his attention dropped from whispering to lower, and he nibbled on the curve of my neck, making me want to ignore everything and everyone outside my house. Want to take him upstairs and do bad things to him in my sleigh bed. Or maybe here on the couch? I hadn't made up my mind when his phone buzzed.

Sighing, he lifted his arm away from me and pulled his phone up to read the text. He keyed in a reply, then kissed me quickly on the head, pushing me off of his lap. "Gotta go, honey. We can talk more tomorrow."

"Or you could come back after you take care of that." I pointed to his phone.

Greg shook his head. "I'm heading out to The Castle, again. This time the night watchman has a couple of teenagers locked in his office." He stood and patted Emma on the head as she stretched. "I think the kids went a bit too far tonight."

I walked him to the front door and watched the truck pull away from my house, lights flashing. The man loved using his lights. I hummed a bit as I went about cleaning up the living room after our date night. Being in a relationship with a local detective had its advantages at times, like when I needed gossip. But I paid for the ready gossip on nights like this when he could be pulled away at a moment's notice. Greg's first wife hadn't been able to deal with the long hours and since the divorce had been dating a banker. Who, incidentally, also made a lot more money than a small town detective.

Me, I liked my time alone, even if it did get me in trouble at times. Like when I didn't have an alibi for Craig's murder. After tossing the pizza box and letting Emma out for one last time, I sat on the back porch in a swing Greg hung last weekend. I'd lit the citronella candles to keep away the mosquitoes and other flying nasties. Using the porch light, I opened my notebook and reviewed my list of suspects. A list Greg would be none too happy to find, but I'd needed to write it anyway. On the page titled "Craig's Murder" I added the unanswered questions from the day.

When I finished, I realized I'd written the names of most of the townspeople due to one or more conflicts with Craig. The man did know how to create enemies. Sighing, I closed the notebook and gently pushed the swing back and forth with my foot. Emma tired of chasing rabbits out of the yard and lay at my feet, ready to call it a night.

My thoughts were on Craig and Josh when I heard Emma's low-throated growl. I focused on the backyard, but didn't see anything, not even a wayward deer or one of the coyotes who ran the foothills. Emma stood, her nose pointed to the back of the property, back where the wall sat. I couldn't see the wall from the house.

I reached for Emma, her body shaking under my touch. "What's going on, girl?" I whispered, not wanting to bring more attention to my location. Even though I sat in the middle of the porch, candles and the porch light were making me the perfect target, if someone was aiming at me.

Slowly I reached into the doorway and turned off the porch light. In the dim candlelight, I made my way down the porch and extinguished each one. Once it was totally dark, I sat back on the porch swing and focused on the yard.

Nothing. Even though Emma still stood at attention. I trained my gaze on the spot where she stared. Still nothing.

Feeling foolish, I stood and opened the screen. I called for my dog. "Come on, time for bed."

Emma turned her head, made sure I was watching, then turned back and barked into the night. Satisfied she'd made her point, she trotted into the kitchen.

As I locked the door, I glanced out the window in my door. Was that a glimmer of light? Leaning forward and squinting, I focused, but no, it must have been a reflection from the moon or something. Turning away from the door, I headed up to bed. Tomorrow I needed to go visit with my favorite business owner, neighbor, and the one guy alive who stood in the way of certifying the Spanish mission wall site: Josh Thomas.

A smile curved on my lips. Greg couldn't even complain about my visit since Bill at the Business to Business meeting had asked me to bring Josh up to speed on our organization. I was doing my job. Sometimes being council liaison was a good thing.

Saturday morning came bright and early. Glancing at the clock, I had a couple hours before I needed to open the shop. People apparently didn't want their caramel lattes quite as early on the weekends. I pulled on my running clothes, and as I tied my shoes, Emma sat patiently. Well, as patient as a dog could be when she can read my actions and know we were heading outside for a run. Her body quivered as she waited, reminding me of the weird incident last night. Before I took off for the shop this a.m., I'd walk back to the wall and make sure no kids were using the place as Friday night make-out central. I lived at the edge of town, so the mission site had been the perfect place for kids to meet up before I moved into Miss Emily's house. My friend had been a firm believer in the early-to-bed-early-to-rise theory of life, so the local teens took advantage of the one place their parents wouldn't look for them.

When I'd gone to fence the property after Miss Emily passed on, we'd found the remnants of the old Spanish mission where South Cove's existence had begun. Now I was fighting for the historical commission to certify the site so I could ensure future generations would know the sordid history of this part of the California coastline.

And have the funding for a decent fence to protect the site. I stood on the porch, watching the birds circle over the road, and stretched. Emma, already on her running leash, sat and watched me. I loved my dog.

Remembering our run from yesterday, I wondered if Brenda had come for Fifi yet. I'd meant to ask Greg last night, but with him in such a bad mood, I thought better of bringing up anything about the case, even the homeless dog. If he didn't show up at the coffee shop, I'd give him a call once I got off. A car slowed and my paper flew onto the sidewalk in front of my house. Just inside the fence. Emma barked a greeting and I waved at Henry, my paper boy and the owner of one of the local art galleries. Everyone did whatever they could to make ends meet in the small tourist town.

A run down to the local beach, a hot shower, a glass of orange juice, and I was ready for my day. When I put Emma out in the fenced backyard, I glanced out at the area where the wall sat. Nothing looked different or out of place in the light of day. After work, I'd head out there anyway, just to make sure. Emma curled up on her bed on the porch and laid her head down. The run had tired her out. Exactly my evil plan. I locked up the back door and, grabbing my purse and a travel mug filled with strong, black coffee, I headed out the door to open my shop.

I owned the building where my coffee shop sat and my aunt lived in the apartment. Well, I and the bank owned the building. I liked having my aunt close. Since my mom died, Aunt Jackie was the only relative I had or at least I'd known about. For years, it had been me and Mom against the world. Then one day when I was off at law school, the world won and Mom had a heart attack in Albertson's produce section.

I shook back tears, no need to get emotional now. The ocean fog covering the town late last night while I slept had burned off in the bright sunshine only a California morning could bring. When I was interning in Boston, I'd experienced all four seasons. Here, the world stayed bright and color-blocked the entire year. Flowers bloomed in the city-maintained planters down Main Street. And the small town seemed like a village straight out of a fairy tale. The Disney version, not Grimm.

A kid on a skateboard flew toward me. He slowed and grinned when he recognized me, stepping off the board when he got close. It was Nick Michaels. "Miss Gardner."

"Nick, I thought you gave up your skateboarding once you got your license." I wondered if Sadie'd stripped the kid of his beat-up truck or if he'd loaned it out this morning.

"A guy's gotta get to work." He shrugged, his black hair falling into his eyes. "Mom had a cow when she heard I was late to my job so I kind of got grounded."

I bit my lip, trying not to smile. "Sucks."

"Totally. To work, and back." He shook his finger in the air. "Otherwise, you need to come straight home."

"Your mom thinks she's doing the right thing." This parenting gig was hard. I wanted to sympathize with the kid, but I knew Sadie would kill me.

"Yeah, I know." His eyes brightened. "Although I'm going to break the rules on my way home tonight. You got the latest Robert Jordan I ordered yet? I can spend my prison time reading."

"I'll have it waiting so you don't have to stay long," I promised. Sadie might not even know the kid stopped if we were quick about it. Although I don't think stopping at my shop for a book would get him into much trouble, even if his mom found out.

"Cool." He stepped back on the skateboard. "Catch you later."

I watched as he flew the next few blocks down to Lille's. Curving around the flower planters, the kid appeared more like a downhill skier more than a skateboarder. I turned back. One more block and I'd be at the shop. As I crossed the road, a man stepped out of a doorway and stopped my forward movement.

I looked up into the off-white button-down shirt, buttons straining that could only belong to one person. Josh Thomas.

"Miss Gardner," he started.

I held up a hand. "Look, I've got to get my shop opened." I glanced around the large man and noticed a woman standing in front of the door, peering in. "I've got customers waiting."

"We need to talk," Josh called after me as I scurried away.

Pulling my keys out of my purse, I called back, "I'll stop in this afternoon, after my shift."

The woman stood as I approached.

"Sorry, I'm late. Busy morning already. No one ever talks to me on the walk in to work and today, I see three people. Must be some kind of record." I realized I was chattering. But the woman didn't seem to mind.

"You're not that late, besides I wanted to stop in and see you before I left anyway."

I swung open the door and flipped on the light switches. Stuffing my purse under the counter, her words sunk in. She stood across from me, a year older, but her eyes were still a brilliant blue. Her eye color was the only thing that hadn't changed over the year. Instead of mousy brown hair, now she was a shiny blonde. More importantly, the woman had lost at least a hundred pounds. "Brenda?"

"In the flesh. Of course there's a lot less flesh of me now." Brenda Morgan spun around, her figure trim in jeans and a cool flowy shirt. "You didn't recognize me, did you?"

"Not at all. Not being married to Craig agrees with you." The words were out of my mouth before I could stop them. I slapped a hand over my offending lips and could feel my face heat. "Oh Brenda, I'm such an idiot. I'm sorry for your loss."

She patted my arm. "No worries. We both know my ex was a miserable son of a biscuit and he probably deserved what he got. I'm sad Fifi got hurt in the process."

"How is she?" I pulled on an apron and put coffee filters in both the coffee brewers. Turning on the machines, I'd have hot coffee in minutes.

Brenda slipped onto one of the bar stools by the counter. "The vet says I can take her home at the end of the week. Although I'm going to have to get a new place. No way would she be happy living in my tiny apartment."

"I know Emma would have the walls chewed by the time I returned from my shift. I'm glad I spent the extra money to fence the entire backyard. Although I suspect she spends most of her time on the porch sleeping." Finished with the must-dos, I stopped in front of Craig's ex-wife and smiled. "So what can I tempt you with today? A slice of banana bread? Or a slice of one of Sadie's pies? My treat."

Brenda laughed. "Neither. I'd have to do a second run on the beach to burn the calories off. How about a cup of that hazelnut coffee I smell brewing?"

"As soon as it's done. You sure you don't want some food? I've got a fruit cup Aunt Jackie added to the menu. She's always pushing it to our customers."

"Sounds good." Brenda set her phone on the countertop.

As I grabbed the fruit from a fridge behind the bar, her phone buzzed. She glanced at the display, then stood.

"Sorry, I'll be right back. Work." She stepped outside the shop and as she talked, I finished the rest of my morning prep. I didn't want to pour her coffee until she returned, not knowing how long the conversation would last. When I glanced out the window to check on her, she appeared agitated at the person on the other end of the line. What would get her so worked up on a work call? When she lived here, she was working part-time for the English department at a college over in Bakerstown. Maybe a student upset at a grade?

The bell over the door chimed and a couple walked in. They weren't locals so I put on my best customer service smile and called out a greeting. The two stopped at a carousel near the door where I kept local author books. Local being from the entire California central coast. We did have one author in town. Bill not only ran a bed and breakfast and served as the chair of the business council, he also wrote historical California gold rush romance novels. But the rest of my books ranged from cozy mysteries to real crime, a few craft books, and the ever-popular New Age self-help books. And the damn things sold. I was always refilling that display, probably because the tourists wanted a taste of the local culture.

I was pouring two large coffees and boxing a pie to go from the back when Brenda finally returned to the store, her eyes red like she'd been crying. "Hey, I'll be done in a second."

She shook her head. "I've got to go. It was nice seeing you."

I took a step toward her. "Hold on, are you okay?"

"Not really." She forced a smile, then almost sprinted out of the shop. The couple glanced at her and then back to me.

"Looks like she's just been told her dog died," the man joked.

Since I knew that wasn't true, I wondered who, besides her dead husband, could have Brenda that upset.

CHAPTER 6

Counting down the minutes, I was almost at the end of my shift when Esmeralda swept in the door. Thirty more and I would have been on my way home. My luck always ran bad. At least this time she'd left her cat at home.

She sauntered up to the counter, her multicolored skirt swishing due to the honest-to-God petticoat she wore underneath. Chains circled her neck and hung loosely on her white peasant blouse. She wore her salt-and-pepper hair long and loose over her shoulders. And, even I had to admit, the woman rocked the gypsy look. Since her "profession" was the town psychic when she wasn't answering phones over at the police station, she knew how to stay in character.

And the tourists loved it.

"Double-shot vanilla latte? Or is it a chai tea day?" I asked, trying not to make eye contact. After Amy's warning, I knew this could be more than a social call.

Esmeralda waved her hand and the diamond rings on all four fingers and her thumb glittered in the bright lights. "Whatever. I'll play your game. I'm here to talk to you, but you already knew that."

I made the double shot latte, making sure to use skim milk and sugar-free flavorings. The woman was constantly counting calories even though she probably wore a size six. Maybe her vision showed her what could be if she let herself gain weight?

Handing her the cup, I called over to Toby, who had already arrived for his shift. "I'm taking a break. Yell if you need something."

Esmeralda held out money for the drink. I poured myself a cup of black and waved her money aside. "On the house." I pulled off my apron and stepped around the counter, my inside screaming, urging me to run. Instead I nodded to the empty couch over near the mystery section. "Let's sit."

She followed me and I cringed with each step but pasted on a happy face by the time we'd settled on the old leather couch. I took a sip of the black gold to steady my nerves, then asked, "What's up?"

Esmeralda set her untouched drink on a coaster on the coffee table. When she leaned closer, I could see the worry on her face. "The spirits are trying to contact you."

"I haven't missed any calls," I quipped.

"This isn't a joking matter. I've been woken three nights in a row by a woman who says you're blocking her." Esmeralda's eyes narrowed. "Has anything weird happened lately?"

"Besides Craig Morgan being killed?" My mind flashed on Emma and her sudden fascination with the back of the yard the last two nights. And that puff of white. I pushed the questions away. If some spirit was trying to reach me, they needed to be more up front in their communication style. I didn't have time for guessing games.

Esmeralda frowned. "Maybe it's about that. Although I don't think so." She leaned closer. "You have seen some things recently, I can tell by your denial."

"If that's true, you should work full-time at the police station. I'm sure Greg could use a human lie detector." As soon as the words left my mouth, I felt bad. "Look, I don't mean to upset you, but really . . ."

She leaned even closer and took my hand. "Really, you're scared. There's no reason not to open yourself up to the other world. They are there to guide us, not harm."

"That's not what I've heard." I shook my head. "I'm not ready to believe this stuff, sorry." I glanced back at Toby, who now had a line at the counter. "And I need to get back to work."

She tightened her grip on my hand. "Go see the place you've been watching. The woman will contact you there."

Great, now I was part of an old spy movie? *Go along with it,* I told myself, *and she'll leave.* I started to speak, but Esmeralda waved my words away. "Just promise me you'll try."

As I stood, she watched, her face focused on mine, pleading for me to listen. "Weirder things have happened. I'll go to the place after work."

"You'll learn to trust me one of these days, Jill." She picked up her latte and the newest edition of *People* and started reading. Apparently I was dismissed. I grabbed my coffee cup, took a sip, and thought about my morning. Only in South Cove would the local psychic track you down at your job to bring the news of the other world.

I washed my hands when I went back behind the counter. Toby glanced at me. "Something I should know about?"

"You handle the strange and unusual now?" I smiled and shook my head. "Everything's fine. She's delivering a message from the other side."

"Craig Morgan's not harassing you from the dead now, is he?" Toby kept a straight face but his lip twitched.

I threw a clean towel over my shoulder. "Would you believe me if I said yes?"

Toby's eyes widened. "Seriously? I was kidding."

I started the espresso machine. "That's funny, so was I."

The lady standing at the counter snickered. "She got you."

Toby raised his eyebrows and focused back on the customer. "This time. I'll get her back. Just not when she's expecting it. What can I get you, sweetheart?"

For an hour, the business kept steady, and before I knew it, the line disappeared. I glanced toward the couch. Esmeralda was gone, as well, having left during the rush. I still felt her presence, pushing on me to follow through with my promise. Aunt Jackie slipped in next to me. "I need to talk to you."

"You and everyone else today." I nodded at Toby. "You okay here for a while? I've got to step out and visit our new neighbor."

He glanced at the clock. "You're done in fifteen minutes anyway. Take off early, isn't that the perk of being the owner?"

"Yeah, I hear rumors like that." Nodding to Jackie, I added, "Though maybe I'm just the person who thinks she's the boss."

"If you want to say something, spit it out." Jackie put her hands on her hips.

I put my arm around my aunt and pulled her to the door. "I'm kidding with you." Kind of. Aunt Jackie was a bulldozer when it came to getting what she wanted. No matter what the cost.

"Well, be that as it may, I need another check signed for the travel costs for our mystery author." Jackie shrugged off my arm and held the door open for me. "So before you leave, come into the office."

"Seriously, you need to tell me what's going on. I can't be signing blank checks all the time." I narrowed my eyes at my aunt, trying to gauge her determination.

She didn't even blink.

"At least, could you tell me how much the check's going to be? I might have to add funds to the account." I tried to bargain with her.

"You think I'm an idiot? We have plenty in the operating fund and by the time you do the monthly bookkeeping, the secret will be out." She put her hand on my arm to still me. "Wait, where are we going?"

"I told you, to visit with Josh Thomas."

Jackie stopped walked. When I looked back to see what was going on, she shook her head. "No way am I walking into his store. The man looks at me like I'm a daily special down at Lille's diner."

"Whatever." I pulled her arm. "You're imagining it."

"The man wants me. I'm not so old I don't see it when a man lusts for my body." She shook off my hand. "I am not going over to that old fart's place."

"Aunt Jackie . . ." I started but she shook her head.

"I'm not subjecting myself to being objectified. You just come back into the office when you're done telling him how to act at the business meetings. The guy needs to keep his mouth shut. The meetings will go a lot faster that way. You tell him to stay quiet." Jackie turned, then called after me, "And come sign my check when you're done."

"As if I could have forgotten in the last three minutes." I watched my aunt power-walk back to the shop. She made a zipper motion on her mouth when she saw me watching, then pointed in the general direction of Josh Thomas's shop.

The woman was a nut. When I turned back around, Josh stood in the open doorway to his shop. I waved and he stepped back into the shop, apparently trying to avoid me. After almost sitting on me to make me listen this morning, now he plays vanishing games with me? I lengthened my strides and pushed open the heavy wood and glass door into the antique shop.

A bell rang over my head, and I blinked my eyes, trying to focus in the dim light. The man kept the shop dark. I'd heard serious antique sellers were concerned about the damage electric light caused to the merchandise. Personally, I thought it was a way of keeping down the utility costs. A musty and dusty smell engulfed me and I sneezed. Pulling a tissue out of my purse, I called out, "Josh? Can I talk to you?"

No answer. My eyes adjusted to the dim lighting so I gingerly stepped around the displays, heading deep into the building. Boxes lined the walkway, more as I walked farther into to store. The man needed to unpack his merchandise and get it displayed. No one ever bought something out of a box.

He had an antique cash register sat up on a high bar. I took a peek behind the bar to see if he was asleep in his chair. No Josh, but it looked like he'd been working on some paperwork. I stepped closer and a receipt caught my eye. The Castle's logo was on the top. On the receipt, Craig had written "appraisal and estimating service, $1000." I flipped through the file; there must have been twenty more, with the amounts all in four digits. What had Craig needed appraised that often that he would pay these kind of fees for? I remembered Aunt Jackie mentioning the crate at the dock. Would there have been this much stuff to appraise?

I slipped one of the receipts in my pocket as I heard footsteps coming from the back. Stepping away from the counter, I scanned the darkness farther into the store.

"Josh Thomas, show yourself or you're not invited to the next meeting." I called, my voice shaky.

A breath on my shoulder made me spin and there he stood. "No need to be controlling, Miss Gardner. I've been pulling some boxes for a private client who's coming in this week."

I shuddered, hoping the action wasn't as obvious as it felt. "Sorry. I'm here to talk about the Business to Business meeting. To answer your questions about our process?"

Josh started digging in the box he'd set on the counter, his voice muffled. "I don't have . . . questions."

"Then maybe you can answer one for me. Why were you and Craig trying to stop the certification on the mission wall?" Anger flared through me. Trying to tamp it down, I waited for him to answer.

"Who said I was part of that?" Josh poked his head up over the edge of the box. "I've been staying home, keeping an eye out for those ruffians. Day in, day out. I've been watching those boys."

Yeah, and that's not creepy at all, I thought. "My consultant on the commission. He says you have some kind of proof." I watched his face for a response.

"The man talks too much." Josh took some statues out of the box and set them on a shelf next to him. "I don't have anything to tell you."

Frustrated, I ran my hand through my hair, trying to think of the right combination of words to make him talk. Imagining a duck with a ruler, I went into my "we have ways . . ." mentality. "I need to know what's going on. It's only fair."

Josh took the last few statues out of the box and moved them next to the other items he'd lined up on the counter. He started folding the box and his cold green eyes appraised me. He set the folded cardboard on the top of the boxes already unpacked.

"I'll tell you what Craig had on the wall under one condition." He stepped around the bar and sat in the chair, pulling a rag off the table and polishing one of the figurines, not meeting my eyes.

Why did I have the feeling this deal would be one with the devil? "Which is?"

The room quieted while we waited. Finally Josh spoke. "I want a date with your aunt."

CHAPTER 7

Sitting at my desk, my aunt's face had never been so red. "Tell me this one more time—he wants *me* to go out on a date with *him?* Is the man crazy?"

I raised my eyebrows. I'd signed another blank check for the mystery author book signing. Against my better judgment. At least after the Cloaked in Mystery event went down in flames, I'd be able to tell her "I told you so" with a clear conscience that I hadn't deliberately sabotaged it.

"Oh, give me a break. You know what I mean. It's not like I've ever said one kind word to the guy. In fact, mostly, I've been a grump about him. Maybe he's into M&M stuff."

"S&M, Jackie. M&M's is a candy." I bit my lip to keep the giggles from flowing out of me. "Think of it as a charitable act. You'll be helping save the South Cove mission wall project."

Jackie shook her head. "You're not looking at Mother Teresa here." She tapped her finger on the desk. "Stop making that damn face. I'll think about it. That's all I can promise."

Grinning, I grabbed my purse. "Thanks. I better get home. Emma's going to be whining at the door waiting for me."

"You spoil that dog. You need to get married, have kids, then you'll know what it means to be needed." Jackie focused on the computer and entering yesterday's receipts. Apparently after dispensing her bit of wisdom I'd been dismissed.

"I don't need kids to feel manipulated and drained. I have you and the business for that." I waited but my aunt didn't even take the bait. She just waggled her fingers at me. "Whatever."

Smiling, I left the office and called out a good-bye to Toby (who was explaining the process of roasting beans to a pretty blonde who didn't seem to even see the coffee in front of her). Her eyes were focused on Toby and Toby alone. I don't think the guy even knew the effect he was having on her. Then I saw a glint in his eyes when he responded and waved me off. He knew exactly what he was doing.

When Toby had been attacked on stakeout guarding me and my house, he'd lost not one but two girlfriends when they'd both showed up at the hospital ready to play nurse to the injured Toby. The man was a horndog. And his charming personality had been increasing sales since Jackie hired him. He was like having our own romance cover model in the business.

I'd made it about halfway down the road to my house when a truck pulled up next to me. Ray Stewart leaned over the bench to the open window. "Hey, beautiful, want a ride?"

I walked faster. "No, thank you. I'm fine."

"I'll say so. You are the hottest thing in this town." Ray let the truck coast next to me.

A thought made me stop. "Hey, what work did you do for Craig?"

Ray frowned. "Who said I worked for Craig?"

"You. You said you were waiting for him to pay you when I caught you eavesdropping on Josh and Craig's fight." I folded my arms and stared at him.

"Oh yeah." Ray shrugged. "I just did some stuff for him. Moving stuff from the docks to his place."

"I didn't realize you were in the moving business, too." He was lying. I could tell by the grin he'd gotten when he started to speak.

"You need some help over at your place? I'd move your bed for free." Ray leered and I took a step backward, which made him laugh.

"Leave me alone, Ray. Go see Lille if you want some attention."

My cheeks burned. Man, I wanted to punch the guy. But I didn't need another complaint about my anger issues hitting Greg's desk. Although this one charge might have been worth the trouble.

"You don't know what you're missing, honey." Ray squealed the tires and took off down the road toward the highway. Something niggled at my memory, but when I reached the house Emma distracted me before I could nail the memory down.

An hour later, after our second run of the day, Emma and I sat curled up on the porch, me on the swing and Emma on a blanket. I had a paperback in my hand and had almost forgotten about the world. Or at least this one, where I'd been accused of killing a man I'd admit to hating. But no one would accuse me of stranding poor Fifi out on the beach to drown. Thoughts of Fifi took me to Brenda's visit that morning. The woman had blossomed once she'd gotten out from under Craig's thumb. And now, with him gone, she should be able to enjoy the rest of her life. A single thought rang in my head. *Brenda was better off without Craig around* made me pause. Could she have killed her ex-husband?

Then the idea balloon all but busted over my head. Brenda would never hurt Fifi. The girl was holding back something, though, including whom she was talking to on the phone today. I tried to refocus on my book, but the spell was broken. Now I was ruminating about Craig's murder.

Standing I stretched and slipped a bookmark into the paperback. I'd promised Esmeralda I'd take a walk out to the wall, allowing the spirit to pass on their message I'd been ignoring. Besides, the way Emma kept worrying the place, I was concerned maybe a small animal had been caught in the fencing or maybe the dog was digging an escape hole. Better to get these chores done today so tomorrow I could focus on the housekeeping and laundry. I'd remodeled most of the downstairs in the last few months and I wasn't excited about starting on the second floor. No, once the mopping, dusting, and vacuuming was done tomorrow, I'd be collapsing on the couch with either a movie in the DVR player or a book in my hand. Or probably both.

"Come on, Emma. Let's see what's back at the wall." I stepped off the front porch, then turned to the right, noticing my bird-of-paradise plants blooming. I made a mental note to bring my camera out to capture the moment. I glanced up at the softening light. Maybe tomorrow morning, before the cleaning frenzy began.

I walked away from the house and Emma ran circles around me. She ran to the side fence, then back to me, then back to the house. The dog had way too much energy. I glanced at the lock on the door to the back shed, just to make sure it still was on. The lock appeared fine, but I walked over and jiggled it anyway. Habit, I guess.

Earlier in the year, I'd had some problems with people stealing the artwork stored there. Now the art was at the gallery, which seemed to sell a piece a month. Even at that pace, Miss Emily had painted so extensively during her life, they would still have paintings available for years.

Crossing the rest of the yard, I passed into the tree line and dropped down into a small valley. There, to the right, was a stone wall. Kevin, my fence contractor, had been convinced it was the remnants of the old mission and brought in the historical commission. When we'd found a fortune in Spanish coins in an old trunk mixed in with a pile of old pirate costumes, the find seemed to support Kevin's insistence.

Now, the wall's historic certification was in jeopardy because Craig Morgan didn't want to share the council's marketing money.

Or *had* been in jeopardy. Would Craig's death stop the challenge? Or would Josh keep waving the banner? I sighed. I'd probably never find out. No way would I be able to talk Jackie into dinner with the portly Josh. Her last husband had modeled for a certain hair-care product that kept him looking young. The woman had standards. High standards.

I'd arrived at the wall. Nothing. The fence still stood around the property. No holes had been dug starting Emma's escape. No small animals roved the fence, anxious about my arrival. The place was peaceful and calm.

I sat on the wall, a habit that makes Frank Gleason, the historical guy, cringe. Of course, I was also the kid who ran my hand across the stone tomb of a visiting pharaoh mummy king to the local museum. I heard a guard telling someone not to touch, but I never guessed he was talking to me. I'd been so lost in the feel of the cool stone, wondering about its history and the stories the sarcophagus could tell, I hadn't heard him. How could touching stone be a problem? I kept my hand on the coffin until the guard lifted it off. Was that what I was doing with Esmeralda's spirits? Ignoring them? Feeling foolish, I closed my eyes and whispered, "I'm here. If you want to say something, I'm here. I'm listening."

I slowed my breathing and sat, letting the quiet surround me. I heard Emma lie down next to me and she stuck her cold nose on my ankle. I jerked it back and pain seared up my leg.

"What the heck?" I reached down and felt my ankle. Blood oozed out of a small cut. I pulled my leg up onto my knee and studied the spot. A small line bled red. As I leaned closer, using my T-shirt to wipe away the blood, my cell rang. I pulled out the phone and answered, not checking the display to see who was calling. I held the shirt tight against my ankle, trying to stop the blood.

"What?"

A brief silence greeted me and I lowered the phone away from my ear, checking to see if I was still connected. "Hello?"

"Where are you?" Greg's voice filled my ear.

Tears filled my eyes. Sharp pain radiated from my ankle. I sniffed. "Sitting on the wall."

"You okay?"

I shuddered and took a breath. *Pull yourself together,* I thought. I responded, "I'm fine. I cut my leg on something."

"Can you walk?" Greg asked, sounding like the knight in shiny armor he was in real life and in our relationship.

"I think so, thanks. You must be calling to cancel?" We'd had a standing Saturday night date for months now. Greg said it was upping our relationship status.

I thought it was easier for him than remembering to ask me out week after week. Now, he only called if he wasn't coming. Like tonight.

"Wrong. The front door is locked, no one answered my knock, and I didn't see you in the backyard. I'm almost there." And with that, he clicked off the phone. Within seconds, he came over the hill and jogged toward me. Kneeling in front of me, he took the edge of the T-shirt off my cut and examined the wound.

"Hi," I said, ever the witty conversationalist.

"Hi back." He smiled up at me and I swear the birds sang and a sunlight beam broke through a cloud and shone down on him. The guy was a walking fairy-tale hero. My heart pounded watching him.

Emma greeted him, taking advantage of his lowered position to give him a wet ear kiss. The dog can be a total slut. That's all I have to say.

"Come on, Emma, that's enough," I called to my dog, not that I was jealous or anything. Well, not much.

"Let's get you back to the house so I can clean this cut and maybe pour you a glass of wine?" He swept me into his arms and started carrying me back to the house.

"Umm, I can walk, you know." I turned my head toward him and almost fell into a kiss. Instead, I leaned into his chest, the smell of his aftershave sweet and comforting.

He chuckled. "I know you can, but let me pretend you need me for a second, please? My male ego would appreciate it."

We walked—actually, he walked, I was carried—back to the house. When we got up to the stairs, he slipped me onto a chair. "Your first-aid kit in the bathroom?"

"Well, I have Band-Aids and peroxide under the sink, and a topical cream in the top drawer in the kitchen, I think. Maybe I should go find the stuff." I stood, but Greg pointed a finger at me.

"Stay," he commanded. Emma sat next to me and whined. I sat back in the chair.

"I'm going to pretend you were talking to my dog."

Greg laughed. "Emma listens better than you do." He patted her head and the tongue rolled out. The girl was a traitor. "Keep Jill here."

The dog gazed up at me and smiled one of those doggie grins. Then she scooted in front of me, effectively blocking my path away from the chair.

"Bad, bad Greg." I laughed. "Teaching my dog bad things."

"I've got to have some advantage around here. My wild animal magnetism doesn't seem to be controlling you." He opened the screen door. "I'll be right back. You have beer in the fridge?"

"Does a deer roam the woods?" I responded.

Greg shook his head. "I can't believe you read all those books, but common phrases mess you up. It's does a bear—"

I held up my hand. "I know the saying. I don't like the word the original phrase uses. Why couldn't they have coined a nicer phrase? Like does a bear hunt for berries in the woods? That's as true as the original."

"But not as funny." Greg disappeared into my house.

I absently rubbed Emma's head now as she had placed her chin on my knee for comfort as she guarded me. "I don't think the other one's funny, either," I told my dog.

She woofed a small response that I'd like to pretend was *You are smart and beautiful, I love you.* But probably the woof meant, *I'd like to eat bear crap.*

Greg handed me an opened beer when he returned and gently cleaned my wound, putting on cream and the bandage. "You may want to double your socks tomorrow if you run so you don't irritate the site."

"I may use the excuse not to run." I put my foot up on the table I'd moved in front of me and sipped my beer.

"That's another option." Greg slipped into the chair next to me and ran his hand through his hair. "God, what a day."

"I hadn't heard anything so I figured you were swamped." I knew better than to push. Sometimes if he thought I didn't care, he'd talk. When he knew I did, the man could be an information storage unit for the CIA, but without the leaks.

"You wouldn't believe how many interviews I had to do today. I didn't realize how many people in town hated Craig Morgan." He took a sip of his beer.

"Besides me, you mean."

Greg laughed. "Yes, besides you. Although your name did come up as a kind of folk hero in several interviews. You should have stood up to the guy months ago. The town would have built a statue in your honor."

"I'm not sorry I yelled at him. He was being a jerk." I peeled a corner of the beer label back. "I don't think he should have been killed, though. A lot of people are jerks."

Greg sighed. "Yes, they are. Including Ray Stewart. That man is a piece of work. He says hi, by the way."

"Insinuating that I'm interested?" My gut clenched. Lille could do so much better. Why was she even with the guy?

"Mostly wanting to see if I'd flare and go all Neanderthal to protect my woman." He banged on his chest. "Me man, you slave."

"In your dreams." I leaned back and closed my eyes, listening to the birds chirp. "Hey, talking about cavemen and their wives, Brenda stopped in the shop this morning."

"What did you think of her new look?"

My eyes flew open as I glanced at him. "Seriously, leaving Craig was the best thing that ever happened to her. Her eyes were bright, she didn't look beat down, and she must have lost enough weight to make a second person."

"Apparently they'd been talking about reconciling."

"No." I thought about the difference in the woman I saw this morning and the one who'd left town to get away from Craig. "That would have been stupid. Why would she have even considered coming back?"

"According to Brenda, Craig had changed. They'd been in couples counseling for the last three months. And in front of the counselor, he said the right things. Brenda was doubtful at the beginning, but he knew her weaknesses." Greg finished his beer, glancing at the cell phone. "I'd sure love to turn this off for the night, but with an ongoing investigation, I'd better not."

"I know. Duty calls." I glanced at my foot. "Since I'm on the injured reserve list, does that mean you'll be making dinner?"

"If clams and grilled tuna with roasted veggies sounds like dinner, I'm game." He glanced at my beer. "Ready for another?"

"Sure. But I don't have clams or tuna. We'll have to go to the store." I sat forward. "And one of us needs to stay sober to drive."

"I've already taken care of that. I stopped at the farmer's market on my way here." He nodded at the empty beer bottle. "Besides, I'm playing designated driver tonight. You, on the other hand, are enjoying yourself."

As he walked back into the kitchen for a fresh beer for me and a glass of iced tea for himself, I wondered if plying me with liquor was his way of keeping me from asking too many questions.

Then I wondered if this was going to be my last meal before he told me what he'd came to say: that I was still the one and only logical suspect in the murder of Craig Morgan.

CHAPTER 8

Dinner was on the grill and I'd finished off two more beers before Friday's canceled dinner came up. "What happened out at The Castle last night? You never said who the watchman found." I said a silent prayer, hoping it wouldn't be Nick Michael. Sadie hadn't called, but then again, we didn't really chat except when she stopped by the shop. I was a bad friend. Tomorrow, I'd call her just to chat. "Or can't you talk about it?"

If he couldn't, that would tell me a lot about what action he'd take.

He tossed the peppers, onions, and mushrooms in a grilling basket, then closed the cover, turning the heat down. I smiled. Grilling was like an art to the man. He'd bought me the grill as a housewarming present on our first date. Even though I hadn't at the time known it was a date.

He took a sip of his tea and leaned against the porch railing, his long legs crossed, still in his signature Wranglers, but instead of boots, he had a pair of sandals on his large feet. "Seriously, that watchman has worked under Craig way too long. The man's paranoid. The kids snuck onto the property for a quick swim and probably some other extracurricular stuff." He grinned at me. "Hell, I'd like to go skinny-dipping in that Grecian pool with you some warm summer night."

"So they weren't caught stealing?" Relief ran over me. "I'd been afraid—"

"You were afraid a town kid had turned cat burglar and was fencing priceless antiques?" Greg laughed. "Which kid do you suspect? The one who did their Eagle project down at the homeless shelter in San Francisco or the straight A student with a full ride to Harvard next year?"

"I know we have some great kids in town. It's just that sometimes kids can be led down a path before they even know there's a problem." I thought about Nick and his being late for work because he gave his girlfriend a ride.

"I don't see them as the hooligans Craig and Josh made them out to be. Kids will be kids. You got to let them run free or they'll do stupid stuff when they get out from under their moms' thumbs." Greg ran his hand through his sandy brown hair. He needed a trim, but when he was in the middle of a case, it tended to get longer. I liked it that way.

I watched as he went to check on the fish again. This was our first conversation about our parenting philosophies and even though we hadn't called it that, we both knew we were trotting on shaky ground. I was anxious to change the subject before I said something I couldn't take back, but I needed to ask one more question. "Who were the kids?"

Greg turned off the grill and loaded our plates with the fish and clams and veggies. "The guy was Mike Freeland. One of the juniors on the football team. I don't know if you've met him. His folks live out on one of the local orchards where his dad's a foreman."

The name sounded familiar, but I doubted I could match the face with the name. I breathed a sigh of relief. It hadn't been Nick. Sadie would have been heartbroken.

Greg slipped my plate onto one of the vintage TV trays we used outside when we grilled, which was most nights anymore. I'd found them when we'd taken a Saturday to Bakersfield trip and hit the thrift stores. "The girl's new to town, Lisa Brewer. She works at The Castle and snuck the boy in before closing."

My heart sank. Sadie wouldn't be upset at the news, but Nick would be when he found out his "girlfriend" was playing house with Mike. Maybe the upcoming breakup was a good thing. I knew from personal experience, when you're cheated on, betrayal hits hard, even when you're better off without the person in your life.

Greg waved his fork at my plate. "You not hungry or something?"

I took a bite of the tuna and sighed. The man could cook. The rest of his attributes aside, like the fact he could kiss the shoes off my feet and his wicked sense of humor, I'd keep him around for his cooking skills alone. "Amazing."

Greg smiled and bent his head back over his plate. "That's better. A man likes a little appreciation now and then."

We ate in silence. Then I brought the subject back up after I'd finished the last clam in my bucket. "Nick Michael is or was dating that girl, Lisa."

Greg shrugged. "Not my business who's sleeping with whom. You know that. But I guess by Monday when school starts, the kid will know his girlfriend had a fling. If not before."

"At least Sadie will be happy if they break up. She thinks the girl is trouble." I stood and took his plate. "You want a beer now?"

"I'd rather have one of those brownies I saw in your fridge. And maybe some coffee?" He stood and held the door open for me.

"We can make that happen." I stood on my toes and kissed his lips quickly as I passed.

Greg called for Emma and as he closed the door, I wondered when we'd become this couple. Comfortable in our routines and each other. Both of us were wary of the "m" word, having been married before to people who hadn't taken their vows of monogamy seriously. And we hadn't been dating long. But I couldn't deny we were a couple. A smile curved on my lips.

Greg noticed and came up behind me, putting his arms around my waist. "What are you thinking about?"

I poured water into the coffeemaker and turned the machine on, stalling to think about what I was going to say. Finally, I went with the obvious. "Us."

He turned me around, leaned in, and kissed me. Long, soft, but urgent. The kiss offered so much more. I reached up and locked my hands around his neck and then heard the bell at the front door. Emma barked and ran to sit in front of the door. I heard her gentle whine.

Pulling away from the kiss, I put my hands on Greg's chest.

"Do you have to answer that?" he asked, his voice husky.

"Unless you want a call to the police office reporting our lack of response and Toby showing up here." I smiled and stepped away from him. "She won't give up."

"Who?" Greg followed me into the living room.

I swung open the door. "Aunt Jackie."

My aunt burst into the room and shoved a box into my hands. The good thing about her visits was that she never came empty-handed. The bad thing was it was usually something amazing from the store, so my thoughts of skipping my run tomorrow got revised. I peeked into the box: Chocolate Dream Pie from Pies on the Fly. Kissing my aunt on the cheek, I pointed to the kitchen. "Coffee's started."

She glanced at Greg. "Standing Saturday date has turned into making my niece cook once a week?"

He laughed. "Hey, I cooked. And with everything that's going on, taking off for a real night out isn't doable right now." He shrugged, then added, "If it's any of your business."

"Everything about my niece is my business," Jackie grumbled, then walked into the kitchen, expecting us to follow.

"You'll get used to it." I grinned, taking Greg's hand and pulling him into the kitchen. Emma followed my aunt. The dog loved her. I was starting to feel like the dog loved a lot of people more than me, but maybe I was just always there.

Jackie had already poured three cups of coffee, sat out plates and silverware, and was sitting at the table waiting when we walked in. The woman moved fast.

"So what's up?" I slipped into a chair and removed the pie from the box, handing the empty box to Greg. "Set that on the counter for me."

He complied before slipping into a chair next to me. He watched as I cut wedges of the pie, sliding a plate filled with the dessert over to him. "Sadie does a mean pie."

"She came over to the shop with four of these today. Said she's been unable to sleep lately and wondered if we could take them off her hands." Jackie took a fork and bit into the slice I'd cut for her.

"Poor thing." I said, not meaning it after I took a bite, the creamy chocolate dark against the fluffy whipped cream. Sadie needed a few more sleepless nights if this was the result. "She's probably worried sick about Nick."

Jackie pointed a fork at Greg. "She's convinced you're going to knock on her door, sweep in, and arrest the boy."

"Why would I arrest Nick? The kid's a saint." Greg kept his head down, focusing on the pie.

"Who knows what goes on with that woman?" Jackie smiled at me. "I did get a discount since it was over our normal order."

Leave it to my aunt to make it seem like an inconvenience to take the offered pies. I would have probably paid Sadie double for the pain and suffering she'd experienced; Jackie, on the other hand, asked for a markdown.

"I'm sure we'll have no trouble selling these." I shook my head.

"Not true. We don't open tomorrow and who knows what shape they'll be in on Tuesday." Jackie finished off her pie and leaned back to take a sip of coffee. "But I'm not here to talk about the shop."

"Really?" Greg drawled. "I figured that would be the only reason to show up late on a Saturday night. Uninvited."

"Eat another piece of pie and shut up." Jackie shot back, a smile softening her words.

"As you order." Greg pulled the pie plate closer and served himself a slice. His phone buzzed. Glancing at the display, he groaned. "Toby. I've got to take this."

He stepped into the living room, taking his pie with him. Smiling, I turned back to Jackie. "So why are you here?"

"I've been frantic thinking about going out with Josh. Seriously, could you even imagine us as a couple?" Jackie shook her head.

"You don't have to date him forever." I reached over and put my hand on hers. "Just one date. And then he says he'll show me the evidence against the mission wall."

"Ted Bundy used to tell people just one date, too. And look how that turned out." Jackie raised her eyebrows.

I sighed. I needed to know what Josh had, sooner than later. "Look, would it make you feel better if we did a double date? You and Josh and me and Greg?"

Jackie peered at me like I'd solved an advanced algebra problem. "You sure? I mean, I wouldn't want to put you two out from this cozy domestication."

"I need to know what evidence they have against the wall. I hate to say this, but I'd go out with the man myself if I thought it would help." I leaned back, pushing the plate away, even though I desperately wanted another slice. My ankle throbbed. What the heck had I run into?

"You'd date who?" Greg turned off his phone and put his arm around me. "Do I need to be worried here?"

Bending my head back, I puckered for a kiss. "Only if you forget my birthday. Or our anniversary. Or Saint Patrick's Day. I'm a sucker for green food."

Greg kissed me gently, then took the empty plates off the table and slipped them into the sink. A total keeper. "I'm confused. We have an anniversary? I thought those happened after the whole proposal and marriage thing."

"We have lots of anniversaries." I held up my hand and started counting on my fingers. "The day we met, our first date, our first real party together . . ."

Greg laughed and added, "The day you let me get to second base."

"Whoa, hold on there, way too much information for this old woman." Jackie finished her coffee and took the cup to the sink, where Greg rinsed and slipped it into the dishwasher along with the plates. "I guess I'll see the two of you on our double date."

Greg walked over and got his own cup, filling it from the pot. He held the pot up and with a motion, asked if I wanted more. When I nodded, he walked over and refilled my cup. He glanced down at me. "Do I want to ask?"

My aunt crossed the kitchen and gave me a hug. "You might want to bring the boy up to speed, dear. It's your party."

I watched my aunt leave and waited until I heard the front door close behind her. Then I turned and faced Greg. "Josh is blackmailing me. If Jackie goes out with him, he'll show me the evidence they were going to give the historical commission."

"I don't think that's the legal definition of blackmail." Greg pulled me to my feet. "You want to watch a movie?"

I nodded, limping to the living room with him. "Can you get me some painkillers from the bathroom?"

"Heavy duty or over the counter?"

"Over the counter. Anything stronger and I'll be snoring in ten minutes max." I eased down into the couch.

"So what difference would that be? You usually sleep through our movie nights," Greg teased.

I threw a couch pillow at him. "Snot."

"Angel," he countered.

It's hard to be mad at a man who calls you names like that.

CHAPTER 9

Josh appeared to be having a heart attack, his face beet red. He slipped into a chair next to a large rolltop desk I'd been considering for the shop, until I glanced at the sales price. I didn't want to have to even think about performing CPR on the guy. "Are you okay?"

He pulled an off-white handkerchief out of his pocket and wiped his brow. While he pulled himself together, I peeked over at the counter. The folder with the receipts from Craig had been put away. I quickly refocused my attention on Josh. He was nodding, then he glanced up at me. He swallowed, then in a voice sounding like it came from a squeaky toy rather than the heavyset man in front of me, he whispered, "I never thought she'd agree."

Weird. Then why did he ask me to ask? Pushing the thought away, I took advantage of my upper hand and Josh's apparent shock. "There are some conditions. It's a double date. You can't touch her." My mind raced, thinking of other stipulations to push the situation. "And I get to see the evidence now, before the deal is set."

"What's to stop you from backing out?" Josh narrowed his eyes and watched me, suspicion in his gaze.

"Greg will hold us accountable. No way would he want the mayor to find out he welched on a deal." Which was only partly true. Greg had made his feelings clear on the subject. I already owed him for the outing with Hank and Amy. However, I'd keep my end of the bargain. But I didn't trust Josh to keep his once he got what he wanted. "That's the deal, take it or leave it, I don't care. But we won't be having this conversation a second time."

"Hold on, let me think." Josh leaned back in the wooden chair and I thought I heard the wood groan under his weight. Apparently either it was common or Josh was deaf when he had on his thinking cap.

While he pondered the deal, I pretended to step closer to the cash register to thumb through a box of vintage *Life* magazines. I slipped the receipts I'd copied back at the shop into my right hand, outside of Josh's view. All I needed to do was reach over the top of the counter. I inched my arm upward, then jerked back when Josh spoke. The thick receipt paper slipped through my hands. "Okay. But I get to pick the restaurant. And I'm only buying mine and your aunt's dinner. The two of you have to pay for your own." Josh tapped the desk with his portly finger.

"That's fine. Next Friday night, we'll meet at the shop." I kicked the papers under the counter and walked back toward Josh. "So what were you going to show the commission?"

"Not *going to*, *am* going to show the commission. Just because Craig is gone"—Josh paused and eyed me like it was my fault Craig Morgan was dead. After a couple of beats, he continued—"just because it's only me now, doesn't mean I'm not going to honor his final wishes."

Even if it burns me in the process? I wondered. But I bit my tongue. I was making progress with the man, even if it was at a glacier pace.

He nodded to the back. "I've got the journal in my office safe." He pulled himself to his feet and lumbered to the back of the building. I followed, not knowing if I'd been invited or not, but he didn't stop me, so I must have guessed correctly.

My phone buzzed with a text message. Glancing down, I saw Greg's quick note: *Heading to Bakerstown, will be back soon. Need anything?*

I typed a quick response asking him to stop at the bakery and pick up an assortment of muffins and several loaves of French bread. Okay, so it was a shopping list, but I did text "thanks" at the end. The man knew how to stay on my good side; mostly, it involved food. Fresh loaf bread was one of my favorite things in the world. Besides my boyfriend.

Josh stood behind his desk watching me. When I clicked off the phone and went into the small, dark office, he shook his head. "You need to stop wasting busy people's time. Anyway, here we are."

I glanced at the small, leather-bound book sitting on a piece of parchment on the desktop. Carefully, Josh opened the book and went right to the page he'd been looking for. He spun the parchment around so I could see the hand-drawn map. Leaning down, I could make out the ocean and several crude marks. The words weren't in English.

There in the middle of the page, right where the current court-house would stand if this was a map of South Cove, was an *X* mark and the words, *Misión de estrellas meridionales.* I glanced up at Josh. "You think this is the mission site? City Hall?"

"I don't think, I know. The map shows the location of the mission is a good three miles from your house. Maybe your wall is the residuals of a long-ago barn. But it's clearly not the mission. The mission no longer exists."

Walking down the street toward the diner, my thoughts swirled around Josh's evidence. I'd taken several shots of the page with my cell phone until Josh protested the light from the flash might damage the paper or ink. What should I do with the photos? Greg could send the photos to his university professor friend to verify the wording. I could go to Frank and press him to speed up the certification, but what if Josh turned out to be right?

Then my wall would go back to being a garden wall and I could go back to running my business. Maybe even put up a hammock out near the site for a reading cove.

But what if Josh was wrong, and Frank didn't find out in time? Then a national historic site would have been ignored and destroyed. I couldn't just leave it to someone else to decide. I'd come to love the little stone wall. Stupid, I know, but it meant a lot to me. And if it was the original mission site, it had a right to survive.

Besides, Craig couldn't be right. Not this time. I pulled the door open to the almost full restaurant, waved at Lille behind the counter, who responded with a dirty look. Great, this should be a fun break-fast. When Lille was in a mood, the entire dining room knew it. Often people from town came into the shop for dessert after being run out of the diner by the grumpy owner. I wasn't complaining; bad customer service that threw business my way was good. I felt bad for Lille. Most of the time, her bad moods were caused by one thing. Or, more accurately, one man—Ray Stewart.

I slipped into the booth across from Amy, who was on her cell. She air-kissed me while still talking to Hank.

"A drive down the coast sounds perfect." Amy grinned. "Sure, we can take my truck. I've been meaning to get it out anyway."

Amy was a California girl through and through. She reeked granola. Her Datsun truck was a 1970 something and had fewer miles on it than my aunt's leased sedan she traded in every couple years. I played with my fork, waiting for her to finish her call.

"Look, Jill's here. I'll see you in two hours?" Amy giggled as she listened. "Okay, an hour. But I might be late. Girl talk takes time, you know."

Gag me, I thought as I refolded the paper napkin. How in the world was this guy turning my surfing-loving friend into his Stepford girlfriend? *Keep your mouth shut* was going to have to be my mantra for the next hour. Amy finished her call.

"Sorry about that. Hank and I are taking a drive up the coast." Amy closed her phone and laid it on the table.

"Sounds nice," I said, trying to mean it. I asked another question, just to seem interested. "What else are you doing?"

Amy sighed. "I guess he has a friend who has to move out of his apartment."

I'd taken an unfortunate sip of water right then and I coughed the water out of my nose. Grabbing my napkin, I stared at her. "Your big date is helping someone move? Using your truck?"

"Don't act like that. It's sweet he wants to help out a friend. It's a good trait in a person." Amy studied her menu, avoiding my stare.

"Sometimes I think you're too nice for your own good." I leaned forward, ready to tick off the long list of why Hank wasn't the one and why Amy should run while she still had a chance. A cup crashed in front of me. Jumping back, the steam from the coffee pouring into the cup in front of me felt like it had been brewed on the sun. "Hey, watch it."

Taking my napkin, I wiped up the spilled coffee and looked up into Lille's face. Her eyes burned. "Sorry," she barked. She leaned close to me. "Look, you stay away from Ray, you hear me?"

I frowned and shook my head. "Lille, I'm not interested in Ray. I'm dating Greg. The police detective?"

"So you're using my Ray to make your man jealous? That's mean." The coffeepot in Lille's hand shook, and I saw Amy move closer to the edge of the booth, preparing to run.

"I'm not using Ray. Look, the guy stopped me on the street twice. I told him to go see you and leave me alone. He's the problem, Lille, not me."

Her face turned even redder, if possible. "So you admit to being with him."

"I talked to him. The day Craig was killed, he was outside Josh's shop, listening to their fight. Then yesterday when I walked home, he drove by and talked at me through the truck window. I am not seeing him or even nice to him when he talks to me." I put up my hands in surrender. "What do you want me to do? Ignore him? Tell Greg he's bothering me? What?"

Lille looked like she wanted to roast me over a slow fire and eat me for lunch. "Oh, you'd like that. Getting your man all up in Ray's face—going white knight for you. Stop the games, missy. I'm on to you."

I watched Lille storm away from the table. I felt the eyes of everyone in the restaurant focus on me, trying to see how I would react. Great, now I was Mata Hari trying to steal away husbands and boyfriends from the good women of South Cove. Of course, everyone, except Lille, knew what a jerk Ray was, so maybe I'd be fine.

Maybe.

Carrie stepped up to the booth. "Man, you've got Lille worked up. If you ask me, Ray should be locked up for being sleazy. Everyone knows he's involved in some shady business." Carrie glanced back at her boss, who was fighting with the cash machine. It appeared the register was winning. Carrie sighed. "Well, everyone but Lille. She has too good of a heart. She'd take in a devil in red and believe it when the guy said he was going to a costume party."

Lille, kindhearted? Not my vision of the woman who'd chewed me up and spit me out with a warning to stay away from her man. God, I felt like I was living a country-and-western song.

"Look, can we order? My boyfriend needs some help today so I'm on a tight schedule." Amy tried to move the conversation back to business.

"Sure, honey. I'll even watch your food so Lille doesn't poison you." Carrie pulled out her pad. Seeing what must have been shocked looks on both of our faces, she laughed. "Joking, guys. Man, doesn't anyone on the coast have a sense of humor?"

"Sorry, Carrie." I ordered a mushroom and Swiss omelet along with a short stack of French toast even though my appetite had disappeared. Best new diet around, have someone yell at you twice before breakfast. Three times for lunch. And if you even see another person before dinner, you'll be cringing under your bed and lose weight in no time.

Amy gave Carrie her order, then glanced at me. "Boy, you have her going."

"Wrong." My voice came out louder than I'd planned. I lowered my voice and said, "Ray has her going. I can't believe the slime even told her about him hitting on me. Of course, in his version, I must have been the aggressor. Me. Right."

"Sometimes it's hard in a relationship. You never quite know what's going on even if they say they're telling you the truth." She glanced at the phone.

I held my breath, waiting for her to crack the door open a bit more before I told her Hank was a swine. Then her face brightened and the moment was gone. "So did you talk to the ghost Esmeralda says is trying to reach you?"

I shook my head. Taking a sip of the excellent coffee, I wondered how long, if this Ray thing kept up, that my shop would be the diner's bean source. Lille had a temper and I couldn't afford to be on her bad side long. I paused. "I went out to the wall where Emma's been pointing for the last few days. Nothing. I even did the *woo-woo* open-your-self-up-to-the-cosmos thing. Nada. Not a niggle."

"Maybe you're not sensitive to the other world," Amy mused, stirring cream into her coffee, a habit I'd never see her do before.

76 • *Lynn Cahoon*

"And maybe I was an idiot to listen to Esmeralda." Before we could get into a full-blown discussion of the reality or not of the other side, Carrie came back with our food.

"Here you go. The kitchen has its money on you, by the way." Carrie smiled at me. "The wait staff is backing Lille. Sorry, but she does have the weight advantage."

I salted my omelet. "What are you talking about?"

"The cat fight over Ray. The cooks think you can take her in less than three minutes. Nick even joined in the pool. He's supporting you." Carrie grinned. "Can I bring you anything else?"

"Like a gun?" I smiled. Then her words hit me. "Hey, how's Nick doing? He been showing up for work lately?"

Carrie frowned. "Not sure why you're asking, but yeah, he's been consistently on time. I think his mom read him the riot act. Probably threatened to take away his computer time or something."

I thought about the kid skateboarding down the street yesterday. He'd seemed lighter without the truck Sadie had taken away. Easygoing. Maybe he was thinking being a kid wasn't a bad thing after all.

Too bad his heart would be broken when he found out about his girl.

When Carrie went away from the booth, Amy and I ate in silence, not wanting to say something to make the other feel bad. Finally a safe subject popped into my head.

"Greg and I are going on a double date next Friday." I played with the cheese on my plate. For the first Sunday in forever, I didn't feel like eating.

Amy's eyes brightened. "Toby has a steady girl?"

"Is the moon blue?" I laughed. Toby liked his relationships short and sweet. With no ties to bind him. The man was in love with falling in love. "Actually we're going with Aunt Jackie and Josh."

Amy set her fork down. "Your aunt is going on a date with Josh Thomas?"

I kept my head down, sure I'd burst out laughing if I saw Amy's face. "Yep."

I could feel Amy's scrutiny before she asked, "On purpose?"

I laughed. "There is a bit of coercion. Josh agreed to show me the evidence against the wall if Aunt Jackie went out with him. The double date was her compromise. I think she's hoping Greg will shoot him if Josh gets fresh."

"Could be." Amy dug into her pancakes. "Wait, has he shown you it?"

I nodded and pulled out my phone. Flipping through the screens I found the best picture and enlarged it. "It's a hand-drawn map in some journal." I handed her the phone.

She studied the picture, then handed the phone back. "If that's true, the mission was over by City Hall. That's close to two miles from the site in your backyard."

I pushed the half-empty plate away from me. "Yeah, I know."

Amy took the phone back. "Where did he get this?"

I thought about my conversation with Josh. "I don't know." I glanced at my friend, who appeared lost in thought. "Does it matter?"

"Maybe not. I have a friend who's an expert in California history stuff. He's been champing at the bit to meet you and get a peek at the wall, but he's been on a lecture tour. He's coming into town next week. You want me to set something up?" Amy pulled out a notepad and wrote down a reminder note.

I'd taught her that trick. Before she started with the reminder pad, the woman couldn't remember her own birthday. "I'm home every night except Friday. Have him come over when he can."

I could use all the help I could get trying to fight Josh in his campaign to honor Craig's memory. Seriously, the guy was dead and he still messed with my life.

CHAPTER 10

Leaving Amy outside the restaurant to wait for Hank, I headed over to see Aunt Jackie. Greg was working the case, some meeting with the district attorney or something so our late morning newspaper reading on the back porch had been cancelled. I hoped he would make the "grill whatever's in the refrigerator" traditional Sunday meal. Then we could snuggle on the couch with a movie. It was my turn to pick, and by God, romantic comedy was on the menu. I might have already put the DVD on top of the DVR player.

I climbed the steps to my old apartment, now my aunt's home. I knocked and noticed she'd set out some red geraniums on the porch. There must have been ten pots filled with the cheerful flowers. Not Jackie's usual style, but nice.

I heard the slap of plastic on the hardwood floors. When she opened the door, you would have thought she was leaving to go out on the town. But sequins and pearls were Jackie's everyday casual outfit bling. Today was no exception. The long red halter dress would have been red carpet–worthy, especially with the diamond she wore around her neck. The only sacrifice she made to the comfort gods were the flip-flops on her feet. The woman had stood for years, running her own successful coffee shop in the city. Now she took care of her feet. Or at least kept them off the stilettos she used to wear.

She glanced at me, then her gaze dropped to the flowers. "Jill, I'm glad to see you, but you didn't have to bring flowers. You know I don't have a green thumb."

Confused, I pointed to the pots. "You didn't plant these?"

Jackie laughed, a sound reminding me of a train groaning to pull its load. "Me? Garden? What are you thinking?"

"Well, if you didn't do this and I swear I didn't bring them here, that leaves only one option."

Jackie eyeballed me, daring me to say it.

"You have a secret admirer." I moved around her and went to sit in her living room. "Coffee on?"

Jackie took a long minute before she turned from the door. "It's that man, isn't it?"

"What man?" I figured if I wanted coffee, I was going to have to get it myself.

Jackie closed the door, stared at it, then twisted the dead bolt to keep the flowers from coming inside. She leaned against the door, watching me pour a cup. "That's the new chocolate brew I bought out of a Seattle house. I'm thinking of offering it at the shop, starting with the mystery tour night." She focused on me. "It's Josh Thomas. He's my secret admirer."

I sipped the warm, chocolaty blend with a touch of dark coffee— amazing. "You know this? Or you're guessing?"

Jackie picked up her cup from the coffee table, then motioned to the small table near the east window. "It makes sense. Who else would leave me flowers and crystals?"

"Honestly, Jackie." I slipped into one of the dining room chairs. "You're such a flirt. You may not know who sent you those flowers. And it could have been a different person than whoever sent the flowers."

"You're saying I have two stalkers?" Aunt Jackie sighed. "You sure know how to make a girl feel safe."

"Drama queen," I teased.

She arched an eyebrow at me. "Foster child."

"I wasn't a foster child, but you are a drama queen," I reminded her.

Jackie shrugged. "I wasn't sure what the game was we were playing. I thought it was say-a-random-thought day."

"With you, every day is random-thought day."

"So true." She grinned. "Why are you here today? Where's your hot muffin?"

"I'm going to tell him you said that."

Jackie took a sip off coffee. "Who cares? I'm an old woman. No one corrects an old woman. We can get away with anything."

No truer statement had ever been said. The woman was a natural at getting her own way. "I've never heard you call yourself old."

Jackie shrugged. "Trying it out. Thought maybe you'd feel guilty for pimping me out."

I sputtered in my coffee. "I'm not pimping you . . ." Then I saw her face. The woman knew how to tweak my buttons. I set the cup in front of me and wiped my face. "I came over to visit. See what's going on with you. You know, like family?"

"I saw you last night. So what do you want to talk about?" My aunt tapped her manicured nails on the table.

I ran my finger around the top of the coffee cup, not looking at her. "I'm worried about Amy. This Hank guy has her acting strange. Not like herself at all. She's taking her Datsun to help someone move up the coast."

She paused. "That sounds exactly like Amy. Caring, helpful, willing to give someone her last dime."

"Well, yeah, but . . ." What was I trying to say? "She's doing whatever Hank wants. She thinks whatever Hank thinks. It's like she's been brainwashed."

"More like it sounds like love." Jackie stood and refilled my cup. "I was the same way with your uncle. The things I'd wanted for so long fell by the wayside because I wanted to spend time with him more."

"She hasn't even surfed in over a month." I sipped the coffee, thinking. "I mean, it's like she's changed, inside and out."

"People change all the time. Just keep being there for her. Either she'll find her way back to the Amy she used to be on her own, or the man will do something and she'll realize what she's given up. It takes time." Jackie put her hand on mine. "You changed when you started dating Greg."

"I did not." But something in my brain niggled at the thought. "Did I?"

"Not as dramatically as Amy maybe, but you are more thoughtful about your wild ideas. Maybe even settled in your routine." She squeezed my hand. "It's not a bad thing, dear. People grow up, especially when they are in a relationship."

This wasn't the pep talk I'd wanted when I decided to come over to see my aunt. I'd wanted her to help me stage a "Hank intervention" and cleanse Amy of the demon who had her in his clutches. Instead, I'd been told people change. I decided it was long past time to change the subject.

"So I saw Josh today."

She sighed. "Where are we going? Please tell me it's someplace dark."

I opened my eyes wide in mock astonishment. "Such a bad girl."

Waving my comment away, she smiled. "I can be, but for this, I don't want anyone seeing us and getting the wrong idea."

"Like you're out on a date," I pushed.

"Exactly."

I pulled out my phone. "I don't know where we're going, but it's set for next Friday so be ready." I found the picture of the map and showed it to her. "Have you ever seen this?"

She pulled out reading glasses and studied the photo. She switched back and forth from the several photos I'd taken. Finally she took her glasses off and laid the phone on the table. She pointed to the mission site on the map. "This isn't your property."

"I know."

"Has Greg seen this?" She focused on my face, concern filling her eyes.

I shook my head. "Josh only showed me this morning. Greg's working on the case, big hush-hush detective stuff."

"Then you might want to delete that map before he does." Jackie leaned back in her chair watching me.

"I don't understand. Why shouldn't I show this to Greg? Maybe it would help him with the case."

Jackie stood and took her cup to the sink. She stared out the window to the apartment's view of the ocean. I came behind her and put my cup in the sink, too. "Jackie?"

"That map would help Greg solve the case." She turned and studied me. "Doesn't Amy save old building design blueprints in her job?"

I studied my aunt. She had a faraway look in her eyes. "Yeah. She manages the library of prints for the entire town." I still didn't know where Jackie was going, but I was ready to climb on the train if it meant proving me innocent.

"I'll head over there first thing Monday morning and see if there is any mention in the design plan about the old mission. If they dug to build City Hall, they would have had to tear down any remnants of the mission before they could build." Jackie tapped her polished nail on the table, thinking through her game plan.

"Building records would show that?" I was skeptical.

Aunt Jackie narrowed her gaze on me. "What did you fill out to paint your house?"

Pages and pages of history on the house, the historical paint color of the house, the paint colors of the surrounding houses, and what I was naming my firstborn. "Everything. They wanted to know everything."

"Exactly. What makes you think yesterday's council loved paper any less than today's?"

"What time do you want to meet?"

We talked for a few more minutes, making a plan for tomorrow. For the first time, I felt more in control of the rumors swirling around me. Hell, if I'd been on the jury with this type of circumstantial evidence, I'd be the first to quote the old adage about smoke and fire. Walking home, the cool ocean breeze kept tossing my hair into my face, teasing me into smiling.

I went to do laundry, but didn't have soap. When I went to get a cold drink, I was out of soda. Emma threw up on the living room couch. Finally, I gave up. I decided to quit moping around and put into place the fake-it-until-you-make-it methodology. I got one free Sunday a month, I wasn't going to spend it being a depressed dork.

I escorted the still-heaving Emma out to the backyard with a bowl of water. I cleaned up the mess in the living room. And after checking out the kitchen cabinets and refrigerator, I made a quick shopping list.

Driving north, I turned off the news and tuned in to a soft rock upbeat station and sang in an off-key manner my way to the Shop A Lot on the edge of Bakerstown. Most of the shop owners did their personal shopping on Monday, not wanting to close during the weekend. But once a month, Coffee, Books, and More didn't open on Sundays. We normally closed Monday and then, Toby and I handled the shop on Tuesdays with shortened hours. My chances were slim that I'd run into anyone from town, thereby ruining my pretend happy mood.

As soon as I entered the produce section, Esmeralda pushed her cart forward, blocking my movement. Her cart filled with the makings of a nice salad. I guess I couldn't fault her for not supporting the local farmers' markets up and down the coast, since I was at the same chain grocery store. Pushing up the volume on my fake smile, I greeted her. "I didn't think I'd run into anyone from South Cove today." I nodded to her cart. "Nice salad stuff."

The woman took my arm. Her hundreds of silver bracelets jangled as she grabbed. "You are worried."

"I'm good, really."

Esmeralda ignored me. Waving her free hand over my body, she closed her eyes, then her movements stopped and her eyes flew open in surprise. "You have found a path. But the road will lead others to the wrong conclusion, but you . . . you will find the truth in this journey. Follow it."

An elderly couple gave us a wide berth with their cart. I waved, trying to smile. The woman didn't have any boundaries. When the prophecy hit, it hit. I wondered what she did in the shower. Maybe she had one of those shower notepads I'd seen advertised on late-night television?

"Jill? Are you listening to me?" Esmeralda's voice brought me back out of my mental wanderings.

"Sorry, I thought I knew those people." I nodded toward the couple who now were close to running, trying to get away from us.

Esmeralda glanced at the retreating couple. "Doubtful," she responded. "I think you were ignoring me."

"I was not." My shoulders squared as I faced her. "I'm supposed to follow a road even though it will be wrong."

"No, the road is correct, but others will think it foolhardy."

Shaking my head, I put a hand out to stop her rambles. "Seriously, Esmeralda, I know you believe this stuff, but I've got a lot on my mind right now."

"Just follow the path." Esmeralda glanced at her cart. "Oops, I almost forgot shrimp for the salad."

And she turned and left me. The tornado known as Esmeralda had passed. All I had of the encounter was a general statement to follow some road. "I need to find me a real psychic rather than this wannabe fortune-teller," I mumbled to the Asian pears.

I pushed the cart farther into the produce section and was choosing between several varieties of apples out of the large selection when I heard my name called again. Maybe I should have tried the farmers' market, it might have been less crowded. The person called out "Jill" a second time. Certainly there were more Jills in the world than me? Spinning around I saw Tina Baylor and His Honor the Mayor standing behind her, pushing a grocery cart. I had to say, the cart looked good on him. Like he could do a day's worth of manual labor, something I hadn't believed to be true.

"Jill? That is you. I told Marvin it was you, but he didn't believe me." She turned and smiled at her husband. "Did you, dear? He asked what you'd be doing out of South Cove, but your sweet little shop is closed on Sunday this week, right?"

"Yep. It's a short reprieve, but we enjoy the extra day off." Seriously, I could have opened the store today if I had known everyone from town would want to chat. Fake it, I reminded myself as I pasted back on my smile, my jaw already hurting. "You guys shopping?"

The mayor gawked at me like I was stupid. He opened his mouth to respond, but his wife threw him a look, stopping the words he'd been about to say.

"Just a few things. We're hosting a family barbeque later. Just a small affair. Maybe you and Greg could come?" The woman appeared hopeful.

"Actually, I think he's working tonight and I already accepted another offer." Make it vague, I thought. She didn't need to know my offer was from my couch.

"Too bad, maybe next time. Come along, dear." The mayor started the cart moving.

"Now, hold on a second, the girls aren't done talking here." She studied me. "Men, they act like they are going to be humiliated if they are found in a grocery store by one of their buddies. I had to drag him here. Does Greg help you with the household chores?"

"I think he has enough of his own." *And his ex-wife's,* I added silently. "I'm pretty self-sufficient."

"Oh, no matter, I'm sure that will change when the two of you move in together." She actually winked at me. "Once you get them hooked on the honey, they'll do anything you want."

I could feel my face warm. "It was great talking to you." I shoved four Gala apples into a plastic bag.

"Wait, there was one more thing." She stepped in front of my cart.

"I have to go," I said, even though I didn't.

"This will only take a second." She glanced around the produce section. Satisfied the corn was the only thing with ears, she leaned closer. "Who is the secret mystery author? Tell me it's Stephen King. I love his books."

"Stephen King isn't a mystery author. His work is mostly horror, or sometimes thriller." Of course this woman would know that if she actually shopped for books in my shop. "I've got a great selection of his works at the shop. You should come in and browse one day soon."

Tina Baylor appeared crestfallen. "Oh. I thought maybe since he has a book coming out that week . . ."

"It's a good guess, but even if it was Stephen King, I couldn't tell you because my aunt hasn't told me." I shrugged. "I guess we'll both be surprised."

"You have to be kidding." She glanced at her husband. "You're telling me you don't know? Is there even an author coming in that night?"

"Yes, there's an author. I don't know who it is because my aunt knows I can't keep a secret to save my life." I moved the cart around her. "I do hope I'll see you on the reveal night. It should be fun."

As I walked away, I heard Tina whisper to her husband, "You were right. She doesn't know anything. What a waste. I guess Greg likes them dumb."

I bit my lip to keep from responding. She knew I could still hear her. Now I knew who could stand to be married to Mayor Baylor, the meanest man in South Cove.

Someone just like him.

I kept my head down for the rest of the shopping trip, trying to get through the store without running into anyone who might know me, or my aunt, or even a person from South Cove.

I turned the corner into the laundry detergent aisle and ran my cart right into Mayor Baylor. He stood there staring at me, a box of fabric sheets in his hand. "Miss Gardner," he almost hissed the words. "I wanted to tell you that even though Mr. Morgan has passed on, you're still on notice with the historical commission. I'm sure they'll find that your wall is nothing more than old bricks."

Then he walked to the front of the aisle, where I saw Tina and the cart waiting for him. She narrowed her eyes as he came toward her and without another word, disappeared toward the checkout lanes.

I felt numb. Not only were Craig and Josh part of this campaign against the wall certification, now the mayor wasn't even trying to hide the fact that he supported their bid. I slowly walked through the rest of the store. I didn't want to talk to anyone. I'd reached the dairy section and was standing in front of a selection of cheese with the finish line in sight when I felt a touch on my shoulder.

Greg stood there, a package of steaks in his hand. He kissed me on the top of my head, then asked, "Did you get beer?"

CHAPTER 11

Greg followed me home and pulled his truck into the driveway right behind my Jeep, currently overheating from the drive. Steam poured out from under the hood.

He pulled sacks out of the back of the Jeep. "You need to go buy a new car."

"I know. Hey, I'm going into Bakerstown again tomorrow to talk to Frank, maybe you could meet me over at the car dealership?" I grabbed the last of the groceries out of the car and closed the door with my hip.

Greg held the gate open for me. "Sorry, I've got a meeting with the DA at three and I'm still not ready. This case is becoming a royal pain in the butt."

"Figures. Craig was a pain when he was alive, why would his death be any different?" I grinned as I put the key in the lock and swung the door open.

"Not funny, Suspect Number One." Greg moved past me into the kitchen. I shut the front door with my foot and followed him after tossing my purse and keys on a table in the entry.

"Seriously, the rumor around town is that my boyfriend, the police detective, cleaned up the evidence against me." I opened the back door and Emma charged inside. I knelt down and hugged my dog. "At least you love me, don't you, sweetheart."

He came close and pulled me up into a hug. "She's afraid you won't be around to feed her if you go to jail."

"So not funny." I gazed into his face and he leaned down and kissed me. The stress left my body and I melted into his strong arms.

After thoroughly kissing me, he touched my nose as he stared at me. "I didn't mean it as funny. You still have the strongest motive for killing Craig."

"Everyone in town had a motive for killing Craig." I filled Emma's food dish and took her water bowl to the sink. As I ran water to wash and fill the container, Greg pulled two longnecks from the refrigerator. He opened both, set mine next to the sink, and took a long swig out of his.

"I read somewhere the taste of beer sends messages to the plea-sure sections of your brain." He set the bottle down, then started un-packing the sacks. A part of me wondered if Aunt Jackie was right, that we were too comfortable with each other. The other part of me told that part to shut up and let the man work.

I set the water bowl down on Emma's rug. She ignored it, choos-ing to stay focused on the dog food. "Then I guess all you need is a taste. Seems a waste of the rest of the bottle."

Greg grinned and my heart fell to my feet. The man could seri-ously grin. "So true." He put the package of steaks on the counter. "We're grilling, right?"

"Is there another answer?" I sat at the table.

He joined me. "We could go out."

"We just got back from Bakersfield, now you want to drive there again?" I pulled at the edge of the label on the bottle.

"Not really. We could go to Lille's," he offered.

"I ate breakfast there. I'd rather stay home." I took a sip of the beer.

Greg nodded. "Me, too. I wanted to make sure you did want to stay put. My job forces us to stay in a lot. I hope you don't mind."

"I kind of figured it went with the territory when I started dating you. What am I going to say, quit your job?" Apparently Aunt Jackie's comment bothered him more than I'd realized.

"You wouldn't be the first." Greg reached over and took my hand in his.

I squeezed. "I'm not Sherry." I'd never met Greg's ex but she'd called enough times when we were together I felt like I knew her. And not in a good way.

"Thank God for that." Greg seemed to consider something. "You know I don't think you killed Craig, right?"

I nodded. "I would worry if you did. But am I really the best suspect?"

Greg smiled, but his grin was sad. "You fought with him twice in front of witnesses hours before his death. He was trying to undercut the marketing funding for any business besides The Castle. And there are rumors he was working with Josh to get the mission wall project blackballed by the historical commission."

"Well, when you put it like that, I guess I'd even find myself guilty." I sighed. "Is it going to be okay?"

"I won't let them railroad you. I'm going to find the killer, Jill. I promise." His phone buzzed. "Tox reports are expected in soon. I'd better take this."

I nodded. Watching him walk out of the room, a touch of fear grabbed me. I decided it was time to start cooking. Food cures all fear. Or something like that. I pulled the lettuce and salad ingredients out on the sink. Washing the Bibb lettuce made me think of Esmeralda and her cart filled with produce. And her direction—*Follow the path.* What path was I on? I'd been trying to keep the wall from being called a fraud, keep my aunt in line at the shop, and keep Greg from having to arrest me for Craig's murder.

Which path was my salvation? One or all?

By the time Greg came back into the kitchen, I'd finished the salad, started some water to boil for a pasta salad, and seasoned the steaks with a spicy rub I'd picked up at the store. And I'd made my game plan for tomorrow.

He glanced at my progress and smiled. "I'll go start the grill."

"Did you get results?" I put my hand on his arm, slowing his movement.

He turned back and smiled. "I did. Not sure what they mean, but Jill, I think we have a lead. Finally."

And then he left the kitchen whistling. Apparently, his lead wouldn't be pillow talk.

Jackie's car sat parked outside City Hall when I arrived the next morning. She'd driven less than a block and a half from the apartment. I'd walked almost a half mile. When she slipped out of the sedan, I saw the reason. She'd dressed in a little black dress with stiletto heels. Her spy outfit, apparently.

"Ready?" she whispered.

"After you." My aunt made me smile most days, but she'd outdone herself this morning. She was carrying an honest-to-God briefcase. Probably one of Uncle Ted's that she couldn't bear to part with.

Amy smiled as we approached her desk. "Hey, guys, what brings you out on a Monday? I figured you'd be over in the city today."

I gave Amy a quick hug. "Look, we've got a favor. We need to do some research in the building permits. Can we?"

Amy shrugged. "Sure. I've been working in the back files trying to get everything in order, but I haven't finished the project. Do you know what you're looking for? Miss Emily's house or the shop building?"

Aunt Jackie leaned forward. "Neither. We want to look at the City Hall permits."

"For this building?" Amy pointed downward. "Why?"

"We're trying to confirm or deny what was on this property before the building was built. Have you done any research on the building?" I knew if anyone had researched the building, it would be my friend. Amy was a city planner by profession, but she cobbled together a full-time job here in South Cove by being the mayor's receptionist as well as the city planner.

"Not much, but I can show you what I've got." She keyed the phone so that calls would go directly to voice mail and grabbed some keys and a BE RIGHT BACK sign from her desk.

We followed her down the hall to the last door, Aunt Jackie's heels clicking on the fake marble floor. Entering the room, Amy flipped on the lights and I heard a faint skittering. My skin crawled. Mice. Stacks of boxes lined the room on three sides with a single table and a chair in the middle, the fluorescent lamp hanging loose out of the ceiling over the top. A row of black filing cabinets ran the fourth wall.

"Love what you've done so far," I joked.

Amy swatted my arm. "Give me a break. You wouldn't believe how much stuff I've already gone through. This used to be two rooms of boxes."

She walked over to the filing cabinets. "I don't have many of the early papers unboxed, but what I do have is here." She touched the first cabinet.

"And if it's not there?" Jackie asked, looking down at her black dress in horror, brushing imaginary dust off the hem.

Amy walked over to the far corner of the room. "I'm thinking these boxes. I tried to keep everything together, but I had an intern help with the moving, so who knows where she put things."

I pointed Jackie to the file cabinet. "You take the files; I'll go through the boxes." I grabbed the top one and moved it to the table.

"I'll get another chair." Amy left the room.

Jackie sighed and opened the first drawer. "I guess I was assuming micro-filmed records. Who keeps actual paper?"

"South Cove, apparently." I blew off the dust on the box as Amy slipped in with a chair.

I opened the first box and pulled out a file. "Hey, do you want me to try to sort as I'm going through this?"

Amy smiled. "Sure. I'll bring in some file folders and you can put the paperwork into piles by year." She stood at the door. "The mayor's out today so I have some time. Do you want me to take a box to my desk?"

With Amy's help, we'd be through this a lot faster. "If you don't tell your boss what we're looking for."

Amy grabbed a box and walked back to the hallway. "Believe me, I don't tell my boss a lot of things."

Three hours later, we still hadn't found any records or maps showing the beginnings of South Cove. I glanced at my watch. "I'm supposed to meet Frank over at the historical commission at noon."

"Go. I'll work here for another hour or so, but if I don't find anything, I'll come back tomorrow." Jackie brushed dust off a file she'd brought out of the bottom drawer. "With a mousetrap."

"Call me if you find anything." I tucked the files I'd been collecting into the box and walked it out to Amy. She was on the phone. The last box I'd brought out she'd already scanned and separated into appropriate files, all ready to go into the next empty cabinet. She waved me off, making the "call me" sign with her hand.

My meeting with Frank Gleason was about as productive as the morning had been. He pretended we hadn't had an appointment when I cornered him at the historical commission.

He walked away from me as I approached. "I have nothing new to report. You wasted a trip."

"Have you seen their evidence?" I held up my phone. "I have a peek right here. We need to get ahold of the original document so the paper can be age-tested. You guys do that, right?"

Frank stopped in the middle of the hallway, glancing around me to see if anyone was within earshot. "Look, I'll do what I can. But it's becoming apparent that maybe what we thought was the mission site isn't." He held his hand up to silence my outcry. "I know you're invested in the results. The commission has to examine both sides of the argument. I'm not saying the site isn't old. The coins you found prove the site does have historic significance, but we have to face the possibility it's not the original mission site."

I pointed to my phone. "This is wrong. Either the drawing was manipulated or it's an out-and-out lie. You believe the wall is the mission, I know you do."

Frank put his hand on my arm, a gesture he'd never even attempted before. I didn't think the guy touched anyone. "Sometimes it doesn't matter what a person believes; it matters what we can prove. Right now, the proof is running against us."

The story of my life.

"Look, keep me informed. I'm digging through the city records now. My friend Amy knows a history professor who may be willing to help. You work on your end, and I'll do the same. I'm not going down without a fight." I stared at him. "I'm not kidding."

He sighed. "I'll keep digging. Maybe I can find an earlier map showing the mission location. There has to be one somewhere." Frank walked away without another word.

I watched the man who'd thought his career had moved out of this satellite office into the big leagues of history protectors. He'd talked about writing a book about the find. He probably would have been able to retire and teach as he chose. Now he was about to become the laughingstock of his industry. And he blamed me for raising his hopes.

"I'll call you," I said to his retreating back. I must seem like a love-starved groupie. I didn't care. The sun blinded me when I left the building. I hadn't realized how dark the hallway had been until I'd stepped into the light. The sun's warmth immediately lightened my mood. Maybe not to happy level, but at least I didn't feel hopeless anymore.

I slid my sunglasses on and decided to drive to the car dealership. Time to rip the Band-Aid off.

As I pulled my Jeep into a parking spot at the dealership, a man came out to greet me. "My name's Mitch, and my goal today is to leave you completely satisfied with your visit."

I glanced around at the cars parked nearby. Maybe I'd stopped at the wrong place. No, it appeared to be a car dealership. I glanced at Mitch. "We'll see."

He chuckled. "Honestly, it's the corporate greeting, but I'm getting pretty good at satisfying my customers. What brings you in today? You looking to trade up?"

I shook my head. "Trade, yes. Up, no. I don't need anything fancy. I want a car I can drive and trust. No hidden compartments, no rearview cameras. Just a Jeep, like the one I have now." I slapped the side of my vehicle.

"Well, satisfying you may be the easiest challenge I've had all day." He pointed to the right side of the parking lot. "Let's head over there and I can show you a few choices we have in a 'non-fancy' model."

As we walked through the line of too bright and shiny cars, one thought kept circling. Laboratory results had come back and given Greg a clue. What could have been found in Craig's body? The obvious answer was drugs. Buttoned-up Craig? Didn't seem to fit. The man was so uptight he didn't wear anything unstarched.

"Do you want to look at something else?" Mitch seemed worried. I'd been quiet too long I'd guessed.

I refocused on the here and now. Craig's possible drug use would have to be thought through some other time. "Do you have one in blue?" I loved the simplicity of the Jeep, basic edition. My only up-grade, I wanted a hardtop this time. I climbed into the vehicle, loving the feel of the leather seats. Basic sure had improved since the last time I'd purchased a car. Of course, the price would reflect that. A CD player, stereo, and hands-free phone system, and I was in love. The fact it was a stick made it heaven.

"You want to take it for a test drive?" Mitch regarded me, hopeful. I nodded.

Mitch broke out a smile and sprinted to the dealership building. He called to me, "I'll be right back with the keys."

While he was gone, I sat in my soon-to-be new car and thought about what the tests had shown on Craig. The questions kept circling, giving me a headache. By the time Mitch had jogged back with the dealer plate and the keys, I wanted to cry.

Thank God the test drive gave me something new to think about. The car rode smooth. I loved the acceleration when I left a stop sign, and on the highway, the Jeep wanted to fly. I should have listened to Greg before. Buying a new car wasn't scary. I pulled back into the car lot and parked next to my old Jeep. And my heart sank. How could I give up something I'd loved so deeply? But it was time. I knew it, Greg knew it, and even my new friend Mitch knew it.

I told Mitch I'd take the car and followed him into his office. After signing the paperwork and writing a bigger check than I'd ever imag-ined, I went back to my Jeep to clean out the remnants of almost ten years. I'd bought the Jeep right out of college. My first action as a real adult, getting debt to pay along with my student loans. But I'd paid off the loan and driven the car long past its prime. Now it was time to say good-bye.

Mitch helped me move the stuff. "I'm sure we'll sell this off the lot rather than sending it to auction. For the age, it's in great shape. Some kid will be drooling over this as soon as we put it up."

I didn't respond. Thinking of someone else driving around in my car hurt a little—until I got into the new version, turned up the vol-ume on the CD player, and sang my heart out with an old Dixie Chicks CD. Driving down Highway 1, the ocean to my right and rolling hills to the left, I rolled the windows down to let in the sea air.

As I neared South Cove, I realized I was close to The Castle. The place had been closed right after the murder, but from the sign, Greg must have okayed the reopening. I hadn't been on a tour since my first visit to South Cove. Turning left on the road, I decided it was time for another one.

I parked at the end of the lot, trying to keep my new car as new as possible. I walked up to the entry gate. I slipped a twenty to the girl who sat behind the ticket counter. Her name tag read LISA. This must be the girl trying to break Nick's heart. She wore more makeup than I owned. "One, please."

The girl didn't even look up from her texting. She slipped me a ticket and my change. "Last tour starts in ten minutes. Meet the guide by the Grecian pool to your left."

"Hey, Lisa?" Using the girl's name made her actually look up at me. "Were you here the night Craig was killed?"

Her eyes narrowed suspiciously. "I already talked to the cops. Who are you?"

"Just an interested friend." I wondered what I would ask if she opened up to me. Honestly, I knew she wasn't going to blurt out, "I killed Craig," but I thought maybe she would give me some kind of clue. "So you were here?"

She nodded. "I'd stayed over to help get ready for the weekend. I get a lot of overtime that way, if I want to help set up new exhibits or bring up light stuff from the truck. Craig had gotten in a new truck-load from his cargo bin down at the docks. And boy, was he antsy about the contents."

"Why do you think that? Did he say something?" Now we were getting somewhere. I bet she hadn't told this to the police.

"He made me stay outside until he'd gone through the entire truck. Then he stomped off without telling me where to even put the stuff. Finally, I just shoved everything into the lobby and clocked out. I couldn't even find him to tell him I was leaving." Lisa frowned. "Then the next day, I show up and the cops won't even let me in to work. I lost three days' pay. I needed that money. I'm saving up for a car."

"So you think Craig was looking for something?" I asked, leaning in closer.

"Duh. But he didn't find it. He had a mean streak when he got mad. So I stayed away."

I didn't know what else to ask, so I told her to come in to the shop when I was working and I'd treat her to a coffee. Then I said good-bye.

She nodded and returned to her texting.

I wandered around the perfectly landscaped yard, marveling at the beauty Craig had managed to create. For a man who didn't have a nice bone in his body, he knew how to make The Castle absolutely lovely. The walls gleamed and the flowers bloomed bright against the white buildings. I walked down the steps to the Greek pool and felt like I was on the set of an old Hollywood movie. The stone gleamed without a speck of dirt. Southern California wasn't the only place dealing in illusion. We were pretty good at keeping up appearances here, as well.

An older couple carefully followed me down the stairs. "Can you believe it, Harold? We're at the same pool where he used to have orgies." The heavyset woman glanced around at the flowers. "I bet they walked around here, naked as jaybirds, trying to get a tan while they were fornicating."

Her husband didn't seem impressed. "Let's go on the tour. You've been talking for weeks about this, Marge. Let's not get freaked out."

"Don't you feel the history here?" Marge wasn't letting her fantasy go. She glanced at me. "You feel it, I can see it in your face."

I smiled, trying to keep from getting into the fight. "I'm just waiting for the tour."

Marge didn't take the hint. She even stepped closer. Putting her head near mine, she whispered, "A man was killed here last week. I'm so excited. Do you think they'll show us where he was killed?"

I felt sick. "I don't think so."

The woman pursed her lips. "You're probably right. When we went to Graceland they wouldn't let us upstairs at all. Now, what kind of place holds a tour of half a house?"

"I think there are off-limits areas here, too." I wondered where our tour guide was so he could start taking these off-the-wall questions. I was here to investigate, not deal with Marge's issues.

A tall man dressed in kakis and a polo shirt came up to the pool area and smiled at the couple. "Hey, I'm Daniel. I'll be taking you on your tour. Hey, Jill, you here about the job opening?"

I shook my head. "Nope, I had the afternoon off and thought I'd take a quick tour so I can better sell the site at the coffee shop." As I followed Daniel through the main house, I'd realized I'd missed an opportunity. What job? My mind wandered while I focused on the dark furniture surrounding me. I'd always loved the large meeting room lined with choir pews brought over from Europe. The walls were covered with tapestries taken from castles. The owner had known his history. And the original owner had been a hoarder, gathering up priceless antiques like they were collectible stuffed animals. The place was packed with museum-quality items. No wonder Josh idolized Craig. Managing a place like this must have been an antique lover's dream job.

I thought about Josh in his threadbare suit and shirts, off-white from years of washing. Who would be the next manager of The Castle? Craig hadn't only managed the place, he'd been a part-owner, running the day-to-day operations for the investment group listed on the deed. For a split second, the question of Josh killing Craig for a chance at the job ran through my mind. I moved closer to Daniel, and while the couple admired a set of tapestries, I asked, "The job? Are they already replacing Craig?"

Daniel nodded. "And it's a sweet package. You get the house in the back along with almost a six-figure salary. No wonder Craig could drive such a posh ride."

The couple seemed to be arguing about what story the tapestry was telling. He smiled. "I put in my application, but I think without a degree, I'm a dark horse."

"Do you know who else is applying?" I might as well see what the guy knew.

"The only ones I know for sure, besides me"—he grinned—"are Brenda, Craig's ex. She told me she put in an application. I guess she used to teach at some art school. And that new guy with the antique store."

"Josh Thomas?"

Daniel checked his watch and waved the couple closer. "We need to get this train moving, folks." He glanced down at me. "I can't believe that they might hire the guy, he's a walking heart attack. I think the only thing he wants is the health insurance."

As the tour continued, Daniel pointed out the large collection of

Madonna and Child paintings The Castle owned—a strange collecting hobby. I still was thinking about Craig and his murder. By the time we'd gone through the main house and a separate cottage kept for the wealthy owner's guests back in the day, I'd stopped listening to Daniel's chatty tour. There was something I was missing, but try as I might, I couldn't get my mind to focus.

I slipped onto a stone bench and let the tour pass. Daniel saw me and came back. "You okay, Jill?"

I pulled out a bottle of water I kept in my purse and took a sip. "I guess I just need to sit for a bit." I pointed to the walkway leading to the main gate. "If I go that way, I'm back at the parking lot, right?"

Daniel nodded. "I can walk you there."

"I want to see the guesthouse. Didn't the Beatles stay there?" Marge called out to Daniel, clearly not happy with the delay.

I waved him on. "You finish the tour. I'll sit and get more of this water down me, then I'll head to the parking lot. Probably just too much sun."

He looked at Marge and her husband, who were staring now, then back to me. "If you were anyone else, I wouldn't leave you. So don't make me regret this."

"Thanks, Daniel." I waited for them to disappear down the bend in the path that took them to Casa del Sola. Then I turned left and tucked through a bush, ending up at the manager's bungalow. The place where Craig was killed. Yellow police tape still hung on the trees around the door, but the seal on the door was gone.

"In for a penny," I whispered, then slipped on the rubber gloves I used to wash the floors at the shop.

Opening the door, I found the living room much like it must have been the night Craig was killed. Furniture was upended, couch pillows torn apart, their stuffing coming out like a white waterfall. Whoever killed Craig had also been looking for something. Like the map showing that my mission wall was a fraud? Another clue that pointed to me.

I left the living room and eased down the hall, careful not to touch anything or even breathe too hard. The master bedroom hadn't been ransacked. Craig's bed sat neat and made in the middle of the carefully decorated room. A pile of books sat on his nightstand, and my heart sank. They were all research books focused on the Spanish settlers and early California history.

I opened one of the books. The insides had been carved out to create a hiding space. I shuddered. Who would deface a book like this? Then I realized, the hole in the middle was just big enough to hide a stack of bills. Craig had been making his own safety deposit boxes, hiding money in books he could keep close. I opened another book: same hole, no money.

My cell chirped and I jumped, knocking the books off the table. I hurried to pick them up and answered the phone, holding the cell to my ear with my shoulder. "Hello?"

"Hey, sexy." Greg's voice made me feel guilty, like he knew exactly where I was standing.

"Hey, yourself." I picked up the last book and a sheet of paper fell out. Picking it up, I saw a some sort of drawing on the page.

"Where are you?"

"I took a Castle tour, I'm just coming out. Why?" I tried to keep the defensive tone out of my voice as I shoved the paper into my pocket and headed out of the bungalow.

I hadn't learned anything new, except Craig had liked local history and his killer had been looking for something. Both clues pointed to me as a possible suspect. I quietly shut the door and realized Greg had been talking. I slipped my gloves into my purse, then grabbed the phone. "Sorry, I think I lost you there for a minute, what did you say?"

He chuckled. "I said I'm close by, I'll meet you in the parking lot."

As I followed the path to the exit, I wondered why Greg wanted to meet. He could just want to see me. Yeah, right.

As I stood in the parking lot at the exact place I'd fought with Craig, a motorcycle with a rider dressed in black leather with a full face helmet pulled into the parking lot. Lisa closed and locked the information booth, putting a CLOSED sign in the window. I watched her climb on the back of the bike, wrapping her arms tightly around the man, and the two took off.

"That's Lisa's boyfriend, if you were wondering."

I started and turned. Greg stood behind me, his arms folded and his eyes dark. I couldn't explain away my presence here at The Castle so I didn't even try. "When did Nick get a bike?"

"Nick Michaels? He didn't. I think Sadie would kill him if he tried. That's not Nick. That's Reno Hendricks. He's a mechanic over in Bakerstown." Greg came closer. "I don't see your car. Don't tell me you ran this far."

I smiled. "No, I have a car."

Greg's glance swept the now almost-empty parking lot and settled on the new Jeep. "You finally listened to me?"

Slapping him on the arm, I pouted. "I'm not stubborn. Or stupid."

Greg lifted his eyebrows at my comment. "And yet I find you here, at the crime scene."

"I wanted to talk to Lisa. She says Craig was upset about the delivery the night he died. That there was something missing in the truck full of antiques when she helped move them into storage."

Greg put his hand on my back and walked me toward my new Jeep. "Yes, I know. I interviewed her as part of *my* investigation." He opened the door and motioned me into the driver's seat.

"And did you know Nick thought he was Lisa's boyfriend?"

Greg shrugged. "Some women like to keep a spare on the line, just in case." He leaned in to check out the interior and I could smell his aftershave. "It doesn't mean she's a killer."

"I never said she killed Craig. But I know I didn't do it. So who else does that leave?"

He lifted my face to his and kissed me. "You're going to be okay. I'm going to find the killer. I always do." He smiled. "You did good with the Jeep. It suits you."

I smiled and smoothed my hand over the leather seats. "It's a little more than I wanted to spend, but I fell in love with the beast as soon as I saw her."

"I bet you made some salesman's day, walking in with a cash sale." Greg leaned against the car. "You want to take me out to dinner to celebrate? That little place down on the highway overlooking the ocean?"

"You want me to buy you dinner after spending this kind of money today?" I held my hands out in mock surprise.

"Sure, then you can tell me what you were looking for during the tour." He tapped my nose with his finger. "And your theories about the killing. I know you've come up with at least a few."

I opened my mouth to deny it, but then thought better. If Greg was asking to hear me out, I would lay my cards on the table. He could tell me to stop after I gave him the piece of information that worried me the most. The one giving me clear motive to kill.

CHAPTER 12

The world seemed brighter as I walked down the road the next morning to open the shop. Birds chirping in the trees, the sun warm on my back, I felt like skipping instead of my usual fast-paced stroll. Too many princess movies growing up, I guess. As long as I didn't start chatting up the birds, I'd be okay.

Greg had listened to everything I said, even asking me to repeat a couple of things. When I'd showed him the journal map picture on my phone, he'd shaken his head. But he hadn't told me to stop investigating or trying to prove the journal was a fake. I'd even told him about Amy's friend who was coming into town and he'd asked to be in on the meeting.

When he'd walked me to my door, he surprised me with a quick hug before saying, "You're something else, you know that?" Then he'd walked back to his truck, calling back at me, "Be sure to lock up."

I'd followed his instructions. Locking the door was overkill. As a tourist town, South Cove was more likely to see problems with the day visitors hitting the winery for a few drinks and coming up a little too tipsy to drive home. Break-ins were rare, unless you called the kids swimming in the pool at The Castle a break-in. And even then, the worst that happened was the trash they left behind. Now, with Craig's murder, the town felt on edge.

But today was glorious. Greg believed me and hadn't immediately arrested me as he examined the journal. Or maybe he liked his women on the wrong side of the law? That was me, a rebel coffee shop/bookstore owner with an unused law degree. And a brand-new Jeep.

Maybe the Jeep was my real source of happiness. I didn't care. Today would be a great day.

As I came into town, I saw the cruisers parked near my shop. My heart sank. Aunt Jackie? I started running.

Toby saw me coming and stepped up to meet me. "He's all right. Kind of shaken up, but alive. The ambulance is taking him to County over in Bakerstown for a look-over. But seriously, I think he's overreacting."

"Greg?" I felt confused.

Toby laughed. "No. Josh. Someone broke into his shop. From what I can see, they must have waited for him to come in this morning, then attacked and robbed him. Josh says they only got his petty cash and an antique necklace and tiara set. They probably thought it had real rubies."

"Why would they rob an antique store?" This didn't make any sense.

Toby stared at the brick building. "I hate to say it, but it could have been kids, tired of Josh always dogging them."

"Kids wouldn't do this. Especially not our kids." I paused. "Did you get the call?"

Toby grinned. "The guy set up a security system. Did you know he carried a radio button in his pocket at all times? He pushes the button, the security team calls us. Usually, I get here to listen to him grump about trash or vandalism. This time, I saw the door, announced myself, and the rats scurried out the back. I heard a bike take off before I got to the parking lot."

"A bike? You mean a motorcycle?"

Toby nodded. "I've got Esmeralda pulling video feed from the traffic cams. We might be able to see something, even with that cheap system the mayor approved."

Just then, the EMTs wheeled Josh out onto the street, the stretcher groaning under his weight. His eyes met mine and he waved me over.

I looked at Toby for approval, and when he nodded, stepped over to Josh. He'd stopped the EMTs from loading him up so we could talk. "Hey, I'm sure you'll be just fine." I gave my best health pep talk.

"Look, don't tell your aunt about this. And we're still on for Friday." Josh grabbed my arm, his grip surprisingly strong for someone in his shape. "You owe me."

"We're on for Friday, but if you have to reschedule, that's okay, too."

"No. I'll be there." The EMTs pushed the stretcher into the ambulance, forcing Josh to let go of me.

Toby nodded at the retreating ambulance. "What was that all about?"

I smiled. "I do believe that Mr. Thomas is smitten with our Miss Jackie."

Toby barked a laugh. "Man, I did not need that image in my head. Thanks, Jill."

I glanced over at my shop. "Do you think someone broke in there, too?"

"I already checked. The alarm is still set, no signs of a break-in, but maybe I should walk through, just in case."

I considered his offer then shook my head. "No. I'm just being paranoid. See you this afternoon." I glanced up at the busted door on Josh's store and winced.

I unlocked the door to the shop and picked up the mail that had been dropped through the slot in the door yesterday. Setting the envelopes on the counter, I went to start coffee. Regulars would be popping in for their morning fix on their way to work. I checked the dessert case and put out a new coffee cake, blueberry crumble, and a few slices of a chocolate marble cheesecake. Aunt Jackie must have restocked the display last night after our delivery guys arrived.

I was about to sort through the mail when Bill Simmons came through the door. "Hey, Bill, large black to go?" I grabbed a cup. "Hear about all the excitement this morning?"

I heard him step closer. "Crazy stuff. Is Josh all right?"

Nodding, I said, "I think so."

Bill glanced around the shop. "Is your aunt working?"

"No, she's off today. I'm taking her shift later." Probably more than he wanted to know. I cocked my head, noticing the worried look on the bed-and-breakfast owner's face. "Why?"

Bill nodded at the coffeepot. "I'll take a large hazelnut to go." He slipped into a stool near the barista bar I'd built. After pouring Bill's coffee, I poured a cup for myself and came around the bar to sit next to him.

"What did she do now?" I sipped my coffee, grateful for the dark blend. With Aunt Jackie around town, things were never dull.

"It's this whole Cloaked in Mystery thing. She said the author wants to stay for a week after the reveal. He's apparently on a deadline for another book, so his publisher has given him a week in between signings to finish and then he's back on the road." Bill sighed and took a sip of his own coffee.

I shrugged. "I don't understand. Isn't that a good thing? To have a week's booking? I would think he'd be a perfect guest, quiet, in his room writing most of the time."

Bill leaned into the chair. "That's true, if he's real. I have this gut feeling we're going to show up the night of the launch and there will be your aunt, like some giant surprise party. No author, no launch, no weeklong booking."

"I don't think that will happen." Okay, the thought had crossed my mind, too. Aunt Jackie was all about the marketing. And if she could string us along, she'd figure out a way to do it and try to make everyone happy in the meantime.

Bill stared at me. "You don't even believe what you're saying."

"Okay, say this is a joke, what's the harm?" I glanced at the clock. *Please let another customer stop in.* I didn't like where this conversation was heading at all.

"The harm is, we're deep into tourist season. I don't want to have a room booked without having some method of payment to guarantee the costs if he doesn't appear." He stared at me. "Are you willing to put up a night's guarantee in case this thing goes south? Do you trust your aunt that much?"

I sighed, not answering Bill's question.

"I thought so." He pulled out a five and left it on the counter. "I'm going to leave the booking off. If there's an author, he can take his chances when he shows up."

"Wait. What if I get you a name? Then you can contact the guy directly and get his credit card information. That way you know you're covered."

Bill stood and nodded. "You have a week. If I don't hear from you before next Monday with his contact information or your own credit card number, I'll release the hold on the room."

"Thanks. Look, I know she can be pushy and I appreciate you working with her on the event." I stood and walked him to the door.

"Your aunt has great ideas." He smiled. "I just don't trust her execution."

You and me both, I thought, as Bill waved and left. If I had to pay for a night at Bill's bed-and-breakfast because of her overpromising, there was going to be a problem. I glanced at the clock—7:00 A.M. No way would she be awake yet. I'd go visit with her when Toby came in for his shift at noon. My bright and shiny mood was quickly fading away. I started dusting the bookshelves, losing myself in the titles I hadn't read and promising myself some time for a good long read soon.

The morning flew by after Bill's visit. I almost suspected people purposely stayed away while we talked, except that was impossible. When Toby showed up at noon, both sides of the shop—book and coffee sales—had been brisk and steady. I turned the register over to him and went up the inside stairs to my old apartment. I knocked on the side door.

No answer. I glanced out the hallway window overlooking the back parking lot. Her car was gone. Apparently my aunt had decided to run errands. I scribbled a "call me" note and shoved it under the door. Then I walked back to the house to let Emma out, eat lunch, and fulfill my promise to myself for some reading time.

I'd finished the mystery when the alarm went off on my phone. Time to head back into town to relieve Toby. I glanced at my phone, no missed calls. Where was she? Even if she'd gone into Bakerstown shopping, she should have been home by now. I dialed her cell but my call went straight to voice mail.

Maybe she'd seen Bill and me talking and was ignoring my attempts to contact her. Wouldn't be the first time she'd dodged a touchy issue.

I filled Emma's food and water dishes, gave the mutt a kiss on the head, and left her outside for the rest of the afternoon. "We'll run when I get off work," I promised. *Unless I get a chance to talk to Jackie,* I silently amended.

Walking back into town this time, my mood wasn't quite as light as it had been that morning. The late afternoon wind whipped my unrestrained hair into my face. I walked faster.

Main Street was crowded for a Tuesday. A tour bus sat parked across the street to my shop and I dodged curious visitors as I raced to the store. When I opened the door, the line to the register was up to the edge of the door.

"Excuse me." I weaved through the crowd. Toby was brewing a new pot of hazelnut and had two espressos running along with five to-go orders of pie on the counter. I washed my hands, and sliding an apron over my head, I asked, "Where do you want me?"

"Finish that order. Five apple, two espressos, and three hot chocolates." He nodded to the group over at the mystery bookshelf. "The lady in blue ordered. I've already taken their money. I'll run the register and call out orders."

For the next thirty minutes, the line never seemed to end. I'd pulled out the last of the cheesecake and Sadie's pies from the back. We were going to have to restock for the morning. "Who are these people?" I whispered to Toby.

"A church group out of Southern Oregon. They're heading to a gathering in Santa Barbara from what I've heard. We're their midafternoon break."

I glanced at Toby, who should have been off at four. "You okay staying longer?"

He smiled. "I've already talked to Esmeralda and she's let Greg know. As soon as it slows enough for you to take over, I'll leave. I'm not expected until six."

"You may want to eat dinner or shower or something," I teased. Toby worked harder than anyone. Most everyone here worked a couple of jobs, trying to stay afloat financially, but Toby seemed to feed on the energy it took.

"I'll order to-go from Lille's. It's Philly-cheese night." He grinned.

"Hey, you don't think I actually cook when I'm home anyway, do you?"

"Honey, looking as good as you do, you shouldn't have to cook a meal in your life," replied the woman standing at the counter waiting for her coffee. "I'm sure I could scare up one or two young women from our congregation who'd be more than willing to let you court them."

I laughed. "Believe me, Toby has no trouble finding women."

"Then the boy needs to pick one and settle down. Men aren't meant to walk alone on this earth. Adam and Eve were the first couple and see how that turned out." The woman took the coffee I handed her. She waved and walked out the door.

I glanced over at Toby and noticed a grin on his face. Shaking my head slightly, I warned him not to comment, and we pushed through the last of the tour bus customers. Finally the door closed on the last person and I watched the bus driver load up his charges and then slowly ease the lumbering bus down Main Street to the highway. I poured a cup of coffee and headed to the closest table. "Oh my God. That was unexpected."

Toby grabbed a tray and started cleaning the next table. "I think you sold out of the Central California guide books and the history section on South Cove. Bill's going to be ecstatic we unloaded all of the copies he brought over last week."

I waved him over to the table. "Come sit for a second. We can clean up later."

Toby loaded the tray and nodded. "I'll be right back with my own cup."

He returned a few minutes later with another tray. He sat a carafe of coffee and two pieces of the chocolate cheesecake on the table. "Time for a true coffee break. What do people who work at factories do for their break? It must be boring getting junk food out of a vending machine."

"When I worked at the law office, we had catered coffee and pastries brought in each day. Kind of like here." I smiled. "I guess I've always been luckier than most."

Toby smiled. "You should try the coffee Esmeralda makes at the station. I swear it could cut engine grease."

I laughed and took a bite of the cheesecake. "Heaven."

"You okay?" Toby set his fork down. "I've been worried about you. It's been kind of crazy around here lately."

"Seeing Josh like that, it was kind of a shock. I hate to think anyone would do that." I sighed and took another bite. "I moved here for the peace and quiet. Between this and everyone thinking I hated Craig enough to kill him ... the guy was a pain in my butt. But I don't wish anyone dead. You know that, right?"

Toby put his hand on my arm. "There is no way you could have killed Craig. I know it and Greg knows it. Now we have to find out who did the deed."

I sniffed. "How can you be sure?"

"You made me take a mouse out of the no-kill trap last month and release it over at the park. And I'm constantly being called in to swat a spider in the back room. I don't know if you've even stepped on an ant." Toby took a bite out of his dessert. "So you think you could have stabbed a man enough times to kill him? I don't think so."

"Spiders creep me out. And mice." I regarded the guy sitting across from me. Toby had been knocked unconscious a few months ago guarding my house when Miss Emily's disgruntled family tried to steal back their inheritance. I hadn't known him except as Greg's partner before he'd started working the afternoon shift. But the more we talked, the more I liked the guy. The church lady was right; we needed to find him a steady girl.

"And yet you think anyone who has ever met you could peg you for a murderer?" Toby glanced at the clock and finished the last swig of coffee. "Gotta go make the streets of South Cove safe from any more roving tour buses."

"Or you could barricade the road until I close this evening." I grinned. "Tuesdays are supposed to be slow. I've got tons of work I need to get accomplished in the next few hours."

Toby gave me the littlest violin hand gesture. "Customers are good for business, you need to remember that."

"Yah, yah." I took our plates to the sink and then grabbed the tray Toby'd been using. "Get out of here."

"Yes, boss." Toby grabbed his jacket and headed to the door. "You drove back this afternoon, right?"

"No. I'm walking home. It's still light at nine." I piled cups and plates onto a tray and started wiping down tables.

"You shouldn't until this thing is settled. You know someone killed Craig." Toby stood in the doorway, holding the door open.

"Yeah, and right now, I'm the fall guy. Why would they kill me and prove I wasn't the murderer?" I picked up the full tray.

Toby seemed to consider my point and grudgingly nodded. "I get that. But I'll be here at nine to give you a ride home in the police cruiser." He grinned. "I'll even let you ride in the back like a real criminal."

"Oh, the joy." I started rinsing plates and putting them into the dishwasher.

"See you then." And Toby was gone.

I didn't want to ride in the back of the police cruiser. Maybe I should call Greg and ask him to convince Toby I was fine. No, he'd probably agree with his deputy. Maybe Aunt Jackie would take me home?

I contemplated the ceiling, thinking about my aunt. She still hadn't called or come down to see me. Maybe she didn't get my note. I finished rinsing, turned on the dishwasher, and wiped my hands. Then I called up to the apartment.

Five rings and I got her answering machine. Yes, my aunt still had an honest-to-goodness answering machine hooked up to her landline. Just like me. "Aunt Jackie? Pick up, it's me, Jill. Are you up there?" I waited but then the machine thanked me for calling and clicked off. Then I called her cell. Still no answer. I left another message. Glancing around the empty shop, I took a chance and ran to the back. I opened the back door to the parking lot, but her car wasn't there.

"Where are you?" I whispered as I closed and locked the back door. I grabbed my laptop and headed to the front. It was time to order in book stock and more desserts. I hoped Sadie would be able to fill a double order this week. I didn't want to be totally optimistic, but the tour bus had wiped out my stockpile I'd frozen. I would use up the extra pies even if it meant sending one home with Greg or Toby.

An hour passed and I'd completed my weekly order and sent e-mails to Sadie and Bill. I loved being able to use local suppliers as much as they probably loved the business I gave them. Seven P.M. and the evening temperature outside cooled. I was considering shutting early but instead, I pulled out one of the new releases I'd ordered for the store last week and started in on my research duties. Reading. Sometimes it was good to be an owner.

The bell on the door pulled me out of the book. I'd been lost in the pages. Glancing at the clock, I saw it was already eight-thirty. My stomach grumbled in protest as I'd forgotten to eat the turkey sandwich I'd brought for dinner. I loved it when a book captivated me that way. I set the paperback aside and stood to greet my customer.

"Hey, Jill." Brenda Morgan stood at the doorway. Fifi was on a leash at her side. "You mind if I bring her in? She's been through so much, I hate to tie her up outside."

"It's only you and me, no worries. Come on in. Can I get you something?"

Brenda and Fifi came into the shop and sat at a table. Fifi immediately lay at her owner's feet. The dog was trained. "Coffee. Black and regular. Yes, I know it's late, but I need the caffeine."

I poured coffee into a carafe and took it and two cups out to the table. "Mind if I join you?" I asked as I filled her cup.

"Actually, I was hoping you would. I need to talk to someone beside Fifi." Hearing her name, the standard poodle raised her head and her tail thumped on the floor.

I slipped into the chair across from Brenda. "What's going on? Are you doing okay? I know you guys have been divorced for over a year, but still, it must have been a shock."

"Actually, we never finalized the papers. I'm still Mrs. Craig Morgan." Brenda took a sip of coffee. "Or more accurately, I'm the widow Morgan." She considered her bright blue track suit. "Maybe I should be wearing black?"

"I don't think that tradition holds anymore. Especially since you guys were all but divorced." I considered keeping my mouth shut, but then blurted, "How come you didn't sign? He was a royal jerk to you."

Brenda smiled. "The man could be nice. It was just rare."

When I protested, she held up a hand. "You sound like my sponsor."

"What sponsor?" Had she had a drinking problem?

"When I left, I joined a program. They set me up with a woman who'd really had a bad life." She shook her head. "Vanna's stories about her husband made Craig look like an angel. She's not happy I'm even here."

"But Craig's dead." I didn't understand.

Brenda shrugged. "She thinks I'm going back to my old life. That I'll be vulnerable again. And since we never divorced, I guess in a way, I am."

"You never pursued the divorce?" I would have run straight to a family law attorney as soon as I left town.

"I wasn't the one holding up the divorce. Craig was. He said he wanted to give us another shot. He was working on something that would have given him more time to devote to us, rather than being on twenty-four/seven at The Castle. The man worked way too much."

I guess everyone had a secret side. But to call Craig a devoted family man was going a step too far. At least from my interactions with the guy. I leaned back. "So how are you holding up now?"

Brenda dabbed her eyes. "It's hard. I don't even know when I can plan the funeral or whom to invite. He made a lot of enemies in the town. Do you think anyone would show if I did the funeral here? Maybe over at Oak Street Methodist? I know neither Craig nor I were members, but I was raised Methodist and it would mean a lot to me."

"You need to talk to Pastor Bill. I'm sure he'd help with the arrangements. And Doc Ames, of course." It wasn't like I was an expert in funerals, but since I'd been the one in charge of Miss Emily's earlier this year, I knew whom to send her to. And Doc, as the county coroner and the owner of the local funeral home, would be able to advise her.

"I appreciate your help. I know people are saying things about you and Craig." Brenda tore at her napkin. "That you would have already been in jail if you weren't dating Greg."

"I didn't kill Craig. And there's no evidence proving I did. That's why I'm not in jail, not because Greg and I are involved." I tried to keep my tone from betraying the anger I felt at her words. Greg didn't deserve the slight, and I definitely hated the town's rumor mill.

Brenda put her hand on mine. "I don't mean to upset you. I wanted to say, I don't care who killed him. The murderer did me a favor. Craig dead is the only way I could get my freedom. And for that, I'm grateful."

"Seriously, Brenda, I didn't kill Craig." My voice raised in volume, trying to get her to understand.

"Whatever." Brenda took a sip of her coffee. "I'm just glad Vanna didn't kill him."

CHAPTER 13

Brenda's words shocked me. "You shouldn't talk like that. Someone might think you're serious."

"Honey, I am serious. The guy wouldn't give up, and Vanna hated him for it. I'm not stupid, I know he didn't love me. I just couldn't say no around him. I'm like an addict with the wrong men. And Craig, he didn't want to lose something he owned. So he gave me the song and dance that once this big deal came through, he'd be different. Not as driven." Brenda snorted. "I'm not sure I could have been strong much longer. And then, when he got me back, everything I'd worked for would have gone down the drain. I like my life. I have friends."

"Well, you got away. And you got the last laugh." I reached down to pet Fifi. "You get to start over now. Do you have plans?"

Brenda shook her head. "I've got to wait for the investigation to end so the insurance will pay out. Of course we had savings, a lot more than he led me to believe when I moved into the city. The guy pleaded poverty and now I find he has cash stashed in his apartment at The Castle. No wonder my attorney couldn't find it."

"Did you tell the police what you found?" Greg hadn't mentioned an unusual amount of cash in Craig's apartment. Maybe that was why the guy was killed, someone else knew about the stash.

Brenda's eyes widened. "You're kidding, right? This is my money, or would have been if he'd been honest during our talks about divorce. No way am I going to risk losing it."

"Why would you lose the money?" Brenda's logic sounded reasonable, but something kept nagging at me about Craig stashing money. I tried one more time, "The money may be why Craig was killed. Maybe it's not his?"

"My former husband was pretty good at playing both sides of the fence. If he was holding this cash out of the banking system, I can assure you, he did something he didn't want others to know about."

I thought about the receipts for "services" I'd found at Josh's store. Had Josh been part of this cash business? I watched Brenda take a sip of her coffee. "Do you know whether Craig and Josh had a business arrangement? Was Josh doing appraisals for The Castle?"

She glanced in the direction of Antiques by Thomas, like she could see through the building's walls. "You mean the new antique dealer?" Brenda shrugged. "Maybe. I know Craig was always griping about having to call in someone from Bakerstown. I assume he'd rather use a local guy and save on the travel charges."

"Enough business to pay out thousands of dollars to an appraiser?" I thought of the stack of receipts I'd found.

"I don't think Craig paid over a thousand for a year of appraisals. The Castle didn't buy that much new stuff anymore. New purchases have only been for select pieces that add to their collections." She stood, laying a ten on the table. "That's for the coffee. We're staying out on that chain just before you get into Bakerstown." She gathered Fifi's leash and swung her purse over her shoulder. "Tell your aunt I'll be here for her Cloaked in Mystery night. I'm looking forward to celebrating something. I'll call you about the funeral."

I followed Brenda and Fifi to the door, then turned the open sign over to closed as I locked the door. They crossed the street and passed by Ray Stewart, who must have been at the liquor store down the street. Fifi started barking and pulling at the leash. Brenda grabbed her collar and I saw Ray swing wide around the dog on his way to his truck. "Shut that mutt up," he yelled at Brenda after he'd closed the truck door.

Fifi jerked against her leash again, and I watched as Brenda strained to hold her back. At least the dog had good taste, I thought.

Ray sped away down the street, and Fifi calmed down. Brenda saw me watching and smiled, indicating she had it under control.

I thought the woman was fooling herself about being in control, either with the dog or her life. But who was I to judge? I turned off the outside lights and walked through the shop, turning off lamps and lights that gave the place a homey feeling. I took the cash drawer out of the register and grabbed the book I'd been reading. The rest I'd clean up tomorrow morning when I opened. Locking the drawer in the safe, I grabbed my purse and headed upstairs to the apartment.

Once more I knocked on the door with no response. Now I was beginning to worry. Again, feeling foolish, I checked the parking lot. The only car in the lot was Toby's cruiser. My ride was here.

Toby stepped out of the car and held open the back door. "Your chariot awaits."

"You realize my neighbors are going to think you arrested me for Craig's murder, right? Brenda says everyone is already saying I did the deed." I peered into the back; it appeared clean, black vinyl on the bench seat rather than cloth. Probably so the blood and vomit from prior passengers could be hosed out.

"I'd put you up front, but the computer doesn't move. There's no front passenger seat. You can deal with the back for the two minutes it will take to get you home safely." Toby nodded to the car.

"I could walk," I protested.

Toby shook his head. "I called Greg. He said either you come willingly or I *am* to arrest you and take you down to the station for questioning."

"That's blackmail," I grumbled as I slipped into the back.

Toby shut the door, then climbed into the driver's side. "Nope, that's two people who care about your safety. You want me to use the lights?"

"No!" Then I saw his eyes in the rearview mirror. He'd been teasing. I leaned back, resigned. "Hey, did Jackie say she was going somewhere today?"

Toby pulled onto Main Street heading toward my house. "No. But I haven't seen her since Saturday. Why?"

"I haven't been able to reach her all day." I watched the town pass by as Toby drove. The closed shops' lights twinkled in the gathering darkness. Strings of white lights went from one tree to the next down the street. Soon, we'd be decorating for the summer festival and the street would look like a Beach Boys Revival/Retro Fifties theme.

When Toby pulled into my driveway, I tried to open the door. No luck. He shut the engine off and climbed out of the car. Opening the door, he swept down into a full bow. "Delivered safely."

"You're a nut." I started walking to the fence gate. A thought stopped me. "Hey, if you hear something tonight on the police scanner, or if you're called to a wreck or something, let me know if Jackie's involved, would ya? Even if she tells you not to?"

"Of course. What, do you think I'd hide something like that from you?" He shut the cruiser door. "She's fine. I'm sure she took off because she had the day off. You know, like a vacation day? Where you can do things like visit art galleries or go shopping? Or even"—he fake-gasped—"visit a friend in a nearby town?"

I pressed my lips together, trying to stop the smile. "Okay, I get your point. I'm concerned, that's all."

"I'll keep an eye out to see when she comes home. If I see her, I'll tell her to give you a call." He climbed in the driver's side and then leaned out the window. "I'll even use the lights pulling her over. That should give her a jolt."

"Good night, Toby," I called back without turning around.

He tapped his siren in response. I could kill the kid. Except for the fact he brought in a lot of traffic to the shop. And he had a good heart, and a twisted sense of humor. Thank God my nearest neighbor was Esmeralda. She would give Toby a piece of her mind in the morning if he'd interrupted one of her private readings.

I unlocked the door and turned on the lights. Toby's cruiser still sat in the driveway. He saw me watching, waved, then backed onto the street. I shut the door and set the dead bolt. Then I went to the back door to let Emma in for the night.

She sat at the door, staring. When I opened the door, her tail started thumping. "Hey, girl." I stepped outside to give her a quick hug. She gave me a quick bark, then ran to the back of the yard and grabbed her tennis ball. She'd taken up ball chasing on days when I worked too long to take her for a run. She returned to the porch and dropped her ball. I grabbed the slobber-covered toy and threw it out to the edge of the yard. While she was chasing, I returned to the kitchen, grabbing a soda from the fridge. We'd be playing for a while.

I thought about Fifi and the close call from being tied up on the beach. If someone did that to my dog, I'd . . . I stopped before I said I'd kill them. People already thought I'd killed once. Broadcasting empty threats into the universe wouldn't help the cause. When I returned to the porch, I reached down again and threw the ball farther this time. I sat on the swing, watching the night.

I loved my yard, my dog, my life. Emma bounded back up on the porch and put the ball into my lap. Except this time, it wasn't a tennis ball at all. Gingerly, I picked up the gift the dog had brought and took it into the kitchen, sitting it on the counter out of Emma's reach. She'd followed me and whined when I stopped the game of fetch.

Picking up the cell, I dialed a familiar number. When a man answered, I said, "I think you need to look at this."

Greg had been working on paperwork at City Hall so it took him less than five minutes before he was knocking at the front door. I'd forgotten to unlock it. I went to let him in.

"What's happening?" He gripped my arms as he came through the door. "Are you all right?"

"I'm fine. You need to see this. Tell me if it's what I think it is." I walked back to the kitchen, Greg following close behind. It hadn't escaped my notice he'd kept his hand on the butt of his service revolver. What can I say—I love the strong, silent type. Right now, I was glad I had someone to call when weird stuff happened.

The metal ball-shaped item still sat on my fake granite countertop. Just sitting there. Emma had given up on any idea of playing catch and had taken to her bed in a corner of the kitchen. When she saw Greg, she popped up to greet him.

"Hey, girl." Greg reached down and rubbed behind Emma's ears. "So what did you find?"

"I'm not sure, but isn't this one of those incense carriers they use in Catholic services?" I leaned closer. "It's dirty, but I think that's what it is."

Greg bent down to get closer to the ball. "You're right. It's a censer or thurible—depending on your sect. The altar boys used to carry it before the priest when I attended service as a kid."

"So what's it doing in your backyard?"

Greg, not taking his eyes off the metal ball, answered, "That is an excellent question."

"That you can't answer." I leaned my head back. "Do you think it's from the mission? Could Emma have dug it up somehow?"

"Just because I don't know the answer doesn't make the question not excellent." He led me over to the table. "When is Amy's friend coming by?"

"Tomorrow night. She's bringing him over after they have dinner at Lille's."

Greg nodded, thoughtful. "Maybe he can determine the approximate age of the censer."

I frowned. "But you think it's old?"

"It could be from the mission or"—Greg paused—"I think there was a mention of a missing censer on Craig's list of what was taken from The Castle the night of the break-in."

I swallowed. Every time I thought things were getting clearer, Craig's death popped back into the picture. "So Amy's friend can tell us if it's the stolen Castle item or from the mission site?"

Greg shrugged. "Maybe. I'm always amazed at the information specialists can get off the strangest things." He absently petted Emma, who'd put her head on his leg. The dog was staring at the censer and gave out a short bark.

I inched the relic farther away from the edge of the counter. It might have been Emma's chew toy, but now, it might be much more valuable. I opened the cupboard under the sink and pulled out a bone-shaped dog treat. Emma sat straighter, watching me. I gave her the treat as a replacement. "Good girl. Now go lie down."

The dog headed straight for her bed in the kitchen and started focusing on the bone. Watching her reminded me of Fifi and Brenda's visit to the shop. "Brenda's glad to have Fifi back. She doesn't look bad for almost being sea lion fodder."

"Brenda or the dog?" Greg teased.

"Fifi. Although she is a bit touchy. She went crazy when Ray walked by. I guess she has good taste in people." I slipped back into a chair at the table, opening my notebook and listing off one more to-do for tomorrow—calling Amy to confirm her friend's visit. "I wonder if I should send him pictures before he comes by?"

"Wait, Fifi went crazy on Ray?" Greg moved forward in his chair and tapped me on the hand to get my attention.

"Batshit crazy. I swear I didn't know if Brenda was going to be able to hold him back." I cocked my head and watched Greg's face. "Why?"

"Studies say dogs remember people who were mean to them. Maybe Ray had a run-in with Fifi?"

"Like dragging her to the beach and tying her up kind of run-in?" I ran through the scene I'd witnessed earlier. "Ray did say he'd been working for Craig. Maybe he went looking for the money he claimed Craig owed him."

Greg shook his head. "No. Craig wrote him a check the same day he was killed. I've already got a copy from the bank."

"Maybe he didn't think it was enough?" My words hung in the kitchen for a long time while Greg sat, apparently thinking.

"Or Fifi was reacting to something else," he finally muttered, glancing over at Emma, who had finished her treat and now was gently snoring. "I've got to get back to work."

"Have you eaten?" I glanced at the fridge, wondering what I could whip up quickly.

Greg stood. "Toby brought me over chicken from Lille's after he dropped you off. He wanted to tell me you were home safe."

My lips pressed together. "You mean he wanted to let you know how funny he thought the whole thing was."

"Just the South Cove Police Department taking the safety of our citizens seriously." Greg kissed me quickly, then patted me on the head. "Sorry, kiddo, but there was no way I would have let you walk home after dark when all this is happening in town. You don't know what or who would see that as an opportunity."

I shook my head. "Why would they kill me? Right now, I'm the best patsy to blame Craig's murder on, ask anyone. Heck, Brenda practically came out and thanked me for doing the deed."

He pulled me into a hug. "We're going to figure this out."

I laid my head over his heart and listened to the beats. "Before I go to jail?"

"Hopefully." Greg lifted my chin so he could see my eyes. His lips curved into the smile I loved. "I don't think you'd look as good in prison orange as you do in these sexy sweats."

"Go to work." I pushed my hands on his chest, but his arms tightened around me and this time, the kiss was long and deep.

After it ended, he smiled. "Now I'll go to work. Lock up behind me."

I followed him to the living room, where he stood on the porch waiting to hear the dead bolt click. I parted the curtains and watched him stride to his truck. I knew he worried about me, but my main concern right now was making sure I didn't go to jail. He might not have a choice on arresting me if some hard evidence didn't show up to clear my name. It might be circumstantial right now, but the rumors got one thing right. I was the one with the best motive.

Sleep didn't come easy, and as I tossed, I thought about Craig and Josh. What was in Craig's crate down at the docks? Had Greg already searched the crate? Or did he even know about it? Frustrated, I kicked the covers off and turned on the light. If I was going to be living a mystery, I might as well read one. Maybe I'd get some good hints on whodunit as I read.

I ran downstairs to grab the paperback I'd picked up at the shop and put the teakettle on to boil. I let Emma outside and read while I waited. Five minutes later, I was back upstairs, tucked into bed, a cup of cinnamon apple tea on the nightstand, Emma sleeping on her bed under the window, and before long, I was lost in the pages of the book.

CHAPTER 14

The alarm buzzed loudly and I reached over to hit the snooze button. Sleep finally made its appearance a few hours ago and now I felt like a train had hit me. I like my eight hours. Seven's doable. But three? I was going to be the walking dead most of the day. Unless I took a nap after my shift.

The thought of a nap later cheered me, and I rolled out of bed and headed downstairs to grab coffee and let Emma out.

Thirty minutes later, after a shower and a piece of toast covered with crunchy peanut butter, I was on my way. I kept glancing behind me when I saw a car, hoping it wasn't Toby's cruiser or Greg's truck. No way was I going to hide in fear or see a murderer around every corner. But I did walk faster than normal, watching my surroundings carefully.

The morning was clear and beautiful. I could smell the ocean on the light breeze that kept tossing my hair into my eyes. I'd grab a clip at the shop and pull the mess back, but leaving it down meant by the time I reached the shop, it would have air-dried from the walk. As I listened to the birds chirp, my mood rose and I didn't feel as tired. Two hours later, with the morning rush from the commuter crowd complete, I curled up on the couch and opened the book to where I'd finally pushed it away last night. I loved this mystery author. She painted a picture of the small town and the crazy people who lived there so completely, you felt like you knew the characters as they moved from book to book. And murder to murder.

The bell chimed and Sadie Michaels walked in. Her face seemed a little pale, but when she saw me, she grinned. "I heard you had a special taxi ride home last night."

Toby. I was going to kill him. "Seriously, people are already gossiping?" I stood and gave Sadie a quick hug. "Want some coffee?"

"That would be heaven." Sadie walked with me to the coffee bar. "I swear, if I'd known raising a teenager would be this hard, I wouldn't have had any kids."

"You know that's not true. You adore Nick." I poured a large hazelnut, Sadie's favorite, and topped off my own cup. I glanced at the display case. "You hungry?"

"No. And stop tempting me." She sipped on her coffee while I moved around the counter and we walked back to the couch. "I swear I ate most of a chocolate cream pie last night when I couldn't sleep."

"Something happen?" I watched Sadie.

"Like Toby bringing him home in the police cruiser?" she teased, then shook her head. "Nothing recently. I'm just worried about this girl thing. And now, with the murder and everything. I'm a mess."

"Nick's a good kid. You know he's not involved in anything bad." I could no sooner see the boy killing Craig than I could see him stealing from the collection plate at church.

"Kids do stupid things. I just pray he's not into something that will mess up his future." Sadie sighed, then glanced at me. "Sorry, I should be asking how you are. I hear Brenda's been singing your praises for saving her."

"I know. Sometimes the woman gets strange ideas. I didn't even know they were still considering reconciliation, did you?"

"I haven't seen Brenda since the volunteers from that abused women's shelter came and moved her stuff out of The Castle and she disappeared into the city."

I sat straighter. "What are you talking about?"

Sadie glanced around the empty shop. "I guess it's not a secret. I was at the church when the volunteers showed up that day. She'd been planning the escape for some time by then. She came to the church, handed her keys and a list of things she needed to the woman in charge, and then they took her to the city."

"Pretty cloak and dagger." I eyed my friend. "How come you never mentioned this before?"

"I guess I thought everyone knew. You know you can't keep anything a secret, not in South Cove." She grinned. "But I did hear that Craig went all aggrieved spouse when he found out. He claims Brenda was crazy and he never hurt her or controlled her life."

"Of course he did. Probably afraid he'd lose his position at The Castle."

Sadie laughed. "I don't think that was possible. I heard his father or someone was on the board, that's how he got the position in the first place."

"Jackie says he was a trust-fund baby." I shook my head. "From what Brenda told me, their finances weren't in that good of shape. Maybe rumors are just rumors?"

"Sometimes, but I saw the volunteers whisk Brenda away, so we know that's true. Or at least her side of the story is true." Sadie glanced at her watch. "I've got to go. It's my turn to deliver the monthly donations to the homeless shelter."

I stood and followed her to the door. "Lunch next week?"

"Sure." She waved and disappeared out the door. I watched her as she headed toward her house, probably to get her car for the delivery. The woman was a whirlwind. She got more done in a day than I did in a week. I returned to my place on the couch and started reading.

I'd finished the book and was feeling pleased with myself since I'd figured out the murderer before the big reveal, when the phone rang.

"Coffee, Books, and More," I chirped, glancing over the shelves for a new release.

"Just checking in to see if you still want us to stop in tonight. Wait, hold on." Amy mumbled something else I couldn't hear, then came back on the line. "Esmeralda says the ghost wants to know if you got her present."

"What?" A chill started down my back, and my mind raced to the censer sitting in my kitchen. The one my dog had found after being in the yard for months.

"I don't know—she stopped by my desk, asked if I was talking to you, then told me to ask. Then she went down the hall to her office." Amy sighed. "The woman gets weirder every day."

I didn't answer, thinking maybe Amy wasn't right about our local psychic. I thought about the censer showing up in my yard. Esmeralda was my neighbor. She could have thrown it over the fence without me even knowing since I'd been at the shop most of the day. Everyone in town knew my schedule. A picture of the woman sneaking across the road with a stolen religious relic made me snort. I was grasping at straws.

"Hey, did I lose you?" Amy's voice brought me back to the conversation.

"Sorry, just thinking." I went back to the couch where I'd been sitting. "Actually, I did find something I want your guy to look at tonight."

"He's not my guy," Amy shot back, maybe a little too quickly.

"I didn't mean anything. What's going on?" I watched a bird fly into the tree right outside my large window. I'd found the robin's nest up there in the spring, and then the bright blue shells broken on the sidewalk once the babies hatched. I felt like a proud mom when I'd watched the tiny birds fly away.

Amy sighed. "Hank's not happy about me going to dinner with Justin. I mean, I told him we're just friends and he went off on me. I don't get it. He stands me up last Sunday after making these plans about borrowing the truck, then he gets put out because I'm going to dinner with a friend from college?"

Trouble in paradise, and I couldn't be happier. A smile curved my lips. I pushed it away before I answered, hoping I sounded outraged. "He stood you up?"

I heard her breath catch on the other end of the line. "Seriously, I waited for hours. I'd almost called Greg to see if there had been any accidents between here and Frisco. Finally, he picked up and acted like I'd misunderstood. That he'd made plans for next weekend."

"That's weird." I pumped my fist up and down. Not that I didn't want Amy to be happy, but this guy wasn't the one. Maybe she'd see now without me opening my big mouth. Again. I couldn't see us doing barbeques together for the next twenty years. I'd probably kill him and then Greg really would have to arrest me.

Amy sighed. "I know. Then he said he was coming by tonight and I told him I wouldn't be home." She paused. "He yelled at me, called me all kinds of names, then hung up."

"You don't deserve that." I pressed her, trying to get her to agree.

I heard a sniffle on the other end of the line. "I know. Anyway, I'll see you tonight? About nine? I'd cancel with Justin, but he's so excited about the mission find, I don't want to disappoint him."

"There's no reason to cancel. Hank will have to realize that you have friends. Male and female. And you have a life. You can't drop everything when he calls. What does he think, it's nineteen-fifty?"

Amy finally laughed. "I guess. Look, I've got a project I've got to get done today for the council. I'll see you later."

"I'll be home."

"Hey, Jill?" Amy stopped me from hanging up.

"Yeah?"

"Thanks for not telling me Hank's a jerk." Then the line went dead.

I smiled as I hung up the phone and went back to finding my next read. Amy would be all right. Even she saw Hank's true colors. I hoped his behavior would be enough to cause her to break it off before the guy broke her heart.

By the time Toby came in to take over, I'd had one additional customer, who mostly wanted to pick up several books for her weekend. I'd cleaned the display case, restocked the desserts, cleaned out the coffeemakers, and spent the rest of my shift perusing the online bookstore for new releases and old favorites to order.

It was only then I realized I still hadn't heard from my aunt. Fear crept over me as I took the stairs up to her apartment. I hesitated, then knocked. No answer. I knocked again, louder. I closed my eyes and prayed quietly, "Please let her be all right."

The door swung open and there she stood, in a robe, her hair wrapped in a towel. "Seriously, Jill, you need to start calling before you drop in." She leaned on the door frame. "What did you want?"

"Did you get my note?" I peered around her, but no one else seemed to be in the apartment.

"Yes, but I got in late last night from the city. A friend had a dinner party." She raised her eyebrows. "Then I went to City Hall for your wild goose chase."

I tried not to laugh. "Sorry. I'll talk to you later."

I headed down the stairs and ran straight into Mayor Baylor. "Oh sorry. Were you looking for me?"

He blushed. "I've got a meeting with your aunt, if you must know."

Shock must have shown on my face because he blundered on.

"She wants to discuss the festival." He stepped past me. "I don't know why I'm even trying to explain myself."

I stood, shocked, on the stairway until I heard his knock on the door. When the murmuring voices faded, I realized that Aunt Jackie must have invited the man into the apartment. My skin crawled. *Please don't let my aunt be the mayor's something-something on the side,* I prayed. Then I thought of Tina. The mayor's wife would kill Jackie, then probably castrate her husband, if they were having an affair.

I power-walked home, trying to get the image of my aunt and the mayor out of my head. Then Emma and I took a run down to the beach. The afternoon weather had stayed amazing and the run cleared my mind. Thinking about Amy breaking up with Hank turned my smile into a wide grin. Running by the cove where Greg had found Fifi made me consider Brenda and her on-again-off-again relationship with Craig.

So much was hidden from others when two people were intimate. Good and bad. My mind was jumbled when we finally arrived back home. Instead of focusing on what would happen if Greg stopped finding my tendency to find trouble cute, I headed upstairs to take a shower. He would be here at six to grill dinner.

By the time Greg came over, I'd finished my domestic goddess duties, namely cleaning the downstairs where people would be, and had even baked a batch of peanut butter cookies to serve Amy and Justin with coffee. I had brought home a cheesecake, as well, but it never hurt to have a couple of choices.

"Smells amazing in here." He snagged a cookie, kissing me before biting into the still warm treat.

"Those are for later, when Amy's friend visits." I swatted his arm.

He grinned and nodded to the plate. "You baked enough for an elementary school bake sale. I don't think they'll miss one." He picked up another three and sat at the table. "Or a few."

I laughed and grabbed my own. I did run today. One wouldn't hurt my diet. I didn't count the cookie dough I'd tried while baking. "So how was your day, dear?"

Greg winced. "So we've come down to that? Ward and June Cleaver conversation?"

"Not unless I've forgotten and Ward was a police chief solving murders." I glanced at the fridge. "Beer or iced tea?"

Greg glanced at his watch. "Toby's officially on, so beer me up, please."

I grabbed two out of the door. You wouldn't think beer went with cookies, but it was a surprisingly great match.

"I've got Amy's favorite wine chilling, as well." I sank into my chair. "She's been having a bad day. Hank troubles," I added.

"We can only hope." Greg rubbed his hand against his forehead. "Man, I don't like to judge, but I don't know what she sees in that loser."

I nodded. "I'm trying to keep my mouth shut, but I danced around the shop while she cried on my shoulder over the phone."

"You are a horrible friend." Greg smiled. "And I love you for it."

My breath caught. I think he realized what he'd said as soon as I did. The *L* word had been spoken. He stood and opened the fridge. He didn't meet my eyes. "You got the steaks ready to grill?"

"Yep, and I'm making a spinach and avocado salad to go with it. You okay with that?" I stayed seated, my legs shaking a bit. At least my voice sounded calm.

By the time we'd finished preparing dinner and had dished up plates to eat outside on the small table on the porch, Greg finally spoke. "Look, about what I said earlier."

I stopped him. "The phrase slipped out. I understand. I'm fine with the way things are now. We don't need to move forward into something else."

His gaze focused on me and then he dropped his glance. "But what if I want to?"

My heart pounded. "I guess that would be okay." This time my voice did shake, just a bit. I focused on cutting the steak.

"Okay then, we'll table the discussion until later." Greg grinned.

"Later?" I cocked my head.

He poured steak sauce on his plate and cut a bite off. Dipping it into the sauce, he paused his fork and watched me. "When we don't have company showing up any moment. I'm happy we opened the door and you didn't slam it shut."

"It's not wide open, yet," I amended his analogy.

Greg didn't look up when he replied, "Not yet."

By the time we'd finished dinner and cleaned the kitchen, Amy and Justin had arrived. I carried a tray filled with plates, forks, cookies, and cheesecake into the living room while Greg got their drink orders.

"Before we talk, can I see the wall?" Justin's eyes glowed with anticipation. "Since the light is fading?"

"Oh yeah, I guess we should." We walked to the kitchen door, where Emma sat on the porch. She greeted Amy with a wag of the tail and then sniffed Justin's pant leg. He must have met muster because he got a wag and a slurp of a kiss on the hand, as well.

"Justin, that's Emma." We made sure the door was shut behind us and started walking through the backyard. I could feel Justin's excitement oozing out of him as we walked.

"I can't believe this." Justin ran in front of the rest of us and knelt down by the wall, reaching out to touch it like it might disappear in front of him. "When did you find this?"

"When I moved into the house. The city was pushing me to do upgrades so I hired some help. The contractor doing the fence actually found the wall and called in the historical guys. You think it might be part of the actual mission? Could you tell the commission that?" I pressed. I figured it was good news the way the guy was almost salivating.

"I'm not certified in this type of historical artifacts, so I doubt any testimony I would give would hold any credence." Justin took out his cell phone and snapped a few pictures, moving up and down the wall to get a better angle.

Damn. I'd been hoping I'd be able to bring in the big guns and force the commission's hand. Still, he did seem interested. "I don't understand, I thought you were a history professor."

"I am. But California history is a hobby, not my profession. I teach European history. That's why I took up studying California in my spare time. You wouldn't believe the history in almost every town up and down the coast. Sure, we have cowboys, but we were settled from adventure ships the kings and queens of the European courts sponsored. Everyone was looking for the lost city of gold." He went over and stood by Amy, giving her an impromptu hug. "You're the best. I appreciate you setting this up."

Something in his tone made me watch the two of them together. Amy was actually blushing, right up to the roots of her hair. She liked him. That was obvious. Hank might be a jerk, but he'd been right to be worried about this visit. Justin appeared to be into Amy, too. I wondered if my friend even realized the effect she was having on the man.

Greg cleared his throat and the two sprang apart like jack-in-the-boxes. "It's getting dark. If we're staying out much longer, I'll have to get some flashlights from the house."

Justin shook his head, grinning. "I'm done. But I'd love to come back after I've had some time to dig into some research. This is truly historic, if you're right. A lot of the missions down the coast had been considered lost."

"You're welcome anytime." I leaned into Greg as we walked back to the house, Emma trotting in front of us.

Justin paused as we reached the steps. He glanced back at the area where the wall sat, even though it couldn't be seen from where we stood. "What else did you want to show me?"

We went back into the kitchen where I'd set the censer out on the table. "Emma found this in the yard the other day."

Pulling out a chair, he sat and put a pair of wire-framed glasses on that should have made him look like a super geek. But he was more super geek on sexy steroids. Or the male version of sexy librarian.

He frowned and bent his head closer to see the item, inching it closer to him by tugging on the edge of the napkin I'd set it on. He took his phone out again, and took several shots.

Amy slid into a chair beside him. "So what do you think? Does this prove the mission wall is real?"

Justin took off his glasses and glanced at her, then at me. "I don't know. It reminds me more of the ones used in medieval England, not Spain. I'll have to do some research."

"At least we have the coins verified." I took cups out of the cabinet. "Blueberry cheesecake and coffee?"

"Sounds divine." Amy stood. "What can I help you with?"

I shook my head. "Nothing. Tonight you're a guest. Hey, did you talk to Jackie today?"

"Yep, but she was in a foul mood when she left. At least today she wore jeans, but I swear her tank was designer. She was covered in dust from head to toe. I know I saw the original building permits before. I would have sworn that they were already in the file cabinet. Maybe the last intern pulled them and didn't get them filed back." Amy leaned against the counter.

Maybe I should have mentioned the mayor's impromptu visit to Jackie's apartment, but before I could decide, Justin interrupted our prattle. "What coins?"

"Hold on a second." Greg pushed his chair back and left the kitchen. When he returned, he had the coin case I bought to show off a set of three of the coins. Not valuable enough to make the house a target for random gold thieves, but a nice keepsake nonetheless. He handed the case to Justin.

"Bob's pirate gold?" He read the inscription on the box out loud.

I smiled and put a cup of coffee and a plate in front of him. "Kind of an inside joke, kind of a memorial to the son of the woman who left me the house. He actually played pirates with the coins after he found them as a kid. Then they were shut up in a chest and forgotten until we cleaned out the loft over the shed."

Justin snapped a picture of the coins, as well. I didn't know if he'd get anything but the glare from the glass, but I saw him check the shot, so I guessed he must have been happy.

"Hey, what do most antique dealers charge for appraisals?" I settled next to Greg.

Justin slipped his phone back into his pocket. "I guess it depends. The university is considered a deep pocket, so our contracts run from two hundred to four hundred dollars, depending on the number of items we're getting looked at."

Greg frowned at me. "Are you finally going to get someone over to look at Emily's stuff?"

I decided to put a card on the table. "Actually, yes, but that's not why I'm asking." I retrieved a file from my office. "I found these receipts on Josh's desk and thought they seemed high for appraisals."

I opened the folder and handed the copies to Justin. Greg waited for Justin to look, then slid them over the table to examine, too.

"A thousand's pretty high." Justin whistled. "Even for a place like The Castle. I didn't think they were buying much lately."

"And how did you get copies of these?" Greg was staring at me.

"I plead the fifth." He didn't chuckle.

I tried to refocus the conversation and asked Justin, "So this wouldn't be a normal appraisal fee?"

"I wish. I could pay off my student loans doing appraisals like that." He picked up his fork and took a bite of the cheesecake with whipped cream topping. "This is amazing."

I put the back of my hand on my forehead and sighed. "I'm glad you like it. I spent hours in the kitchen today."

"Whatever." Greg folded the pages and slipped them into his pocket. He gave me the "we'll talk about this later" look as he dug into his own dessert. "Tell the truth. You got it from the shop. The box probably says Sadie Michael's Pies on the Fly."

"I cut the slices." I pointed my fork at him.

Justin laughed. "My mom was the best cook in the world. Or at least I thought she was. When I found out she ordered in most meals, I was shocked. I guess I should have realized KFC didn't mean Katherine Francis Coulter."

All three of us broke out in laughter, and the rest of the evening was spent telling stories and making jokes. When Greg and I walked Amy and Justin to the door, minutes after eleven, I wondered why the two weren't a couple. They seemed right together. And, selfishly, it made double date nights more fun.

Justin kissed me on the cheek. "Thank you for a terrific evening. Next time I'm in town, I'll buy us dinner."

Greg shook his hand. "We'll take you up on that."

I sat on the porch swing and Greg stood next to me. "Let me know what you find out about the wall," I called out to the retreating couple.

"Believe me, I'll be on this first thing in the morning." Justin opened the car door for Amy. And as I watched, for a second I thought he might lean in for a kiss. But then the moment passed and the car backed out of my driveway. They turned back toward South Cove Bed-and-Breakfast, where Justin had a room for the night.

Greg slipped in next to me on the swing. "I like him."

I watched the road and the taillights until they disappeared. "Me, too."

"Hank's going to be yesterday's news if Justin plays his cards right." Greg laid an arm around my shoulder and I snuggled closer.

"We can only hope." I thought about Amy's voice when she told me Hank stood her up this weekend. It was like she didn't want to admit to anyone, especially me, she had doubts. But the woman was solid gold, inside and out. She deserved better than what Hank could bring her. I liked Justin. I couldn't see holiday dinners at the house with Hank. My head hurt at the image. The words flew out of my mouth before I could stop them. "Hey, are we doing Thanksgiving?"

Greg didn't answer right at first. Then he asked, "You mean, as a couple?"

"I guess. I want to invite Amy, of course, and Aunt Jackie. You don't already have plans, do you? I'd love to host my first year in the house. I think Miss Emily would like the idea, don't you?" I absently drew circles on his jeans with a fingernail as I thought about the menu. Turkey, definitely. And I could make a pumpkin pie. At least I was pretty sure I could. If not, there was always Sadie.

"You know it's still summer, right?" Greg cocked his head and stared at me.

I shook my head. "Nothing wrong with planning ahead."

"We haven't done anything as a family for a while. After Mom died, Jim and his wife used to host since Sherry was too busy with her career to bother. Then Marsha died and it became another day with too many memories." Greg's voice was low. "Jim's never recovered from her accident."

I'd met Greg's brother, Jim, when his company took the job painting my house last spring. The man made it clear he believed I was the only reason Greg wasn't reconciling with his cheating wife. I was sure having him at the Thanksgiving table would be just as pleasant as inviting Hank, who, if he and Amy were still dating, would have to be on the guest list. But for Greg, I'd suffer through. Heck, I'd even invite Mayor Baylor and Tina, if he asked.

Crap, I had it bad.

CHAPTER 15

Wednesday was lunch day with Amy, but when I arrived at the shop the next morning, I had a message on the answering machine. I hit the PLAY button and Amy's voice filled the empty dining room.

"Hey, Justin's hanging out for another day so we're hitting the beach. Waves are supposed to be amazing right after dawn. I've called Baylor and told him I'm taking a personal day, we'll catch up Sunday." She laughed at something in the background I couldn't hear. "Anyway, sorry to bail on you. Later."

I smiled as the machine clicked off, and then I started the coffee-makers. When everything was set, and the shop was still empty, I grabbed the book order sheet and glanced at the customer requests. Greg had ordered three new Civil War mysteries. He'd begun moving away from only reading nonfiction. I glanced through the new catalogue and added ten or so new releases. Then I took the paperback out of my purse, poured a cup of hazelnut, and cuddled into the easy chair by the window where I could see the street and the front door of the shop.

I was still there when Toby showed for his afternoon shift. Six hours of uninterrupted reading bliss. Of course, Aunt Jackie would see it differently. She'd complain about being open all those hours without a single sale. But I knew Wednesdays were historically slow.

We'd be busy enough sooner than later. A slow day here and there wouldn't kill us.

I was almost out the door when Darla Taylor, owner of the South Cove Vineyard, burst into the room.

"Jill, I thought I'd missed you." She gulped in air like she'd run from her winery at the end of Beal Street, almost a mile away.

"You almost did." I set my purse on the counter. "You want some water?"

Darla came up to the counter and nodded. "Thanks."

I waited while she drank down a full cup of water. She wiped her mouth. "I don't think I've run in years. This trying to get into shape is going to kill me."

Her words made me reconsider my thought of offering her a piece of the strawberry cobbler we'd gotten in that morning. I'd estimate Darla to be five feet tall, and almost that wide. The thought of her running didn't make any sense. But I guess every diet started somewhere.

"Sounds like you're on the right track," I said, trying to be supportive.

Darla waved off my words. "Anyway, I needed to talk to you. I'm doing a story on Craig's murder for the *Examiner*. Do you have any response to the rumor that you're suspect number one? I tried to get Greg to confirm or deny, but that boyfriend of yours is uncooperative with the press."

"You think I killed Craig?" Now I regretted offering her water. I wanted to kick her out of the shop. I felt Toby stand behind me.

"Of course not, silly. I know you wouldn't do anything like that. You're too much of a sweetheart. But a girl's got to follow the leads and rumors. I'm the best reporter Tom has at the *Examiner*. I can't be showing partiality. Especially to friends." She pushed the glass toward me. "Can I get more water?"

I wanted to tell her no, but Toby grabbed the glass and filled it before I could speak.

"Thanks, doll." I swore Darla batted her eyelashes at my barista. She took a long drink, set the glass down, and focused on me. "So, where were we?"

"You were explaining why you're even here." I crossed my arms and focused on the woman drinking my free water.

"Don't get upset. I wanted to get your side before I took this to print. We won't name names, but the article is going to mention the rumors." Darla pulled a notebook out of her fanny pack and flipped a few pages. "The widow says the two of you talked recently and she told you that you saved her life."

"That's not what happened. And I didn't kill Craig." I could see the headline now: *Bookseller denies role in wife's scheme to kill local tourist attraction manager.* And the worst thing was that instead of hurting the business I got from townies, it would probably increase my foot traffic. I should let Darla say whatever she wanted. "Look, you know Brenda can get carried away. I couldn't kill anyone."

Darla scribbled in her book. I was digging my grave deeper. She glanced up at me. "Can you tell me why Greg hasn't charged you or even brought you in for questioning?"

"Because I didn't kill Craig?" This was getting us nowhere. "Look, Darla, I've got to leave." I focused on the part-time police officer slash barista at my elbow, making sure I didn't go postal on the woman. "Toby, why don't you get Darla a piece of that double Dutch chocolate mousse cheesecake on the house?"

I grabbed my purse and walked around the serving bar. Planting air kisses on Darla's cheeks, I pleaded one more time to her rational side. "Don't run the article, please?"

Distracted, Darla stared at the plate of chocolate yumminess Toby had set in front of her. "What?"

"You know it can't do anything good for my business." I held my arms out to engulf the entire store. "And I've kind of grown attached to being part of the community."

She sighed. "I'll think about it."

My smile deepened. "That's all I can ask."

"Later, boss," Toby called after me as I walked out the door. As I left, I heard Darla trying to get Toby to spill anything he knew about me, or the murder, or me and the murder.

The girl didn't know what she was up against. Toby was like a human Fort Knox. I straightened the sign announcing the Cloaked in

Mystery event. I was glad Aunt Jackie was taking this on, because I'd have been over it two weeks ago. I hated event planning. Getting the players together for the next business-to-business meeting had been on my to-do list since the last meeting. I vowed to send out invites when I got home today. I needed to make a standing first Tuesday of the month announcement for the meeting rather than pretend like it was going to be any other day.

The Summer Festival decorating committee had been busy over the last few days. The streets of South Cove looked like a garden gnome had walked through the village vomiting summer flowers. Merchants had a wide berth on how they decorated their shops for the festival. How, not if. The only restriction was there had to be something mentioning the festival in shop windows or Darla would come decorate for you. Jackie had designed a Cloaked in Mystery barbeque theme to promote our upcoming event. Josh Thomas re-created a historic trip to the beach with mannequins in long, striped swim clothes.

Running through a mental list of must do's, I nearly jogged home. When I got there, I threw some laundry in the washer and listed into my notebook the things I'd been thinking about. I dialed Jackie's number.

"Why was Mayor Baylor visiting you yesterday?"

The line was quiet. Finally, she sighed. "I'd hoped you hadn't seen him. It's not what you think. I wanted to see if he knew anything about the building permits for City Hall."

"And you thought he'd just tell you? The man knew Craig was trying to shut down the mission funding. Why would he admit to being in on the fraud?" Sometimes my aunt didn't think.

"Give me a little credit. I have a way with men."

She was right, she did. "So, what did you find out?"

"Not one darn thing. The man is a lech and thought I'd invited him for a tête-à-tête." Jackie laughed. "You should have seen his face when I said he needed to leave or I'd call his wife."

"You need to be careful."

"Pish, I can handle myself." Jackie paused. "I guess I'll head back down to City Hall today for a few hours before I come into the shop.

I've almost gone through all the boxes. If it's still there, I'll find the paperwork today."

"Just be careful."

After saying good-bye, I felt a nudge on my leg. When I glanced down, Emma sat and put a paw on my thigh. "Time for a run?"

Her response to the word was immediate, and she ran to the back door, whining for me to meet up with her. I let her outside and headed upstairs to change into my running clothes.

Thursday morning came and the coffee shop was slammed. I'd been busy from the moment I'd opened the door with my first two customers having to wait for the coffee to brew before I could send them off to their day with their large blacks and a morning cinnamon roll. Jackie's new flyers sat on the desk with handwritten instructions on the top for Toby and me to slip one into every bag we handed out—and if they only ordered coffee, with the receipt. *The marketing maven strikes again,* I thought after I'd handed out the first batch and went into the back for a new pile.

Jackie had divided the flyers up into packets of fifty, probably so she could monitor how many we actually handed out versus the number of sales we had that day. You didn't mess with her marketing plans or you never heard the end of it.

Toby's arrival came at the same time as a tour bus stop, so my six-hour shift turned into seven before the traffic slowed enough for me to leave. We'd had several customers return to the line with books after getting their coffee. I'd sold more books today than I had in one shift ever. The flyer appeared to be working, at least in the short run. Jackie would be ecstatic, even though when she'd started working with me, she'd suggested we'd do away with the book side of the business entirely. Now you would have thought the section had been her brainchild. I had to admit, she knew her marketing stuff.

As I took off my apron, loud voices near the front of the shop drew my attention.

"Look, you're cute and all, but really, you couldn't have thought I was serious? I mean, look at me." Lisa Brewer ran her hands up and down the front of her body, showing off her assets. "With all this, I don't have to date high school boys for real."

Nick Michaels look stunned. "But you said—"

Lisa laughed and shrugged. "I needed a ride into the city. You had a car. Mystery solved." Her attention was diverted to the street where a motorcycle was double-parked in front of the store. The rider, sans helmet this time and wearing a doo rag with a skull hand-painted on the front, revved the engine, obviously his idea of knocking on his date's door. "Sorry, Reno's here. I've got to go."

"Lisa, wait . . ." Nick grabbed at her arm, but she twisted away before he could catch her.

She stopped and turned back, kissing him on the lips, then wiping her lipstick stain off his face. I saw her glance out the window to see if Reno was watching. He was, and even at the distance where I stood, I could see his face darken.

"Toby," I called in a hushed voice. I felt him standing behind me before I heard his words. A habit he'd come to perfect in the last few months. Why was drama always happening here in this peaceful shop?

"I'm watching." Toby's response was as quiet as my call had been. Even the customers seemed to be holding their breath, waiting to see how this love triangle would end. I hoped it wasn't with a dying Nick calling out for his love from the black-and-white tile of my coffee shop's floor.

But Lisa seemed to be done playing both men and smiled at Nick. His face beamed with hope at what he thought the kiss had meant. The hope disappeared with her next words. "Thanks for everything. Maybe we can hook up again."

And with that, she flounced out of the shop, her miniskirt flowing in the light wind outside. She climbed on the back of the motorcycle, put her fake cowboy boots on the foot holds, and wrapped her arms around Reno's stomach. A stomach that I would bet boasted a six-pack once you stripped off his rider leathers. I could see the attraction—who didn't love the bad boy? But my heart ached for Nick.

He stood at the glass window and watched the couple leave. As they started up the street, Reno gave him a little wave to add insult to the injury.

Toby tossed his towel on the counter. "Poor kid. I'd like to murder that jerk and I don't even know him. I'm going to go talk to Nick."

I sighed and put back on my apron.

"You don't have to stay." Toby paused, looking at me, probably realizing my shift had ended a while ago.

"You can take over when you get back. I don't think this will be a quick chat." I smiled and nodded to the phone. "I've got some orders to finish up anyway. You think I should call his mom to give her a CliffsNotes version?"

Toby nodded. "Nick won't like it, but he knows he lives in a small town. South Cove isn't the place where you can have something like this not get back to your mom. Man, I'd hate to be in the locker room next week. Those guys are going to give him such grief."

I watched as Toby put his hand on the boy's back, then the two of them walked out of the shop. I'd noticed men weren't usually the ones to sit and talk about a problem. They did things, then the talk got mixed around in the doing. Give me a group of giggling girls crowded on a sofa any day. At least the words got said, eventually.

I waited for them to walk out of eyesight, then picked up the phone. When the other end picked up, I said, "Sadie, Nick's got a problem."

Thirty minutes later, Toby returned and put his apron on, pouring himself a cup of coffee. I gave him a pointed stare.

"What?" He pretended to be focused on how many pieces of cheesecake were cut and ready in the display case.

I blew out a breath. "How is Nick?"

Toby stopped rearranging the case and leaned against the counter, his arms crossed over his chest. "Frankly, I'm worried. He wouldn't tell me everything, but he let it slip Lisa talked him into doing things he knew were wrong. What that means? I'm not sure."

My heart stopped for a second. "You don't think Nick had anything to do with Craig's murder, do you?"

Toby shook his head. "That's the thing, I don't see him doing something illegal for any girl, but he wouldn't tell me what he did. I guess me being a cop doesn't make me the best one to confide your secrets to."

"You have to tell Greg." I stated the obvious, the words coming out before I realized.

Toby swung a clean towel over his shoulder and then took a sip of coffee. "I know."

We ended the conversation there, and finally, two hours late, I started walking home. I stopped in at Diamond Lille's, ordered a turkey Reuben to go, and then slowly made my way to the house. Any thought of Greg showing up with a movie later had been dashed with the incident with Nick and Lisa.

And if there had been something worse than breaking into The Castle grounds for an after-school party, Sadie would make Nick do the right thing and confess. There wouldn't be any hiding behind lawyers. Nick would tell the police everything. I hoped his good sense had kept him from ruining a perfectly good life.

When I reached the house, I set my sandwich on the table, let Emma out, and picked up the phone. The kid needed a friend.

"Jimmy Marcum's office," a cheery receptionist answered.

A few hours later, my phone rang. I didn't even look at the display. Greg would be hot because I hired Jimmy. I might as well face the music.

"Grab your purse and come with me." Aunt Jackie's voice surprised me.

I turned off the television. "Where are you?"

"In your driveway. Come on, I found out where Craig's crate is stored."

I stood and opened the front door. My aunt waved at me from her open window. "Come on," she said into the phone.

I held up a finger, then let Emma outside, tucked my camera into my purse, and locked up the house.

When we'd reached the highway, I asked, "So, who told you about Craig's crate?"

"Brenda was in the shop last night." Jackie whipped the sedan around a slow-moving truck that had been going the speed limit. I gripped the door handle. "The girl talks up a blue streak when you let her."

I watched out the window, thinking about how calm the ocean

looked today, knowing under the smooth surface a whole 'nother world existed. Just like small towns. "I'm thinking it's probably locked."

"There's a hidden key, according to Brenda. Or at least there was one. She kept one just in case so she didn't have to drive back to South Cove if she forgot to grab Craig's when he sent her for items." Jackie grinned. "People like to tell me things. They think I'm like a bartender, advice central."

We listened to Jackie's all-Sinatra, all-the-time station, and by the time we'd arrived, even I was feeling mellow. Frank could do that to a girl. We parked near the harbor and headed toward the docks. Shipping containers sat in a fenced area, a guard station at the gate. I raised an eyebrow, but Jackie approached the security guard without any hesitation.

"Crate four-five-nine. We'll be fast." She smiled and waved at me. "Or we will be if my niece will stop dawdling. You'd think she'd never visited a shipping yard before."

"Sounds like you know where you're going, then." The security guard tapped his baseball cap and then went back into his shed. I heard the televised voices of sports announcers talking about the upcoming baseball game that evening.

"You are amazing," I whispered as we got out of hearing distance. Jackie grinned at me. "Look like you're supposed to be somewhere, and everyone leaves you alone. How do you think I get into all the best parties, by invite?"

I was learning more and more about my aunt. Some things I wasn't sure I wanted to know.

Finally we found the correct crate. Jackie looked around the dusty metal container as long as a long-haul truck body. She picked up several rocks, abandoning them one after another, then slid a key out of the bottom of the last one. "And you doubted me."

We unlocked the door, and I cringed at the loud creak. Jackie pulled a flashlight out of her Dooney & Bourke tote. She clicked it on and the beam illuminated the dark crate. Piles of furniture, tapestries, and oil paintings in frames. Antiques. Just like you'd expect to find in a collector's crate.

Walking through the narrow walkway, I reached out to touch a tapestry, only to have my hand slapped. "Don't touch. Fingerprints!"

I glanced around the crate. "I don't see anything here that shouldn't be here."

Jackie sighed. "Me, either." She shined the light onto the ceiling. Nothing. "I guess I thought maybe this was the clue."

"It was a good thought." I heard voices outside the crate. "We better go before your security guard realizes we're not at crate four-five-nine."

Jackie relocked the crate, hid the key in the rock, and as we walked toward the gate, seemed thoughtful. She looked at me. "I just can't figure out why someone would want Craig dead."

"Besides the obvious, you mean." I turned and saw the fake rock still in my aunt's hand. "You probably should leave that here."

She glanced down at her hand. "Oh, I hadn't realized." She turned, but I stopped her.

"I'll take it back. Meet you in the car." I grabbed the rock with my sweatshirt. "Fingerprints, right?"

"Just hurry. I need to get back and relieve Toby." Jackie turned back to the car, and I watched her for a few seconds. She seemed so disappointed that the idea hadn't brought any new information. But it was one more place we'd checked. Soon the mystery had to be solved. I walked back to the crate, but heard voices before I turned the corner.

"He had a fake rock somewhere around here, I know it." Ray Stewart stood, yanking on the lock we'd just clicked. A big man stood near him.

"Maybe you took it so you could come back later," the man growled.

Panic made Ray's eyes widen, and I almost felt bad for the man. Almost. It was nice seeing the bully get what he gave. "I promise, Sarge, I wouldn't do that."

I stepped back away from the crate and sprinted to the car. Even though Jackie and I hadn't seen it, the clue had to be in the crate. We'd come back this weekend and search the items from top to bottom with gloves. I tucked the fake rock into my purse and made my way to Jackie's car.

"Let's get out of here," I said, glancing over my shoulder to make sure I hadn't been seen.

We'd found the reason for Craig's death, we just didn't know what we were looking for. Yet.

CHAPTER 16

Greg picked me up right at five-thirty Friday evening, his usual jeans and uniform shirt replaced with black jeans and a button-down shirt, collar open to show a touch of his tanned chest. I opened the door and motioned him in. "I can't find my black clutch."

I turned back to sprint back upstairs when I felt him grab my arm and swing me into his arms. He held me close, one hand on the low of my back and the other sweeping my hair off my neck. Then he kissed me, long, hard, and sweet. I leaned into the kiss, smelling the freshly showered skin, the scent of his soap still lingering.

"Wow," I breathed when he let me go. I felt his gaze drop and then rise again to meet my own. I was glad I'd chosen the black dress with the *V* neckline. It clung to my curves without being too slutty. Sometimes that was a fine line.

"You sure we have to chaperone?" He smoothed back a curl that had fallen into my face.

I touched his cheek. "She'd kill me if I let her go alone. Although it might be worth the trouble."

He smiled. And the slow, sexy smile almost changed my mind. "We haven't had a lot of time together the last few weeks. It's too bad we have to spend the little time we do with your aunt and her star-crossed lover."

"Don't let her hear you say that. She's livid she even has to go. Something about prostitution being illegal." I nodded to the stairs. "So can I go get my purse?"

Greg crossed the room, flipped on the television, and sank into the couch. "Just don't take too long. We still have to pick up your aunt and drive into the city. Josh made the reservations for seven."

"If I don't find it in a few minutes, I'll bring a different one." I kissed him on top of the head and started up the stairs.

"Why don't you use the one you can find?" he called after me.

Emma followed me up the stairs and stood watching as I dug on the top of the shelves. "He doesn't understand girls, now, does he?"

Emma cocked her head as she watched. I think maybe she agreed with Greg. Ten minutes later, I had the right purse, finished the makeup painting and jewelry selection, and was ready to go. I padded back down the stairs barefoot, my pumps in my hand.

"Ready."

There was no answer from the couch. I could see the back of Greg's head, but he didn't turn. I spun around to show him the final product, pulling on the last shoe as I started the turn. "Greg?"

Still no answer. Then I heard a gentle snore. I couldn't believe he'd fallen asleep. I stomped over to the front of the couch and shook his arm. "Greg, wake up!"

All of a sudden I felt myself being pulled onto his lap. He pushed back my curly hair, set in a wild, untamed look, and kissed me again. This time, I didn't even question the contact, I just enjoyed.

He peered at me and finally slapped me on the butt. "Seriously, you have to stop kissing me. We're going to be late picking up your aunt."

"Hey, buddy, you started it." I laughed and stood, pulling him to his feet.

"Not the story I'm telling." Greg whistled to Emma. "Okay if I put her in the back?"

"Perfect. She'd hate to be locked up all evening while we're gone." I walked around closing windows and was waiting at the front door when Greg returned. He took my keys and locked the dead bolt as we left the house. I scanned the sky, but it seemed cloudless. We might just have a nice evening in store.

Jackie was waiting on the sidewalk when we pulled up in my new car. She glanced at Greg in the driver's seat as she slipped into the back. "I guess I should be thankful I'm not riding in the back of the truck."

Greg flashed her a grin. "Well, my other car is the police cruiser and Toby's using that tonight. But I guess we can track him down and trade if you want. I think he'd love chasing down speeders in Jill's new ride."

I slapped his arm. "You are not letting Toby drive my new car." I glanced at my aunt. "Sorry, I guess I should have considered passengers when I bought a new car."

Jackie shook her head. "Stop treating me like an old lady. I can climb into the back as easily as either of you."

Wait, hadn't she just complained? I glanced at Greg to see if I was the only one who saw the irony. I wasn't. He bit his lip, then headed the Jeep down the highway. I keyed the address into the GPS system and leaned back, willing to let Greg drive and the mechanical female voice I called Dora do the navigating.

We were on the highway when Greg said, "So Jimmy Marcum stopped in the station when we were questioning Nick last night."

My heart stopped for a beat or two. "Oh?" I stared out the window, not able to look Greg's way.

"Yeah, he said he'd been hired to represent the kid, but funny thing, neither Sadie nor Nick had called him." I could see Greg through the reflection in the window glass, staring straight ahead, not looking at me.

The car got quiet. Finally I saw him turn and look at me. "You know anything about that?"

"Would you be mad if I said yes?" I didn't want to turn.

"Oh my God. Would you two talk directly? Jill, tell him you called Jimmy. Greg, get off her back for it. She was trying to protect the kid." Aunt Jackie leaned forward. "How do you guys ever have a conversation? This seems more like a dance."

"Aunt Jackie." I glared at her.

She glared back, her stare hard, and then she nodded at Greg.

"Fine. I called Jimmy. I knew Sadie wouldn't hesitate to have him admit to anything if it was the truth. And he needed someone who knew the law on his side. Truth or not." I settled back in the seat and crossed my arms.

Greg took one look at me and laughed. "I knew it was you. You're the only person in town who has Jimmy on speed-dial."

He didn't sound mad. I pushed for more information. "Tell me Nick didn't kill Craig."

"Nick didn't kill Craig." Greg turned off the highway following Dora's instructions.

I turned in the seat to look at him. "Seriously? But Toby said Nick was upset over what he did for Lisa. What did he do?"

Greg seemed to consider his answer for a long second, and I could feel Jackie's attention focused on him, matching my own scrutiny. "I guess it's not confidential, especially since the district attorney has decided not to file charges. He helped her cut the fence on the back of The Castle property so a group of kids could sneak in to swim."

I laughed. "That's all?"

Greg pulled the car under the screen and a valet approached his door. "The kid was pretty upset. He felt it violated his moral code. He said he might even have to surrender his Eagle Scout badge." Greg handed the keys to the valet and walked around to the passenger door, where he opened the door for me. Then he helped me out, holding my hand until I got steady on my too-high heels. As he reached back to offer his hand to Jackie, I watched her consider slapping it away, but she accepted his help. Finally we were on our way through the entry door.

Josh sat on a bench next to a tank filled with live lobsters, a bouquet of cut flowers in his hand. He glanced up at the door as it closed, then jumped up when he saw it was us. Pointedly looking at his watch, he approached us. "You're late."

"Traffic." Greg put his hand on the small of my back and started me forward toward Josh. "How are you feeling?"

Josh glared at him. "Fine, no thanks to your department. I take it you haven't found my attackers?"

"Not yet," Greg growled.

"Pretty flowers," I said, trying to change the conversation.

Josh glanced down as if he'd forgotten he held them. He shoved them at Jackie. "These are for you. Thank you for accepting my invitation."

Jackie nodded and gingerly took the flowers like he'd offered her a live snake. A hostess approached.

"Oh good, you're all here. The table is ready." She held our menus in her arms and led us deep into the restaurant. When we stopped at a table set by the window overlooking the bay, I sighed. I loved even looking at the ocean. I didn't understand Amy's surfing obsession, but I could sit on the beach and watch the waves for hours.

"Nice," Greg commented. Jackie harrumphed and quickly sat before Josh could pull out the chair. He squeezed into a space next to her and the wall, no view for him. I was starting to feel sorry for Josh since my aunt was being a total pill and he seemed lost in her female charms. If he liked her now, rude and obnoxious, I didn't know what would happen if she was actually nice to the guy.

We ordered a round of drinks and appetizers. Greg and Josh kept to soda, but Jackie and I both ordered a glass of wine. The restaurant specialized in seafood with a nice listing of fresh fish items. Since we'd ordered crab dip and stuffed mushrooms to share around the table, I decided to go with a blackened halibut for my main course. I couldn't help notice my aunt ordering the lobster. I guess she thought if she had to be here, she was going to get what she wanted, no matter what the cost.

"My shop's doing well this quarter. I'm so glad I made the move to South Cove. My receipts are up fifty percent from my location in the city," Josh bragged. I glanced at Greg and noticed his eyes glazing over. Out of the three double dates we'd had in the last month, the only one where he'd enjoyed the company was when Justin and Amy had come over to the house. And that hadn't even technically been a date.

I owed him big. Again. I reached under the table and found his hand. I rubbed the palm, as I answered Josh. "South Cove is known for quirky shops. I'm sure Antiques by Thomas will fit in fine. It's nice having you as our neighbor."

"So what kind of business does your shop do? You pull in anything close to your expenses?" Josh shook his head. "I can't believe you make enough to afford two employees."

Greg squeezed my hand. He knew I wanted to inform Mr. Thomas that asking what kind of money a store owner made was rude. And frankly none of his business. Instead of the things I wanted to say, I finally came up with, "We do all right."

"I don't know how. And this new Cloaked in Mystery campaign. Really? You think anyone will even show up if they don't know the draw? And at the beginning of July? People have lives, you know." Josh kept pushing.

Jackie's face grew darker, but she didn't respond.

I put on my sweet, usually-saved-for-the-mayor smile and answered, "We see it as a great way to escape the summer heat and get your beach read autographed by a famous mystery author." I nodded to my aunt. "Besides, the praise needs to go to Jackie. This is her brainchild."

Josh glanced at Jackie and his face went white. "Of course, I don't know anything about book marketing or coffee stuff. Just normal sales, I guess."

"And books and coffee aren't normal sales?" Jackie asked, acid in her tone.

Josh was saved by the drinks arriving and, a few seconds later, the appetizers. When everyone started eating, the salads arrived. The waitress kept our table moving from one course to the next. And I noticed, Aunt Jackie's wineglass got replaced and refilled several times. She'd be a blast on the way home. I hoped she'd fall asleep rather than rail the entire trip.

Just as we were considering the dessert menu, Greg's cell rang.

"Sorry, I told them I was off the clock." He stood and answered. As he walked away, I heard him greet Esmeralda. She worked the late shift on Fridays and Saturdays so she could schedule readings during the day for her clients. The woman had a knack for telling people want they needed to hear to keep coming back. Many of my drop-in customers were heading toward Esmeralda's house for their weekly readings.

"I'm trying the chocolate liquid cake. Molten Chocolate? Yum." I glanced at Jackie. "What are you getting?"

"Besides a headache?" she grumbled, then sighed. "Fine, I want the pumpkin caramel cheesecake."

"Bring two." Josh smiled at the waitress. Then focused on me. "What would Officer King want?"

"Greg, just Greg tonight." I studied the menu. He loved his chocolate, so I ordered him the marble cheesecake, knowing if he didn't want it, we could trade.

We added a pot of coffee to the mix and then the table went silent. I'd just thought of a conversation topic when Greg sat back down.

"Look, I've got to go to the harbor." He glanced at Josh. "Can you give the ladies a ride home?"

"Jackie," Josh offered. "My Porsche doesn't have a backseat."

"Besides," I countered with my fork covered with the chocolate cake just delivered, "you drove my car. Or did you forget?"

Greg considered me. "You have to stay in the car. With the doors locked. No tramping over the crime scene."

I took a bigger bite of the cake. "Scouts' honor," I mumbled around the food.

"Did someone else get killed?" Josh appeared stricken. "Craig had a crate down at the harbor. Did someone break into that?"

"Sorry, can't go into details." Greg regarded my almost-empty plate. "You ready yet? Or do you want to take my cheesecake, too?"

"Great idea." I waved down a waiter and asked for a to-go box. When the desserts were safely ensconced in pretty boxes, I kissed Jackie on the cheek. "Have fun."

"Wait, you're leaving me here?" Jackie seemed like she'd just woken up. She leaned toward me and whispered, "I told you something was off about the crate."

"I'll call you later," I whispered back, then I nodded to Josh. "He'll see you home."

As we walked away, I heard my aunt call after me, "This wasn't part of the bargain."

Greg chuckled as he opened the door for me. He gave his number chip to the valet. "I thought I'd have another crime scene to clean up back there."

I climbed into the Jeep and pulled off my heels, slipping into some flip-flops I kept in the backseat. "She deserves it. The man was being nice, or at least as nice as Josh knows how to be, and she was a grump. Maybe on the ride home she can learn some manners." What I wasn't saying was that maybe Jackie could find out why Craig was paying Josh thousands of dollars over market rate for appraisals.

"If Josh isn't our killer." Greg shut the door and walked around the front of the car, tipping the valet.

I waited for him to pull away from the parking lot before I spoke. "You don't think Josh could—I mean, he loved Craig. A bit too much, if you ask me."

Greg smiled. "Just keeping you on your toes. No, Josh has an airtight alibi for the night Craig was killed. When you gave me those receipts, I decided to take a second look. He was at an estate auction up north. He stayed over and I even have him on camera in the hotel at exactly the same time as we estimate the murder occurred. We cleared him days ago."

"You're mean." But I mulled Josh's alibi around in my head. Why couldn't I have been somewhere a camera could have proved I wasn't the killer?

Greg punched a new address into the GPS and Dora quickly routed him. He sighed and searched my face for something. "I don't think you take this seriously sometimes. It's not one of your books, Jill. People do bad things. And when they think they're going to get caught, they do more bad things to hide their guilt."

I peeked up from the ring I'd been twisting. "I get it. I'm to stay in the car. Even if I have to pee."

That made Greg laugh. "If that happens, go to the nearest police officer on duty and ask to be escorted to a convenience store in the area. I won't make you suffer."

"Thanks." I watched the road pass by as we drove closer to the docks. I knew we were close when the lights from the police cars started brightening the darkening night. Then Dora instructed Greg to turn right, and we were at our destination.

CHAPTER 17

Greg had only been gone twenty minutes and it felt like hours. If this was a quick stop in, how did they get through stakeouts? No wonder Toby had fallen asleep the first time he'd played guard dog for me when everything was blowing up around Miss Emily's death. I took the fake rock out of my purse and fingered the key, wondering if I should mention Jackie and I visiting the crate yesterday. But I knew exactly how Greg felt about me getting involved in police investigations, and besides, we hadn't actually found anything that would point toward Craig's killer.

I'd read the new manual that came with the car, learning the new options including the fact I didn't have to keep track of oil change time anymore, my car would tell me. And it would tell me if I was running low on gas. A handy feature since I didn't like stopping and filling the tank. It was the one thing I missed about being married. My ex had been a fanatic about keeping the tank at least half full at all times.

I watched the red and blue lights flashing on and off and thought of the ocean. I imagined waves coming in with every flash.

Greg's hand shook my arm, and when I opened my eyes, I didn't see the flashing lights anymore. We were sitting in my driveway, the rock in my hands. I scooted up in the seat. "Wow, I guess I was tired."

"The SF cops were calling you Sleeping Beauty." He nodded to the house. "You want me to walk you in?"

"If I make coffee, will you tell me what we were doing there?" I stretched.

Greg smiled and pushed a wayward curl out of my face. "Do you have cheesecake? Someone ate mine from dinner."

"And it was amazing, but yeah, I brought some home from the shop today." I leaned my head on the headrest and watched him. "I thought maybe you'd want some for breakfast."

He chuckled. "Not tonight. I'm heading straight to the office after coffee and cheesecake. I think we finally have a lead."

That made me wake up. I opened my door and grabbed my purse. Crossing over to the fence, I opened the gate and stared at Greg, still sitting in the car. "What are you waiting for? Let's get brewing."

He climbed out of the Jeep, grinning. "I don't know whether to be insulted or proud."

Confused, I stared at him. "What?"

He pulled me close and kissed my forehead. "You tossed aside the idea of a night alone with me for solving a murder case. You're either the perfect match for a local cop, or a crime junkie."

Pushing aside the compliment—at least I thought it was a compliment—I unlocked the front door. An envelope fell to the floor when I opened the door.

Greg reached down and peeked inside.

"Hey, what if it's a love note from my other boyfriend?" I teased as I clicked on lights and put my purse and keys on the front table. Greg absently turned the locks on the door and followed me into the kitchen, still reading.

"You don't have time for another boyfriend. Between being the South Cove primary crime stopper and seeing me, your days are pretty filled." He tossed the letter onto the kitchen table and greeted Emma, who bounded into the living room, ready for human company after chasing rabbits and other wildlife out of the yard for the last few hours. "Besides, Emma wouldn't like it if you brought someone else over. She's bonded to me."

Pouring water into the coffeemaker, I laughed. "That dog can be bought with a dog treat. I'm sure she'd trade me in for two."

"Sad, but probably true." He scratched Emma behind the ears. "You want me to help with the cheesecake?"

"Stay there. I'm perfectly capable of dishing up two slices without brute force." I grabbed two small plates with the rose design from my cabinet. Greg might complain about the tea party feel, but I loved this china and used it every chance I got. I set a fork and plate in front of him and then slipped into my seat. "What's this?"

"You said it was a love letter." Greg started eating, not looking up at me.

"Brat." I took a bite of the cheesecake and the vanilla swirl hit my tongue. Heaven. Sadie Michaels was a genius. I started reading the letter. Looking up, I said, "This is from Justin."

"Yep." Greg took another bite, but now he was watching my face.

Sometimes the strong, silent type only goes so far. I kept reading. Then I froze. I reread a paragraph.

Greg polished off my slice of cheesecake, too. The guy could eat through anything. "Someone could have planted the censer to throw us off track."

I grabbed the letter. "If Justin could put this together in what, a day, then the mayor's going to be asking you what your malfunction is and why you haven't arrested me."

Greg stood and reached for a to-go cup. "He already asks me that every day. Why should this evidence make it any different?"

"Because this says Emma's new chew toy was discovered missing from The Castle." I shook the letter. "Then it winds up in my yard?"

Greg set a cup of coffee in front of me, then pulled his chair closer so he could hold my hand after he pried the letter out of my grip. "Do you think I'm stupid?"

I frowned. His question confused me. "No."

"I'd have to be pretty dense to see this as anything but a frame job. If you killed Craig"—he held his hand up to stop me from talking— "I said *if*. Why would you bring a souvenir from the crime scene, then give it to your dog to play with? That doesn't make a bit of sense."

I thought about his logic for a few minutes. "But it does mean someone is trying to make me the fall guy for this. And the person who's trying, isn't thinking things through."

"Or is dumber than a box of rocks." Greg smiled. "So do you want to know what was in the crate?"

"I'd assumed Craig's antiques?" I tried to sound casual, hoping something I owned hadn't fallen out of my purse while I'd been sneaking around.

He nodded. "The only unit broken into belonged to Craig Morgan. The harbor master verified the ownership before we entered the box. And yes, it had antiques."

I waited, but Greg seemed to be waiting for me to guess. "And what? Antiques, and what?"

"That's just it, nothing. What was there wasn't as important as what was missing."

I sipped my coffee, but my body was beginning to betray me. I needed sleep. I covered a yawn, then asked, "What was missing?"

"The drug dogs say cocaine from their reaction. Although how the trainer tells the difference based on yips and barks, I'll never know."

I felt stunned. "Craig was importing cocaine?"

"That's what it looks like. Which adds a whole 'nother line of questioning to the witness interviews." He glanced at his watch. "The crime techs from the scene are showing up at the station in ten minutes. I've got to get down there."

I followed him to the front door. "Look, be careful."

"I'm working with the geek squad, I think I'm fine." He put a finger under my chin. "It's you I'm worried about."

"Back door is already locked. Front will be as soon as you leave. Besides, why kill your best patsy?" I put my hands on my hips and posed.

Greg laughed and pulled me into a hug. "Because you wouldn't look like a murder. If this was my playbook, you'd be committing suicide or having an accident to keep you out of the picture."

My eyes widened as I studied this man I'd thought I'd known. "Sometimes you scare me."

"In a totally good and sexy way, right?" He kissed me again and then stepped out of the hug. "Stay inside. Tomorrow we'll take the case apart piece by piece. Just you and me."

"Promises, promises." I pushed him toward the door.

He stopped inside the doorway. "I mean it, Jill. Stay inside."

I watched him pull away from the house and for once, I felt alone, vulnerable. But if I'd said that, Toby would be camped out on my doorstop and the last time that happened we both wound up in the hospital. Emma whined next to me.

I bent down and wrapped my arms around the big golden retriever. Listening to her heartbeat made my own slow a bit. Wiping the back of my hand across my eyes, I stood and checked the locks again. "Let's go to bed."

Emma trotted up the stairs behind me. When I reached my bedroom, I put the cell phone on my nightstand, propped a chair under the doorknob blocking the door, and turned on the shower.

Half-expecting to be a leading lady in the *Psycho* movie, the warm water failed to do any magic on my tense muscles. If anything, when I got out and climbed into pajama pants and a tank, I felt more wound up. I opened the soda I'd brought with me and slipped between the covers. There was no way I would fall asleep anytime soon, so I reached for a gothic mystery and got lost in the creepy goodness.

The phone woke me to a sunny Saturday. Bleary-eyed, I glanced at the clock and jumped out of bed, knocking the half-read book off my chest. I'd slept through my alarm and in ten minutes I was supposed to open the shop.

I clicked the phone on, using the speaker function. "Hello?"

"I thought you might still be asleep." Aunt Jackie chuckled. "No need to hurry in, I've already opened the shop and made coffee. Snuggle back with that hunk of yours."

I pulled my pajamas off as I talked. "Greg isn't here."

"Oh. Well then, get your butt down here. I shouldn't have to cover your shifts, too." Aunt Jackie paused, then asked, "Did you get in a fight?"

"No. Greg and I are fine." I shook my head at the phone, not caring she couldn't see my action. With my aunt it was all or nothing. She made no bones about the fact she thought Greg should man up and ask me to marry him. Even though I'd told her time and again, I liked our situation right now. "Look, I'll be down in a few minutes. We can talk then."

I hung up the phone before she could respond. Sometimes conversations with Jackie were better handled with bluntness. That way I got my point across. At least half the time.

I pulled on jeans and a T-shirt, pulled my hair back into a ponytail, and finished my morning bathroom ritual. Emma was already sitting at the door, staring at the chair blocking her way.

"Better safe than sorry," I said to my dog, who looked at me like I was the crazy one. As soon as the door opened, she bounded down the stairs and sat at the back door, waiting for me to let her out.

I filled her food and water dishes and then locked the back door. Emma loved staying outside while I worked. Looking longingly at the empty coffeepot, I grabbed my keys and purse and after locking the front door, half-jogged up to the shop.

The smell of cinnamon, spice, and strong coffee hit me as soon as I opened the door. Jackie stood at the counter, talking to Brenda.

"There she is." Jackie smiled at me. "Your friend stopped by to see you. I told her you'd just be a minute."

"Actually that was a half hour ago." Brenda glanced at the clock. "Your aunt is entertaining."

I kissed Jackie on the cheek as I buzzed by, stashing my purse in the back office before I returned to fill a cup with our dark blend. I held up my hand to stop any additional comments, then took five sips. Finally, with the caffeine starting to run through my body, I felt close to normal. I took a stool next to Brenda. "I didn't expect to see you today. Don't you have to get back to the city?"

Brenda's smile widened. "No, actually. I'm thinking about staying. I took a short vacation. They think I'm broken up about Craig's death, they didn't even question my need for two weeks. I'm looking around for a place here in South Cove."

I took another sip of coffee. The day was becoming much more interesting. "Wow. I thought you hated it here."

Pain shot through Brenda's eyes, and I wished I could have taken the words back. "Sorry, I didn't mean to question. Let's forget what I said. How about, 'Wow, you'll love it here in South Cove'?"

"And I will. Especially with Craig not around to tell me how stupid I am or how fat." Brenda held up her hand. "I know I shouldn't have let him get to me, but when the man who says he loves you treats you like that, it's hard to separate truth from fiction."

"Well, you're definitely not fat now. And you were never stupid."
I reached over and gave Brenda a quick hug. "What were the two of
you huddling about when I came in?"

"Cloaked in Mystery. I was telling Brenda we already have over
fifty people confirmed. I can't believe it. We'll have to take out the
tables to make room for more chairs." Jackie glanced around the coffee shop, already moving things around in her mind.

"I can't believe it's next week." I finished my coffee and handed
my cup to Jackie. "More, please."

"You always were a polite child." Jackie smiled as she refilled my
cup and set it in front of me. "You want something to go with that?"

"I'll grab a bite later." I turned my attention back to Brenda. "So
you'll be here for the uncovering."

She frowned at me. "What?"

"I think she means the uncloaking." Jackie put a piece of pumpkin
pie in front of me with a fork. The pie had been drowned in whipped
cream, exactly the way I liked it. "Eat, your brain cells will thank us."

Brenda nodded. "I've got some things to settle with Craig's estate.
The good news is, he never changed anything when we separated,
and I still have access to our accounts. Tomorrow, I'm driving into
Bakerstown to finalize things with Doc Ames and empty the safety
deposit box."

I'd been scarfing down the pie, but Brenda's mention of a safety
deposit box got me thinking about Craig's hollowed-out books.
"What did he keep there?"

Brenda shook her head. "No clue. The man never even told me we
had one, and according to the paperwork I found, he's had this since
we moved here."

I finished the pie and brushed my hands together. "Maybe you're
a wealthy merry widow."

Brenda barked a laugh. "A life insurance policy would be amazing, but I'm hoping I'm not a broke widow. Do you think Craig had
any clue he might die before me?"

She had a point there. With Craig's arrogance, he probably thought
he'd live forever. "Sorry, forgot who we were talking about."

Brenda glanced at the clock. "Damn, I didn't realize it was that
late. Look, I need to ask you a favor."

I almost said "anything" but thought better of it. "What do you need?"

"I need someone to watch Fifi for a couple of days. I've got to go in to the city and get some of my belongings. I've scheduled a mover to come and put my stuff into storage until I figure out where I'm going to go." Brenda's eyes filled with tears. "I'd take her with me, but I can't have her at my apartment. And I don't need the landlord to have any reason not to give me back my deposit."

I thought about the fenced backyard and considered Emma's territorial reaction. "When are you leaving? I need to see if Greg will take her or Emma. Having them together wouldn't be the best idea."

"I don't have many friends I could even ask." Brenda watched as Jackie sprinted toward the back room. After she'd disappeared, Brenda smiled sadly at me. "See what I mean?"

"She probably . . ." I paused, trying to think of an excuse.

Brenda laughed. "She doesn't want to have to tell me no. That's okay, I get it. I'm heading back in to town on Thursday after the party. Then I should be back next Monday."

"We'll figure something out." I patted her on the arm. "No worries."

But as Brenda left, I wondered if her life with the less-than-petite Fifi would be the heaven she'd always imagined. Craig could take care of the large dog mostly because he lived on site at The Castle and the property backed up to national forest land. Fifi had lots of room to wander, hunt, and just be a huge dog. No apartment Brenda could afford would give Fifi the same life.

Not my worry, I thought as I started my day at the shop. Soon, tourists started flocking in, keeping me busy making coffee drinks and serving up treats. Customers were buying more books today, especially mysteries.

"So, this is the author who's coming this week, right?" A local teenager smiled and handed me a twenty.

I glanced down at the paperback. It was a cozy author who wrote knitting mysteries set in Colorado. I loved her stuff and now brought in the hardbacks for her die-hard fans, like me. "This book is great. Have you read her other stuff?"

The girl peered at me like I'd grown two heads. "Duh. I'm in here as soon as I know it's available. I have the entire collection." She pulled up her phone. "I keep her digital editions on my phone in case I need something to read."

I glanced down at the paperback she was buying. "This came out a year ago, are you sure you don't have this already?" I hated buying something I'd already read.

"I have it. This is a gift. And I'm coming in from Santa Maria with a friend for the Uncloaking." She glanced behind me. "So is Toby working today?"

Now I knew why I didn't know this frequent customer. She was one of Toby's girls. The guy brought in more traffic during his shift that I did on the morning rush when people really needed coffee.

"He's coming in at noon." I glanced at the clock; it was almost that time now. Funny, Toby usually showed up early for the Saturday shift, knowing I was often busy.

The girl took her change and her coffee and nodded. "I guess I'll browse for a while. Maybe there's another book I need."

She wandered off and I focused on taking the next customer's order. Toby was a lady-killer, that was for sure. I had to admit, hiring him was the best decision my aunt had made when she first showed up and took over the day-to-day shop management.

Fifteen minutes after noon, Toby rushed in. He glanced around the nearly empty room and sighed. "Sorry."

He stepped behind the counter, slipping his jacket off and throwing it into the back. As he washed his hands and put an apron on, he focused on me. "I would have called, but we kind of lost track of time."

"We?" I dumped out coffee and added more to the espresso maker. Double shot latte—caramel—one of my favorites and it appeared it would be the last drink I'd make for the day. Traffic had been slow for a Saturday, and Toby could take over without a problem.

He stood next to me and heated milk for the latte. "Greg asked me to come in this morning and go over the results we got from the crate break-in last night. I hear you slept through the whole thing."

I reddened. "Hey, it wasn't like he even let me get out of the car. What would you have me do?"

He grinned and poured the coffee into the cup, then topped the drink with whipped cream and a cover. Toby handed it to the waiting customer. "There you go."

I leaned against the counter watching the few stragglers wandering around the shop scanning the shelves. I liked my life. Toby stood next to me. "Did Greg tell you the drug dogs found a trace?"

I nodded. "I would have never guessed Craig was into that scene." I didn't like the guy, but being a drug supplier? That fell into a whole 'nother category of slime.

"I know, right? I've been arresting DUIs and breaking-and-entering kids for years and there was a drug dealer living right in our town?" Toby shrugged. "He must have kept that part of his life out of the town. I wonder what other secrets are hiding in our little community."

I wondered that, too. "I guess there's at least one more."

Toby cocked his head and focused on me. "What's that?"

"Someone murdered Craig." I glanced around the quiet shop. "And unless they came from the outside to do the deed, they live here with us."

CHAPTER 18

Greg's promised day together failed to materialize on Saturday so after I took Emma for a run on the beach, I sank onto the couch with a book and settled for canned soup for dinner. Locking up the house when I went to bed, my thoughts went back to Greg's parting comment Friday. I guessed now that they'd found a drug connection, I'd lost my status as Suspect Number One, as Greg teasingly called me. At least, I hoped he was teasing.

As I climbed the stairs, Emma on my heels, I considered Craig's murder. Killing a successful drug mule was like killing the goose for the golden egg. Craig had kept this part of his import business under wraps. The only reason anyone knew now was because he was dead. So why would he be killed after one shipment? Someone would have to be stupid to cut off the supply.

Brenda's face floated into my mind. "What if he was trying to change for her?" I asked out loud. "He'd have to go straight if he was going to repair the marriage."

Sometimes Emma could be a great sounding board. Tonight, the dog glared at me like my idea was the stupidest thing she'd ever heard a human say.

I slipped the chair back under the doorknob and patted her on the head. "You're right. Craig wasn't the changing type."

Emma let out a quiet yip like she agreed with my statement, then went to lie on her bed, pawing at the cedar shaving–stuffed pillow making it just right before she plopped down.

Sunday morning came quickly, my sleep having been dream- and crisis-free. I moved the chair, feeling stupid for the extra security, and Emma raced me downstairs.

After letting her out and starting coffee, I sat at the table with my notebook. I wrote down the day's chores, mostly because I knew if I didn't, something would be forgotten. I only had two days to get the home stuff done before I went back to the grind on Tuesday.

Of course my job now was enjoyable, not like when I'd been a lawyer and had kissed the floor of my apartment every Friday night when I walked in the door. I'd loved the weekends then. Now I loved most days. I still put off most of the chores until I had a day to myself. Today, Toby had volunteered to take my shift and I'd let him.

A knock sounded at the front door. Glancing through the window, I saw Amy with bags from Diamond Lille's in her hands. When I opened the door, she breezed through past me and toward the kitchen.

"Great, you already have coffee going," Amy called out. I closed and locked the front door again, feeling stupid for the extra precautions. I expected Greg sometime today, and I knew he'd check before he knocked. I didn't feel like getting a lecture on personal safety.

"Come on in," I said to the empty living room. By the time I got to the kitchen, Amy had plates set out, orange juice and coffee poured, and an assortment of breakfast items laid out on platters in the middle of the table. "Whoa, are we expecting the guys?"

Amy's face screwed up and she burst into tears. She plopped down into a chair and, covering her face, sobbed. I grabbed some tissues from the box on the counter and pulled a chair up next to my friend. Rubbing her back, I handed her the tissues and she loudly blew her nose, wiping her eyes with a clean tissue. Finally, she took in a shuddering breath and the tears slowed.

"Was it something I said?" I figured this had to be about Hank, but I'd let her tell me in her own time.

Amy took her juice and drank down the full glass. She squared her shoulders, then said, "Hank broke up with me."

I tried to put a shocked look on my face instead of the smile that wanted to fight its way out. I'd hoped the couple wouldn't be long for this world, but I'd always thought Amy would be the one to wake up and realize what she was doing to herself. I thought about my next words, finally going with, "That's awful. What happened?"

Amy picked up a piece of toast and smeared raspberry jam on the top. "He thought I was sleeping with Justin. Can you believe that?"

Well, I could, but this was Amy's story to tell. And she didn't wait for an answer anyway.

"He said he didn't trust me to even surf alone because he knew I'd slept with some of my surfing buddies. The guy totally went off on me, accusing me of the most terrible things." She pointed the toast at me, and I saw a drop of jam fly off onto the kitchen wall. I watched it slide down the wall, wondering if jam hurt paint.

Amy poked me with the toast. "Look at me. Hank accused me of sleeping with the mayor."

I burst out laughing. "Mayor Bird? He thinks you slept with him? What is he, crazy?"

"I know, right?" Amy fell back into her chair and sighed. "I guess he didn't understand me or my personality. I'm not a total flirt, am I?"

Smiling, I pulled a plate closer and started loading it with eggs and bacon. "No. You aren't a total flirt. You like people. It shows when you talk to anyone."

Amy nodded to the bacon. "Hand that this way. After the morning I've had, I deserve some fat. Crunchy, pork-filled fat."

"Hank's an idiot." I took a bite of the scrambled eggs and smiled. Maybe we had a chance of getting Justin as part of our group sooner than later.

A knock sounded at the door. "Busy place this morning."

Aunt Jackie stood at the door this time. She whipped in, kissed me on the cheek, and sniffed the air. "Good, you've already made coffee." She took her bags and went into the kitchen, as well.

Seeing Amy sitting there with all the food didn't even faze my aunt. She pulled out three different coffee cakes, set them on the table, and then went to get a plate and a cup of coffee.

"You won't believe who came by Saturday during my shift." Jackie cut a larger-than-normal slice of the blueberry coffee cake.

Amy was lost in thought, shoveling food in, one fork at a time, so I answered. "Who?"

"Josh Thomas brought me a box of chocolates and more flowers." Jackie sniffed. "He said he had a marvelous time and wanted to thank me."

I put a slice of coffee cake on my plate, then handed one to Amy. She picked it up with her fingers and ate it without a word. I turned back to Jackie, who was sampling the French toast. "So, that was nice."

"Nice?" She snorted, then stood and went to the pantry. Pulling out the maple syrup, she poured some into a cup and put the cup into the microwave. While the machine did its magic, she stared at me. "You know, he's just going to ask again."

"Would that be so bad?" I knew my aunt was lonely. She needed some companionship, even if it wasn't from someone who would be the love of her life.

Jackie seemed ready to tell me all the reasons having Josh court her would be one of the signs of the end of the world when a knock sounded at the kitchen door. She went back to her chair, pouring the hot syrup over the butter she'd spread on the French toast. This time I could see Greg standing in the window, holding a bag from the Bakerstown Bakery. Bagels and cream cheese. I wouldn't have to cook for days.

I stood and opened the door, kissing him on the cheek. Emma stood at the door, sniffing the food odors wafting out. I put my foot out to keep her from jumping into the middle of the table. "Stay."

Greg slipped in the door and glanced at the two women sitting at my table, both focused on the food. "I didn't realize you were throwing a party this morning."

I took the bag of bagels and placed them on a plate. I nodded to the cabinet. "Better grab a plate and some food before it gets cold." Although at the rate Amy and Jackie were going, having leftovers might not be in my future.

"Amy, Jackie." Greg nodded at the women, who both grunted rather than spoke. He looked at me, wide-eyed.

"You're the wrong sex." I smiled as I set down his coffee. "Toby said you guys were working on the case yesterday?"

"I would have him chasing down leads this morning but apparently he's taking your shift today?" When I shrugged, he took the coffee and kept his eyes on the women eating next to him. "Lab tests confirmed there was cocaine in the crate. Apparently the ATF had been watching Craig for a while but couldn't get anything on him. They even interviewed Brenda last year. She was clueless."

"Did they tell her why she was being questioned?" I thought about Brenda's calmness when she heard about Craig's death.

"Everything they could. They tried to get her to go undercover, but she was too afraid. They kept an eye on her for the last year, too." Greg finished off the scrambled eggs and handed me the platter since I was standing. Jackie glared at him. He held up his plate. "I'm sorry, did you want some of those?"

She shook her head. "I do want another slice of bacon." She pushed the rest of the bacon on her plate and handed the second empty platter to me. If I didn't fill my plate soon, there wouldn't even be crumbs left. My stomach growled as I sat and grabbed the leftovers.

I spread jam on a piece of toast. "Brenda didn't even mention this and we've talked twice since she's been back."

"Would you tell a friend the feds were investigating you?" Amy asked, slowing her grazing.

"Probably not." I poured syrup over the French toast and thought about Craig. Obviously he had ticked off more people than me. "So you think he was killed for the drugs?"

Greg shrugged. "We don't know yet. Good news is the district attorney's crossed your name off the suspect board." He bit into the coffee cake. "This is good."

"My name's on a suspect board?"

Jackie waved away my question. "Of course it is, dear. You were the last one seen fighting with the dead man. Don't you watch any of the murder shows? It's always the cute, quiet ones whom you have to watch out for."

Greg laughed. "You got that right." He spread cream cheese on a bagel.

"Just for that, you're taking Fifi next week when Brenda goes out of town. I was going to let you have Emma, but now you can deal with the crazy dog." Fifi had been known to take her frustrations out by chewing. On anything. Greg's furniture would be prime targets.

"Now, wait." Greg put his hands up. "Who volunteered me for puppy duty? That dog is worse than Craig ever was. I can't believe Brenda wants to keep her."

"She needs someone to watch her, and you know Emma doesn't get along with Fifi." I polished off the French toast and gazed longingly at the empty blueberry coffee cake plate. Instead of trying one of the others, I stood to get the coffeepot. Filling my cup, I went around the table and warmed up the rest. Funny little ragtag group, and I loved each and every one of them. They were my family.

Amy's phone buzzed, and she quickly grabbed the cell, checking the display. She leaned back in the chair and answered, "Hey, Justin." She stood and walked into the living room to continue her conversation.

Greg caught my eye and smiled.

"What's wrong with her?" Aunt Jackie asked. "I've never seen her without a smile and she's totally Debbie Downer today."

I peered around the corner, judging Amy might be outside of earshot. "Hank dumped her," I whispered.

Greg shook his head. "The guy's not only a jerk, he's stupid, as well."

"That's not charitable. Some people are born dumb." Jackie tapped the table with her finger. "Like the man the two of you let drive me home Friday night."

"Here we go," I mumbled. I knew Jackie wouldn't let that one go.

"Now, you know I had to work. And I can't be dragging civilians with me to crime scenes." Greg tried to appease her.

Jackie pointed at me. "You took her."

I raised an eyebrow. Technically, I took him. "It was my car."

"Did you tell him about Ray being at the crate on Thursday?" Jackie asked, an evil glint in her eyes as she ratted us out.

"What?" Greg stopped eating.

I sent my aunt what I hoped was a withering look. I'd get her back somehow. "Okay, so Jackie thought it would be a good idea to check out Craig's crate."

"You agreed." She pointed a slice of bacon at me.

"Anyway, she found out Brenda had a hide-a-key rock at the crate," I continued.

"Brenda knew about the crate?" Greg sat up straighter.

"Do you want to hear the story or not?" I shushed him. "So anyway, we got there, Jackie talked us past the guard, and we unlocked the crate. We didn't see anything, so we locked it back up and left."

"So when does Ray come into this picture?" Greg's voice sounded tight, and a muscle twitched in his jaw.

"Jackie took the rock," I said.

"I forgot I had it!"

"Jackie forgot she was carrying a fake rock, so I told her I'd take it back to the crate. When I got there, Ray and this other guy were looking for the rock."

"Tell me you weren't seen." Now Greg had his eyes closed.

"I didn't even get close." I stood and went to the cabinet and pulled out the rock from a drawer. "So I still have this."

Greg took the rock and stood. "I'll be right back." He got on his phone and I heard him call Tim to come pick up the rock.

Jackie watched Greg leave the house and shrugged. "If we didn't live out here in the boonies, we could have taken a taxi."

"We live in a tourist town, not out in the boonies. Besides, you got home safe and sound," I challenged. "You didn't need to tell Greg about our trip."

"I think you needed to tell him, but apparently you didn't. So sue me." Jackie glared at me. I started to respond, but Greg had returned to the kitchen.

"Tim will run the rock for fingerprints. I take it the two of you will show up?" He looked at Jackie, then at me.

"I kind of wiped it off, so maybe." I thought about the days the rock had stayed in my purse. "Mine will be on the rock."

"I still don't understand why you let a possible criminal drive me home," Jackie jumped into the conversation.

He cleared his throat. "His background check came back clean. If I had thought you'd be in danger, I wouldn't have let him drive you home."

Jackie preened. "You ran a background check before the date?"

"Of course. You're a valued member of the community and part of

Jill's family. I'm not going to let anything happen to you." Greg smiled killer smile number fifty-eight and my aunt was lost.

She grabbed her purse and excused herself to powder her nose.

I watched her leave. "Nice touch making up that background check thing." I started clearing the plates. Obviously our impromptu family breakfast was drawing to a close.

"We'll talk about the road trip later." Greg stood and carried dishes to the sink. "I honestly did a background check on Mr. Josh Thomas."

"Seriously? It was a double date." I opened the dishwasher and started unloading plates.

Greg brought more items off the table. "I did a background check as part of Craig's murder investigation. She doesn't need to know that. Right now I'm looking pretty heroic in your aunt's eyes."

Bottom rack empty, I started unloading the cups on the top. "So nothing in Josh's past screamed serial killer, huh?"

"Sorry, no. I would love to have this case over. Now we've got more questions than answers." He glanced at Amy's plate. "You think she's done?"

I nodded. "If she's not, she can get a clean plate. Of course, there's not much food left anyway."

He brought the plate over and scraped the few crumbs of toast and scrambled eggs into the garbage disposal. "Would I be a bad guy if I said I'm glad Hank's out of the picture?"

"Only if I am. I'm happy he's gone. I can barely talk about it without grinning. Of course, she wouldn't like it if I broke out into song." I took the plate from Greg and rinsed it. We loaded the dishwasher with rhythm and speed. By the time Amy and Jackie returned to the kitchen, the table was clean, the leftover food was wrapped up and either in the fridge or sitting on the countertop. And a new pot of coffee was brewing.

Amy picked up a cup and filled it with the half-done coffee. "Justin asked if you got the envelope he left the other day."

"I did." I didn't say the evidence Justin had found led the investigation directly back to me. I sat down next to her at the table. "So when is he coming back into town?"

"Hank?" Amy frowned.

I groaned inwardly. On the outside, I put on a Barbie doll smile and shook my head. "Not Hank, Justin."

"Oh, he's coming in for Jackie's murder thing this week." Amy smiled. "He says I need to get out of the house and not fret so much."

"Sounds like a smart man." Jackie joined in the conversation but remained standing.

Amy grinned. "Oh hey, I found the building plans for City Hall."

"You did? Where?" Jackie frowned. "I swear I went through every file in that room."

Amy looked at me. "The mayor had the file in his desk."

"That snot. When I asked him, he said he didn't handle building plans and that I should talk to you." Jackie pointed at Amy. "And he knew where it was all the time."

Amy pulled a folder out of her purse. "I made a copy for you before I returned it to his desk."

Jackie leaned over my shoulder as I read the description. "It doesn't mention a wall, or the mission being on site. But just not saying something, doesn't mean it's not true." I pushed the pages toward Greg. "Another false alarm."

"You'll figure this out." Greg tapped the pages. "And this is the kind of mystery you should be solving instead of my murder investigations."

Jackie laughed and then kissed me on the cheek. "I'm out of here. I've got some errands to run in the city, so don't freak if I'm not at the apartment."

"I didn't freak. I was worried about you." I wondered if Toby had ratted me out to my aunt.

Jackie rubbed off a spot her lipstick had left on my cheek. "I'm a big girl, hon. I'll be fine, no matter what."

She waved at Greg, who stood by the door, watching out the window. And then she disappeared. My aunt had a lot in common with Houdini and his vanishing act.

"What's that about?" Amy leaned toward me.

"Greg believes I should keep my doors locked at all times. So he's following her to lock up after she leaves." I felt silly and expected Amy to laugh, but she didn't.

"Reasonable." She closed her eyes for a second, then they flew back open. "I almost forgot. Esmeralda wants to know if you're still on the road."

"You mean the path," I corrected her.

Amy's eyes widened. "Yeah, that's what she said. Are you on a path?"

"My personal fortune-teller seems to think so. I feel like I'm stumbling through the day." Trying not to be killed, I added silently.

CHAPTER 19

The impromptu breakfast meeting broke up soon after Aunt Jackie left. Amy hung around for a few minutes, talking about Hank, and then she got a text.

"Justin wants me to meet him down the coast. I guess the waves are amazing." Amy glanced at me like she needed permission.

"Why are you looking at me?" I waved my hands. "Fly little bird, go ride the ocean's waves."

Amy grinned. "We said we were shopping today. Remember?"

Crap, I'd totally forgotten about our monthly trip to Bakerstown's shopping mecca. And I needed new capris. But the more time Amy spent with the friendly Mr. Justin, the further away she was from Hank and his manipulations. I would sacrifice my fashion needs for the good of my friend. And future encounters with her dates. "Sorry, Greg and I made plans, but I guess if you want to . . ."

Amy almost jumped out of her chair. At first I felt a tad offended, but remembering Justin's big blue eyes, I forgave her.

"We'll go next weekend." Amy grabbed her purse and headed to the front door, with Greg on her heels to lock it after her.

When he came back into the kitchen, Emma whined at the door. "Hold on, I can only play doorman one door at a time."

"But you do it so well." I opened my notebook and crossed off breakfast with Amy. Although I should have added Jackie and Greg's names to the item before I crossed it off.

"What else do you have to do?" Greg glanced at my list. "Want to add one more thing?"

I studied him. With his sense of humor, he could be asking me on a real, official date, or to help him clean the grease traps over at Diamond Lille's. I never knew what to expect. And I liked it. My lips curled upward, my voice husky and low, as I asked, "What did you have in mind, cowboy?"

He chuckled. "Apparently not what you were thinking. Although your idea may be more enjoyable than mine will be."

"What do you want to do?" I had a feeling it started with a couch, a television, a twelve-pack of beer, and, at least one, if not all of the professional baseball games.

"I think we need to play tourist." Greg spun his keys around his finger.

I watched the silver chain go around and around his hand, mesmerizing me. "I think our cover would be blown the first time we entered a shop. Not many of the town's owners don't know me, even if they hate going to the business-to-business meetings."

"I don't want to go into town to play tourist." He picked up Justin's letter. "I want to go to The Castle and take the grand tour."

On Sundays the tours were combined, and for the price of a ticket, you got to wander the house, the grounds, and even partake of a wine and cheese tasting with the manager. I wondered who was hosting now that Craig had left the building. I peered closer at the man standing in my kitchen. "What are you looking for?"

"I'll know it when I see it."

When we pulled into the parking lot, the Sunday crowd seemed thinner than usual. Maybe having a murder at The Castle had diverted some of the traffic. I glanced at my watch. Or it could be too early for the big crowds. I'd held an impromptu brunch and now, I was playing undercover investigator with Greg, and it wasn't even noon.

He came around the truck and opened my door, holding out his hand. The first time we'd gone somewhere together, I'd hopped out of the truck, not waiting for him to come around. When he groused, I thought it was cute. I'd never had a boyfriend who wanted to treat me like a princess. Now I just enjoyed it.

Lisa Brewer wasn't working the ticket stand when Greg paid for our entry. So far, his plan of being incognito was kind of working. We strolled along the sidewalk, admiring the well-tended flower gardens on either side. The previous owner loved to entertain, so there were several guesthouses alongside the main house. Greg turned me toward the one closest to the house. It was reserved for the caretaker, formerly known as Casa Craig. He glanced behind us, then instead of turning left into the open guesthouse, we turned right and disappeared behind the other cottage.

"For someone who wants me to stay out of the investigation business, you're leading me into temptation, Detective." Whispering, I took a step closer to Greg. If we were going to get tossed out for trespassing, I wanted to be right next to my police officer boyfriend. Although I think Toby would have a hard time arresting us; he'd be laughing too hard.

"Craig's body was found in the woods, so we released the house early. We've searched it, but nothing was found inside. The Castle's attorneys told us to back off." Greg stared at the outside of the building.

"Won't it ruin the investigation if we break in? Chain of custody and all?" I didn't tell him about my own visit to The Castle a few days ago. He'd already learned enough about my extracurricular activities for one day.

I saw Greg bite back a smile. "We aren't going to break in. I told you I just wanted to look."

I studied the back wall of the cottage. "I don't see anything."

Greg didn't answer. Instead he walked closer and knelt next to the dog door Craig had installed for Fifi. The plastic that kept out the heat and cold but let the dog come into the house had been pulled away from the top panel. He took out his cell and took a picture. He studied the woods behind the house.

Finally he stood and motioned me back around the way we'd come. He blended us in with a group of tourists who were heading down to the steps to the Grecian pool. The same pool where Nick and the town kids swam when they'd broken onto the property this summer.

On Sundays, The Castle staff served drinks poolside, allowing visitors to pretend they'd been invited to a party by the owner to see and be seen with the California elite. The man would roll over in his grave if he knew riffraff like me were drinking frozen alcoholic beverages around his pool.

The sun gleamed off the imported tile as we claimed a table near the back by the columns surrounding a spa-like pool house. A waiter arrived, offering a choice of frozen margaritas, draft beer, or chilled water. I took the margarita and Greg, the beer. When they delivered the drinks, they also dropped off a basket of chips and fresh salsa.

Greg pulled at his beer, then dug a chip into the salsa. "Fifi didn't go willingly."

I sipped my drink. "So the person who took her, she didn't like."

"Or didn't know." Greg leaned back, his sunglasses hiding his eyes so I couldn't tell what he was thinking.

I thought about Brenda at the shop and the way Fifi reacted to Ray. I leaned closer. "I told you about Fifi going all pit bull crazy on Ray the other day, right?"

Greg lifted his glasses and glared at me. "When were you hanging out with Ray again? I swear, Lille's going to take you out. You need to stay away from him." Greg fell silent, and I didn't push it. He had the cop look on.

"You told me about the dog incident. Sorry I overreacted." He drained his beer and ate the last chip. "Ready to get back to our date?"

I took a big gulp to finish off my drink. As the frozen delight went down my throat, my head exploded. Too cold, too fast—brain freeze. I put my hands up to my nose and breathed the warmed air in slowly. Slowly the pain went away. I sighed, then smiled. "I'm good."

"You don't lie well."

"Sorry." I stood and waited for him to join me. The sunlight bouncing off the clear blue water of the pool caused me to slip my sunglasses off the top of my head and cover my eyes.

Greg took my arm in his and kissed the top of my head. "I'm not."

Monday morning I found my latest novel and Emma next to me on the mattress and the sun shining in the windows. I never set an alarm for my days off. Ever. I took the early bird shift at the store so on my days off I deserved a few more winks of sleep. Unfortunately, my internal clock usually went off earlier than I'd like.

Today was no exception. Six A.M. on the dot according to my Mickey Mouse clock on the nightstand. Emma licked my arm as soon as she saw my eyes open.

"Hold on, I'll let you outside." I walked to the bedroom door and removed the chair from under the knob. Now it was habit, even though Greg had given my house the all-clear last night. Until Craig's murder was solved, I figured a little paranoia couldn't hurt.

Sauntering down the stairs, I let Emma out, transferred the wet clothes to the dryer, and made coffee. Sitting at the table, I started the rest of my weekend list. Jimmy Marcum had some papers for me to sign for the business. It seemed like we were always filing some business license or something. Last spring, Jimmy saved my butt when the city tried to condemn my house without giving me time to repair. Now they only talked to Jimmy. No more process servers showing up at my door.

I didn't think Mayor Baylor had given up on his quest to annex the property. Before, he'd wanted me to sell to a condo developer who actually was being manipulated by a girlfriend who thought the house hid buried pirate treasure. Now rumor was he wanted to build a South Cove tourist center, and since my property was the closest to the highway, I was the logical choice to condemn in order to build his vision.

Except I didn't want to move, sell, or even think about the possibilities. I don't know why whenever he got an idea, it always focused on my house or my business. After the run-in with him and his wife last weekend, I was beginning to think our good mayor didn't care for me much.

Not that I cared a whit what he thought.

Glancing down at my list, I'd written three things: *Jimmy, shopping*, and *laundry*. Since it was just me, housecleaning only hit my to-do list once a month or if I was expecting company. And neither of those two qualifiers were in store for the next week. I did need to get a new dress for the mystery launch party. I'd kept myself from checking over the book order this week. Jackie had handled it all, and even though I could have determined who the author was, I was enjoying the mystery, too.

I poured a cup of coffee and then added one more item to the list. Not that I'd forget, but so I could check it off: *Take Emma for a run.*

By four, Emma and I had run, the laundry was done, and I was on my way back from Bakerstown. Everything had gone like clockwork. To reward myself, I was scarfing down a fish sandwich from one of the fast food heaven places the city council regulations didn't allow in South Cove. I'd turned up the stereo, Dixie Chicks blaring from the speakers, when the speed of my Jeep started to slow.

Frowning, I pushed harder on the gas pedal. Nothing. Then I saw the display where my speed digitally displayed the last time I'd noticed. *Low Fuel Warning,* it flashed. And apparently, the light had been flashing for a while, because now it wasn't just low, but nonexistent.

I eased the car over to the side of the road and pulled out my cell. I got Greg's voice mail. I wasn't far out of town, maybe ten miles. I could walk, but I'd bought ice cream at the store. I'd hate to have that melt and seep over my brand-new carpet in the back. Gritting my teeth, I left a message—*come save me.* I would get lecture number three: "Don't ever pass a gas station if you have less than a half a tank."

We'd been dating less than a year, so we didn't have many stock lectures. But this one was high up on Greg's worry list. I guess him being in law enforcement, he saw the other side to being stranded. Worse than melted ice cream.

I finished my fries and wondered if I should turn off the stereo. How much did it take to drain a battery? I was considering my answer when I saw an older pickup stop behind me.

I groaned. My knight in shining armor was Ray Stewart. I locked the doors and rolled the window down a crack, not enough for him to get a hand inside. I'd seen too many movies where the kidnapped woman had been Tasered by someone they knew. He might be a local, but I wasn't stupid.

I watched in my side mirror as he ambled up to the Jeep, glancing in the back to see my grocery sacks. His smile creeped me out a tad.

When he reached the driver's side door and leaned over, putting his hands on top of the car, his smile widened when he saw me sitting there.

"Well, hello, beautiful." He leaned back and took a second look at the Jeep. "I didn't recognize you outside of that beat-up piece of crap you usually drive. I guess the rumors were true."

I kept my hand on my cell, hoping Greg would call back. Anytime now. "What rumors, Ray?"

"The old bat must have left you some bank." He smiled and the gold tooth glinted in the sunlight. "I figured it was small town rumors."

"I don't have time to chat."

He burst out laughing. "Honey, it looks like you have all the time in the world to talk with me. Where you going to go?"

I held up my cell. "Greg's on his way."

Ray took a step back and held up his hands in mock surrender. "Ooooohhh, I don't want to upset your cop boyfriend. Do the two of you barbeque baby back ribs? Or does he consider that cannibalism?"

"Not funny." For the first time, I glanced at Ray's eyes. He'd pushed back his aviator wrap glasses on top of his greasy, too-long hair when he saw I was in the car. The degree of bloodshot made his eyes almost red, and I wondered if he was coming off a bender or on something worse. I focused on his pupils, but before I could determine whether they were dilated or not, he noticed my interest and flipped the shades down.

"Bright out here," he commented. "Why don't you open your door and we can go wait in my truck for your boy toy?"

I wondered if that line ever worked on anyone. "I'm pretty comfortable here. But thanks."

His lips curved into a smile. "Then why don't you open the door and let me slip into that leather seat next to you." He leaned in closer. "I've never done it in a brand-new car before."

And you're not going to today, either. I stopped myself from gagging. Just then I saw a car coming down the road heading out of town. I reached down and flashed my lights, hoping the driver wouldn't think

Ray and I were talking. The blue crossover pulled in front of my Jeep and Bill Simmons got out.

I let out a breath. Ray stepped back as Bill approached.

"I've got places to be." Ray waved at the approaching Bill, then leaned in again and licked the window. "Maybe next time, sweetheart."

I shuddered, not able to control the physical reaction this time. I thought I'd vomit. Bill stepped in front of the Jeep, watching Ray get back into his truck and speed away. Once the truck was out of sight, he approached the door as I pushed it open and jumped out of the car, needing some fresh air.

"You okay?" He quickly assessed my stance, head down between my knees trying to breathe. He put his hand on my back, comforting and solid. His voice was low. "Jill? He didn't hurt you, did he?"

I shook my head and wiped at my eyes, hoping Bill hadn't seen the tears. It had been stupid. I'd never been in any real danger, but thinking about the uncloaked hunger in Ray's eyes made me shiver again. I started pacing between the two vehicles. Taking one, then two deep breaths, finally I trusted my voice. "I'm fine. Ray's a . . ." I searched for a word.

"Jerk, scary, monster. Stop me if I'm getting warm." Bill took my arm and led me back to the Jeep, pushing me gently into the seat.

I laughed. "Take your choice." I waved my hand at the car. "I ran out of gas. Can you give me and my groceries a ride to my house?"

Bill nodded. "Unlock the back and I'll load the bags in the trunk while you get settled."

The phone rang when I was composing myself. Greg, I saw on the caller ID. "Hey. I guess I don't need you after all."

"What happened?" I heard noises coming from the phone, lots of voices.

"I ran out of gas. Stop, I know what you're going to say, but I'm fine." *Now,* I added silently. "Look, Bill Simmons is here, and he's taking me and the groceries back to the house. Can you come by later and we can pick up the car?"

"I'm sending Toby now. He'll take care of it. I can't leave right now."

I grabbed my purse and waved to Bill, who had finished loading up my groceries. Locking the doors, I leaned against the car, wanting to finish this conversation out of Bill's earshot. "You don't have to send Toby. Come by later, when you're not busy. And before you yell at me for not telling you, Ray Stewart had stopped and was being his usual jerk self. But he left when Bill arrived."

At first the phone sounded dead and I thought I'd lost the connection. Then Greg asked, "Ray was just there? Where are you exactly? And which way did he leave?"

CHAPTER 20

Toby showed up at the house almost as fast as we did. The other part-time deputy, Tim, sat in the passenger seat of the cruiser. Toby helped Bill carry in my groceries. I stood at the counter, putting away my softened ice cream, promising myself as soon as the house was empty, I'd pull the carton back out and fill up a large bowl. Then I'd sit on the porch in my rocker and eat until I didn't feel dirty anymore.

When Bill brought in the last bag, he tapped my arm like we were old college buddies. "Look, if you need anything, let me know." He inspected me. "You're sure Ray didn't hurt you?"

I shook my head. "No, but he scared the crap out of me. Thank you again for stopping. If you hadn't . . ." I paused, not wanting to go any further with the thought. Whips and chains and kidnapped woman's faces on milk cartons went through my mind. I realized Bill was still watching me. "Really, I'm fine. Just not a big Ray fan right now."

At that, Bill laughed. "Besides Lille, who is?"

He nodded to Toby, who stood at the doorway to the living room. As Bill passed by, Toby focused on me. "I'll be right back."

I heard him follow Bill out to the front door, and like what happened with Greg yesterday, I heard the door locks engage. I put the groceries away and pulled out a bottle of wine.

"I'm checking the house, then we'll go get your car." Toby's voice jerked me back to reality.

"Duh. I guess I'll get a glass later." I reached for the refrigerator door.

Toby frowned. "Go ahead. When I said we, I meant Tim and me, not you. You are supposed to stay put until Greg comes this evening. You'll only be alone for twenty minutes tops. I already stopped for a gallon of gas."

"You're staying?" This overreaction of Greg's had to stop. "Look, Ray's a jerk. We know that. But he didn't hurt me. I don't need a babysitter."

Toby cocked his head at me. "I wasn't supposed to say anything, not until Greg got here."

"What are you talking about?"

Toby led me to a kitchen chair and lowered me into the seat. He sat next to me. "Look, Jill, the reason Greg's not here is we're executing a search warrant."

My heart started pounding. "They think they found the killer?"

Toby shrugged. "I'm not sure about that. But, Jill, Greg's over at Ray's. That's where we're searching. And there's a warrant out for him on the breaking and entering of the crate. He's a person of interest."

I felt the blood drain from my face. I saw my reflection in the glass over a framed photo of me and Miss Emily sitting out on the porch. I appeared paper-white.

I wondered if Ray had known the cops were out at his place when he found me. Had he thought he'd run upon a pawn to barter with? Thank God for Bill. I was going to have to send over a few cakes and coffee for his bed-and-breakfast. A "thanks for saving my life" gift. I realized Toby was watching me. If I didn't want him to reach over and feel my forehead for a fever, or worse, rush me to the emergency room, I needed to respond. "Oh."

Toby still looked like he was going to bundle me off to the hospital.

"Wow. That's a lot to take in." Taking a breath, I added to my original statement with a small smile.

This time I saw the guy physically relax. He tapped his fingers on the table. "You going to be okay alone for a few minutes? Should I call Jackie and have her come over?"

My eyebrows raised. "You'll be gone ten minutes. I think I can handle being alone for almost thirty before I do something stupid."

Toby chuckled. "Greg said something similar, but he didn't want me to leave you alone at all. But he also didn't think I'd get you in the back of the patrol car again."

"No way." I cringed. Then I thought of Tim sitting in the front of Toby's cruiser. I narrowed my eyes. "Hey, you told me no one sat in the front."

Toby had the good sense to blush. "I didn't want to move every-thing for a five-minute drop-off. Sorry."

"See if you get a raise next year." I stood and went back to the fridge to pour my wine. "Go get my car. I'll be fine."

Toby stood and started checking doors and closets. I watched him search the downstairs and then upstairs. When he came back down, I asked, "Satisfied?"

"Seriously, Jill, if something happened and I didn't check, my butt would be in so much trouble." He smiled. "It's good to be the police de-tective's girl. Especially since you can't seem to stay out of harm's way."

"Now you're working on a pay cut." I followed him to the door, holding up a hand when he opened up his mouth to speak. "Yeah, I know, lock up and don't let anyone in."

"I love giving my boss orders." Toby tapped two fingers on the brim of his hat. "You might want to keep your cell with you, as well. Just in case."

When I locked the door, I regarded Emma. "I guess it's the two of us."

I curled up on the couch and turned on the television, searching until I found an old movie and got lost in a land of wizards fighting the constant battle of good and evil. Sipping on my wine, I wondered when I'd fallen into the fray. I pulled a crocheted blanket over my legs and laid my head on a pillow.

A banging noise woke me. I clicked off the television, noticing night had fallen. I checked my cell, no missed calls. Had I imagined the noise? It sounded again, and I realized someone was at the door. Groggy from sleep, I walked over and peeked out the window, wor-ried Ray Stewart would be on my porch. My shoulders dropped when I saw Greg standing in front of the door.

I unlocked and opened the door. "What time is it?"

"Late." He pulled me into his arms and kissed me. Gentle yet demanding. When he was done, I closed and locked the door behind him.

"So, you have a bad day?" I led him to the kitchen, grabbing my half-full glass of wine as we passed by the coffee table.

He went to the fridge and held out a soda. "Bad and not over yet. I needed to see you for a minute. I've got to get back to the station. You want one?"

I nodded and took the offered drink. My neck felt like I'd slept on the couch, kinky and out of sorts. I stretched my head one way, then the other, and sat at the table. "You want to talk?"

Sometimes he said yes. Sometimes, when it was bad, we talked about anything but what he was working on. He controlled the conversations—I knew sometimes he needed a break. I would have. This time he surprised me.

"I was worried about you. Bill said it looked like Ray was giving you a hard time." Greg took my hand, rubbing his thumb on my palm.

I wouldn't tell Greg everything; it would only make him mad. But there wasn't a reason to lie, either. "He was a jerk. What's new about that?"

"But he scared you. Bill said you were in tears."

I thought about the relief I'd felt when Ray drove off. Had he threatened me? Or had I only felt scared? Or was there even a difference? "I let him get under my skin. Bullies know how to terrorize you without even saying anything wrong. I wonder if he plays those mind games on Lille. I never understood what she sees in him. Maybe he's brainwashed her?"

Greg chuckled. "Leave it to you to worry about someone else when you were the one in danger."

"Was I, really?"

Greg's hand tightened on mine. "I believe so. But you were too smart for him. Locking yourself in the car, keeping the cell close, even flashing your lights at Bill. You weren't a victim. Maybe that's why he keeps coming back. To see if he can break you."

"Did you catch him?" I wondered if Lille would even let me eat in her diner again. Especially if word of his terrorizing me started running through the rumor mill.

"Not yet."

Greg's words chilled me. He opened the soda and took a long drink.

"Did he kill Craig?"

This time Greg paused before he answered. "I think so. I mean, there's motive and opportunity. But something doesn't feel right. Of course, his disappearing act today doesn't work in his favor. I'm not ready to convict him yet. But I do want to kick his ass for scaring you."

Greg's words warmed me. "And if I need my boyfriend to beat up another guy to protect my honor, I'll be sure to call you."

"Anytime." Greg stood. "Look, I need to get back."

I stood, as well. "I take it my bodyguard is still out in his car?"

"No taking him coffee. No bringing him crosswords. No leaving the house." Greg tapped my nose. "Stay in the house until tomorrow. Is that too much to ask?"

I wanted to argue. Say I wasn't a too-stupid-to-live girl, yet we both knew better. I'd left the house twice the last time there was a homicidal ex-high school teacher stalking me, and the second time, I got a trip to the hospital for my kindness. A thought niggled at me. "So why did you focus on Ray? Just because he worked for Craig?"

Greg stared at me for a long time, then shrugged. "Actually it was the crumpled Diamond Lille's promotional glass with remnants of rum and Coke. Ray's fingerprints and probably DNA were all over the plastic."

"But you said there weren't any fingerprints on the crate door." Or at least that was what I'd thought he'd said the other night.

"There were fingerprints all over the crate, none of them belonging to Ray. He must have worn gloves." Greg talked slowly, like he was explaining the way a revolving door worked to a five-year-old.

"Really? He finished a quart of rum and Coke, throws the glass on the ground, then slips on vinyl gloves for his theft?" I could see the disbelief on Greg's face. He held his hands up, blocking my words.

"Look, I know it's not perfect, but if he was drunk . . ." Greg explained.

I shook my head. "If he was drunk, he would have never put the gloves on in the first place. Ray's not the brightest guy, but does he seem this stupid to you?"

Greg pressed his lips together. "Not your business, Jill. I don't tell you how to make coffee." Ouch, that stung. Anger cleared my head and I wanted to bite back. But I held my tongue. I was tired. He was tired. Tomorrow he would see my side. He always listened to what I thought. Just, apparently, not tonight.

"Wait, did I tell you about the other guy with Ray?"

Greg frowned. "What other guy? When he stopped on the road?"

"No, at the crate. There was another guy." I couldn't believe I'd forgotten. "Sarge, his name was Sarge. Big, gruff guy, but I never saw his face."

"Doesn't mean that Ray's not a piece of crap," Greg grumbled.

"Look, I'm tired. And grumpy. Before I say something to annoy you further, I'm going to bed."

Greg stood there.

I raised my eyebrows. "Which is your clue to leave. You have Toby on guard. I'll put the chair under my bedroom door like I have for the last week, and we'll talk tomorrow."

He threw the soda can in my recycling bin a little too hard. Then he turned and said, "Lock the door after me."

I followed him as he stomped out. Our first fight. I touched his arm as he stepped through the doorway. "Greg, I'm—"

He didn't let me finish my apology. "Just lock the door." His words were hard and he kept walking until he'd reached the fence. When he saw me standing outside on the porch watching him leave, he yelled back, "Go inside and lock the door."

I stepped inside, my insides burning. I wanted to run after him. To put my arms around him and have him tell me everything would be okay. Instead, I turned the locks on the door. Emma whined next to me.

"You're right, girl. Sometimes men are hard to understand." I walked around the house, checking locks and turning out lights. Then I slipped upstairs, but sleep didn't come easily.

A loud knocking dragged me out of the dream that had kept me circling all night. Ray was standing outside my car door, but for some reason, the locks weren't working, so I had to keep holding the doors shut, but then he'd be at another door, and I'd have to grab that door. Over and over, and I knew, if he got in, I would be dead.

I pushed off the antique quilt I'd found at a local flea market last summer. Pulling my hair back with a clip I found on my nightstand, I moved the chair from under the doorknob. The knocking got louder. "Hold on," I called downstairs. Emma jumped in front of me and ran to the front door, barking.

When I got to the door, Toby stood on my porch with a box. I unlocked the door and leaned against the doorway. "What's up?"

Toby pushed in the doorway. Then turned and considered me. "Cute Snoopy pj's. Don't you think you should get ready for work?"

I checked the oversized wall clock I'd found at the same flea market where I'd snagged the quilt, a year later. Five after six. I opened at seven on Tuesday. "Crap."

Toby laughed and sauntered to the kitchen. "I'll make us coffee."

I sprinted to the stairs, then turned back and scrutinized Toby. "Why are you here again?"

"The boss—Greg, not you—told me I'm to stay with you twenty-four/seven unless he's here. And he says to tell you he's too busy to see you for a few days." Toby shook his head. "You two must have had a doozy of a fight last night. The big guy's face was beet red when he stopped by the cruiser. What was it about, anyway?"

"None of your business. Besides, maybe we didn't have a fight." I tried to act nonchalant about the whole thing.

"Yeah, and I'm a monkey's uncle." Toby shrugged. "No worries. I guess it means we're not friends like I thought we were."

"Stop the guilt trip." I turned back and went up to shower and change.

By the time I returned to the kitchen, coffee was brewed and a plate with several varieties of donuts sat at the table. Emma sat on the porch outside the screen door looking in at the treats and drooling. "You stop, too."

I grabbed a maple bar and poured coffee into a to-go cup. I watched Toby flip through messages on his phone. Slipping into a chair beside him, I tried to read over his shoulder. "What's happening?"

Toby clicked his phone off and stuck a donut whole into his mouth. "Nothing you need to know about." He took his cup to the sink. "You ready to go to work?"

"You heading home after you drop me off?" I grabbed my purse and keys, shutting the back door.

He smirked. "Really? You think Greg will let me leave you unprotected?"

"Macho. Even real men have to sleep now and then." We walked through the living room.

"Tim relieved me about midnight. Right after Greg left." Toby held open the driver's side passenger door.

I stood still. "You have got to be kidding."

"You know I can't have civilians up front. And besides, I think you like it." Toby grinned.

"It stinks back there." I stood my ground. "I could walk to work, no biggie."

"Except Greg would kill me when he found out. So, you can go willingly or you can find out what it's like to feel the wrath of Officer Toby." At that, he did a muscleman pose.

I had a feeling it was going to be a long day.

Toby sat at the counter reading the *Examiner* and commenting on Darla's exposé on the murder. His snide comments kept me laughing while I stocked the front and prepped for the week ahead. I'd noticed several boxes from the book distributor stacked in the back. I considered opening one and outing the mystery author, at least to me. But I resisted. One Christmas I'd found the stash of gifts my mom had tucked in the closet. I'd been disappointed when I opened the carefully wrapped packages; even though it had been exactly what I'd asked for, the surprise had disappeared. I moved the boxes behind a door so I wouldn't be as tempted.

When Lille burst through the coffee shop door an hour later, my day got way worse.

"Where is he? Holed upstairs in the apartment or in the house you stole from that old lady?" Lille burst through the door, her blond hair stuck to the side of her head, her eyes wild and red-rimmed, like she'd been crying most of the night.

"If you're looking for Ray, I haven't seen him." I steeled myself for her fury. But deep down, I felt bad for her. It couldn't be easy to be in love with a man like that, always questioning your place in his life.

"Liar." Lille's voice was hard. "I've already heard the two of you were chatting on the highway yesterday."

I couldn't help it; I laughed. Her face burned a brighter red. "Look, I ran out of gas. Ray stopped when he saw my car." Here I stopped for a minute. Did I tell her the love of her life scared me so bad I kept my doors locked and flagged down the next car coming down the road? Would that make her happy? Or crazier? "I didn't even get out of the car until Bill showed up. Then Ray took off. That's the last I saw of him. Seriously, ask Toby, he was outside the house most of the night."

Lille's eyes narrowed. She glanced at Toby, who nodded. I could see the thoughts running through her head. Finally, she formulated the question, and I knew it pained her to ask. "Why were you outside her house? Did someone threaten Jill?"

Toby paused as Lille took a deep breath to steel herself for the answer she knew was coming. He glanced at me, then answered her question. "Lille, you need to know we've been out at Ray's with a search warrant. He's a person of interest in Craig's murder."

Lille's coloring went from beet-red to death-white in a second. "No way. Ray is sweet and kind. Deep down to his soul. He couldn't have done something like this." Her gaze dropped and she seemed like she was processing the idea, trying to come up with an alternative. Her eyes widened, then she pointed at Jill. "Her. She killed Craig. They were probably having an affair or something, like she bewitched my Ray. The woman's a she devil."

Toby put his hand on Lille's shoulder. "Now, there, you know Jill didn't kill Craig." Toby shot her a glance. "As far as an affair, well, I'm not going there."

"Yech," I said before I thought twice and edited my comment. "The guy was a total jerk. No way would I get involved with him. Besides, I'm pretty sure his wife would take me in a fair fight."

Lille narrowed her eyes. "I'll tell Greg that Ray was with me. Where is your boss?" She directed the question to Toby, deciding I wasn't worth the time it took to say the words.

"You can't lie," Toby warned her. "Perjury is a serious crime. Besides, if he's found not guilty, then you have to remember which lie you told."

"I don't care. Ray wouldn't do this. He's troubled, I'm not stupid. He might cheat." She paused and shot a look my way. "But he's not a murderer."

"Maybe you don't know him as well as you think?" Toby asked, then shook his head. "Look, Lille, we can argue this for days, but until Ray talks to Greg and gets this cleared up, he's still going to be a suspect. If you know where he might be, tell us and we can get this over with. You know Greg's a fair guy. If Ray didn't kill Craig, Greg will find out who did."

Lille sighed and sat heavily into one of the upholstered chairs by the door. She pulled out a notebook from her purse and started writing something. "I figured he was with you." She didn't look up before she continued, "But since he's not, the only other place would be his dad's cabin up in the mountains east of here. Take Green Valley Road to the dead end and go left. It's on a lake up there."

Toby took the offered paper, then looked at me. "I'm going in the back to call Greg. You going to be okay here if he wants me to take a run?"

I smiled. "No, I'm totally helpless and useless without your company and protection." I swatted his arm. "I'll be fine. As I told your boss last night."

Lille waited for Toby to leave the room before she stood and pulled her purse closer. "I guess I better get over to the diner. Who knows what a mess they've made without me there this morning."

I felt like I should say something. "Lille, I'm here if you want to talk."

I saw her shoulders shake a bit. She turned and studied me. "I know this isn't your fault, but it's still hard to see you as anything but the enemy. I don't think talking is going to change that."

Then she walked out the door. She was right. Sometimes the pain was too deep to even pretend it wasn't there. I wondered about her on-again-off-again relationship with Ray and whether this time, the switch would stay off. For her sake, I hoped so.

Toby burst back into the empty dining room. "Call Jackie and have her come down and stay with you. Greg wants me to check out this lead on Ray."

"Yes, sir. You want fries with that?"

Toby blushed. "Come on, Jill. You know I'm only repeating my orders."

I thought about Greg's face when he left last night. Frustrated with me ... and something else. Worry. Adding to his concern wouldn't get this case solved; in fact, it could stand in the way of getting it done. For once, I swallowed my pride and picked up the phone.

"Jackie? I need you downstairs." I hung up without letting her argue. I raised my eyebrows. "Satisfied?"

He nodded, then headed out to the street. As I watched him through the large front windows, I wondered if this nightmare was almost over.

CHAPTER 21

The afternoon dragged. Tuesday was my long day, but I typically got a break when Toby came in for the midday shift. Today, everyone kept asking, "Where's Toby?" when I gave them their change. I almost put a sign on the door: TOBY'S DAY OFF. But then I'd lose the customers. It might be a bait and switch, but the guy would be back tomorrow. They could go one day without a hot, handsome barista. Absence makes the heart grow fonder, I thought.

Jackie had been more blunt. "The stud isn't here today. Off chasing bad guys. I'm sure he'll have stories tomorrow."

I'd sent her in the back to make a couple of sandwiches and we ate in shifts, Toby's clientele keeping us busy until five, when Jackie's normal shift started. As the room cleared, Jackie cut a cheesecake for the display case. "I'm feeling jealous of the Toby show."

"He does bring in the business."

"Well, I'm heading upstairs. I've got to switch out these shoes. My dogs are barking." My aunt disappeared with the last slice of the cheesecake. I glanced at the clock; she'd be gone at least a half hour, watching her favorite game show.

My thoughts returned to the day when both Toby and I had been hospitalized from a blow by a two-by-four delivered by George Jones looking for pirate gold. When Toby's girlfriend had rushed to the hospital, she'd been surprised to see another woman holding Toby's hand. And calling herself his girlfriend. I'd heard both girls dumped him right after his release, but apparently the line of women for the Toby show, as Jackie called it, was deep.

I'd been lost in thoughts of Toby's wild ways when the bell chimed. I glanced up to see Lisa Brewer and her new beau, all six foot tall and muscle-bound in black leather, walk through the door. Then he did a strange thing. He locked the door and turned the open sign to closed. My mouth felt dry, and my heart rate sped up. This was not good.

I saw Josh Thomas walk by and look through the window, probably trying to see if Jackie was working. I waved, hoping my action would alert him to a problem. The jerk waved back and kept walking.

Lisa came over to the counter. "If you want to live through the next few hours, stop doing stupid things like that."

I snorted. "I'm not stupid. My chances of surviving are about as good as Craig's. What, didn't like your job?"

"So you think this is the part where we bond and I tell you the problems I had growing up and how my stepfather abused me?" Lisa shook her head. "Sorry, I don't owe you an explanation for Craig or your upcoming 'accident.' "

"Move her to the back," the man said. And for once, I hoped Jackie had snuck upstairs to her television. My aunt didn't need to be a part of this.

"Hold on," Lisa whined and went over to the large man, rubbing her hands on his bare chest under the black leather jacket. "Baby, let me handle this. I want a mocha before we get down to business."

Seriously? My mind raced. Leave it to a teenager. Maybe I could throw the hot drink at one of them and run like hell.

"Kids." Reno glared at me. "You heard her. Make up one of those mocha things. You don't have anything stronger like a beer or tequila back there?"

"We're a coffee shop, not a bar." The words fell out of my mouth before I could stop them. I tried to stand tall, not letting my fear show. I started the motions for Lisa's mocha.

"Probably better anyway." His lips curled into a smile. "I'm not a happy drunk."

I visibly shuddered, trying to keep my mind on the routine actions of making a coffee drink. It could be my last action in this world; I should put some thought into the process.

"So you killed Craig for the drugs. What, was he threatening to sell to a higher bidder?" I kept my head down, not wanting to see the happy couple standing together, a large pistol aimed at me. Bonnie and Clyde, but one of them was at least twenty years older than the other.

"I told you they knew about the drugs." Lisa spoke and I couldn't help looking at her. Her full attention was on Reno, and neither saw my scrutiny. "So this will be easy; she commits suicide with an overdose. A lot of the city people who move here had secret addictions. She'll just be another one."

"I don't know. We have Ray set up for the murder. I think having two suspects only muddies the water. We don't want Ray getting out of prison before the boys have time to reach him. Sargent has this planned out. You don't want to mess with his plan. He's not as mellow as I am." Reno eased into the same chair where Lille had been sitting earlier. "This is comfortable. We should think about getting something like this for the trailer."

I started foaming milk, wanting to scream, run, anything but listen to these two discuss murder and furniture like they were the same thing. The two were classic sociopaths, if I had to label them. My hand started shaking, and I set down the pitcher. Both of them were too far away to do anything but maybe cause them to slip when they came after me.

"I want leather," Lisa whined again.

What this man saw in the brat was beyond me. Unless the fact she was barely eighteen made the childish behavior acceptable. I was putting on the lid when I saw the wince on his face. Maybe Lisa wasn't totally in control. I tried a new tactic.

"I think leather's overrated. Kind of tacky and hot. Not fun to sit on with shorts." I wiped the cup with a napkin, trying to slow down my actions.

Reno laughed. "You got that right. In the heat, leather will rip the skin right off the back of your legs. Or at least it will feel like it has."

His comment got him a not-so-playful arm slap. "Stop agreeing with her. You have to please me, not her."

He grabbed her hand roughly, and I could hear her gasp of pain across the room. "I talk to who I want. You or her, there's no difference. You're both diversions on a long night."

His gaze drifted to me. "Come out from behind that counter. Bring the coffee for Miss Priss and let me see you. Maybe we'll have to take some time on this assignment. You know, have some fun."

My blood ran cold. I glanced out the window toward the darkening night. Tuesday didn't have a lot of foot traffic, and Toby's girls would have returned to their normal lives by now, knowing their favorite barista was getting ready for his nightly patrol. Some days, I didn't get one customer on Tuesday before I closed.

I carried the cup with me and crossed the dining room floor, my hands shaking. Trying to walk fast enough not to seem enticing, but not wanting to get there any faster than I had to. I couldn't think of a way out of this. I wasn't strong enough to break loose if the guy tackled me. Now I wished I'd taken those self-defense classes with Jackie last spring when she'd asked. I handed the mocha to Lisa.

"Ouch, that's hot." She held it with two fingers, carefully setting it down on the coffee table.

"Duh. It's a hot drink." Reno laughed, apparently pleased with his joke. He motioned to me with the gun. "Sit down, take a break with us. I want to hear your thoughts about this decision."

I lowered myself into the chair across from him. "Would my vote count?"

He stared at me, cocking his head as his gaze ran down the length of my body. "Maybe. You a runner? You look like a runner. Lean, strong, and tanned."

I nodded, not trusting my voice. I wanted to run right then. Get up and dash through the door, but I'd have to unlock it first, then get away from the deadly duo without getting shot, then find some shop that was open where I could secure everyone there from being shot. Mission totally impossible.

"So how did you frame Ray?" I leaned back in the chair, trying to appear comfortable.

198 • *Lynn Cahoon*

"I could tell you, but then I'd have to kill you." Reno laughed. "Oh hell, we both know I'm going to kill you anyway, why not? But don't you want to know how we framed you?"

Lisa rolled her eyes. "You can't help bragging, can you? You know I helped. You never would have gotten onto The Castle grounds without me."

"Whatever. I'm trying to tell this lovely woman a story. Stop interrupting." He leaned closer. "Did you even find our little gift, or did that dog of yours bury it in the yard?"

"You're talking about the censer?" My heart was beating so fast, I felt like throwing up. *Hold it together, Jill. You'll find a way out of this.*

"Whatever you call it. So your boyfriend must have hidden that piece from the district attorney. I thought after we'd dropped it off, you'd be carted off to the big house." He leaned forward and leered at me. "I'm sure your boyfriend got some traction out of destroying that little piece of evidence."

"You forgot, my house was the old mission site. Censers were common at missions." I didn't feel the need to tell him that Justin had verified the relic had been stolen from The Castle.

Reno grinned and leaned back. "I never was any good in history class. Too many dates and battles to remember."

"So your plan didn't work," I said, with much more bravado than I felt. "Too bad."

"Doesn't matter. You'll be just as dead. So, you've probably figured out Craig was transporting for us. He brought in the stuff, we gave him a bonus, then the next shipment, same deal. The creep got greedy, cocky even. He went into the city and started nosing around for other buyers. Like that wouldn't get back to Sargent. The man was an idiot."

"So you killed him for being an idiot." I guess I could understand that. Many times I wanted to kill Craig for opening his mouth. I would have thought he would have been more tactful with a drug-dealing motorcycle gang, but maybe not.

He laughed. "I don't know why you keep assuming I was the one who killed Craig. Maybe it was the little girl here. She's a hothead, you know."

"Hey. Stop talking about me like I can't hear you. I'm sitting right here." Lisa shook her head. "Men. You have to keep a strong hand on them, otherwise they think they can do anything."

If we'd had beers and a campfire, I'd think we were best friends. But instead, these were the last people I'd see on this earth. A noise sounded from the back. "No," I whispered and glanced at the clock. Aunt Jackie's show would have ended about five minutes ago. And she'd be walking through the door right about now. I watched the door to the back, willing it not to fly open.

And somehow, my wish was granted. The door remained closed.

CHAPTER 22

"Did you hear something?" Lisa glanced at Reno.

He shook his head. "You're the one who said she always works alone on Tuesday nights. Didn't you check the back?"

Lisa's eyes widened. "No. I mean, I wanted a mocha."

"So go check the back." Reno waved the gun at me. "And you go stand by the counter. We're done chatting."

"And I was just feeling the love." I strolled to the counter. "I take it you're not paying for her mocha?"

"I don't think your heirs will notice one lost coffee drink." He sneered. He watched the swinging door, but Lisa had disappeared and not returned. "How big is that back room?"

He didn't wait for me to answer. "Lisa? What the heck's taking you so long?"

No answer from the back.

He glared at me. "What's going on?"

I shrugged. "How should I know? I've been in the pleasure of your company the last few minutes. Besides, the walls are pretty thick. She probably didn't hear you." Totally true; sometimes when I was in the back, I didn't hear anything that was happening in the shop. Jackie would get so mad, she'd look like she was ready to blow.

He motioned me toward the door. "Go and get her."

I made a small salute. "Yes, sir."

He grinned. "It's too bad we don't have more time. You might be more fun than Lisa. At least fun to break."

I tried to keep the shiver that ran down my body from being visible. *Show no weakness,* I thought. I turned on my heels and headed to the back. I called out behind me, trying to make my voice sound stronger than I felt, "In your dreams."

As soon as I walked through the door, I was pulled to the side, a large hand covering my mouth. I felt a scream bubble in my throat, but then saw Greg standing in front of me, his finger raised to his mouth. I nodded and the hand released me. Toby was standing behind me. He pushed me toward the back door, where I saw Tim motioning me to hurry. I turned back to Greg, and mouthed, "Aunt Jackie?"

He nodded, which I took as meaning she was fine, but then Tim pulled me the rest of the way out of the doorway. In a lowered voice, he pointed toward the building next door, where Josh Thomas was standing, motioning me to the opening.

When I got there, Josh slammed the door. "Thank God they finally got you out." He led me up the stairs to a small office where Lisa sat, handcuffed and gagged, her feet tied together. Aunt Jackie stood over her, a baseball bat in her hand.

"I was worried about you." My aunt nodded at her charge. "We're standing guard until Greg gets the big guy under control. Then they'll both be turned over to the state police, who are sitting in a cruiser at the end of town."

I watched my aunt play prison guard and shook my head. "You know this isn't a game, right?"

Then my sweet aunt smiled and she looked like a grandmother on television, soft and loving. The vision ended as soon as she opened her mouth. "Kicking butt and taking names."

Lisa snorted and Jackie pushed her shoulder with the bat. "Be quiet, child." Jackie examined me. "Are you okay?"

I nodded. I'd figured I'd taken my last breath in my shop. Now I worried about Greg, and whether he'd be able to take down Reno without being harmed himself.

Twenty minutes later, Toby came into the room and collected Lisa. They had Reno in the back of the cruiser, and were taking the pair to the waiting state police officers. Greg came into the office for a minute, hugged me hard, and then left with Toby. I took that hug as meaning he forgave me for our fight last night.

I watched them leave and then sank into the couch Lisa had vacated. "I am so tired."

My aunt sank down beside me and handed me a chilled longneck beer bottle. "Drink this. You'll feel better."

I didn't argue, just took a swig and then another. When the beer was half gone, I leaned back and closed my eyes. A thought occurred to me. "Wait, how did you even know I needed help?"

Josh finally spoke. "You never wave when I walk past. You glower, you pretend you don't see me, or if all else fails, you turn your back to the window. When I saw you waving and the closed sign on too early, I knew those other two were trouble."

I squeezed my eyes shut. The same obsessive tendencies we'd made fun of after the business-to-business meeting had saved my life.

Josh continued, "I'd seen that girl with the hooligans who kept talking about breaking into The Castle." He paused. "I think she was in my shop the morning I was attacked. I remembered hearing a girl's voice, and when I saw her in your shop, I knew she was up to no good as soon. So I called the police."

I closed my eyes. "They killed Craig."

"We kind of figured that." My aunt's voice had a twinge of humor.

Tears fell down my cheeks, and I put up my hand to brush them away. I hadn't expected this rush of emotion to overwhelm me, especially over Craig. I sipped on the beer, trying to clear my thoughts. "And coming down to the end, it was about money. Craig's greed did him in."

Josh cleared his throat. "I don't know if that's true."

My anger flared, and I stared at him. "You're kidding, right? After all this? Me being held hostage in my own shop by a contract killer and his psycho girlfriend and you're still defending him? And why were you taking exorbitant appraisal fees from him? Were you part of this, too?"

Josh had the good sense to blush. "No. I mean, yes, I took the fees. He and I had an arrangement that I'd charge a slightly higher fee for my services, then we'd split the money." His eyes flashed. "We weren't doing anything illegal."

"Maybe not illegal, but probably immoral." Jackie sniffed.

Josh hung his head. "I didn't feel right about it. And I told Craig I wasn't going to do it anymore. That's why we were fighting the day he died."

Another piece of the puzzle fell into place for me. "So you cut off one of his income sources."

"Don't talk about him that way," Josh pleaded. "Craig was a good man. Give him the benefit of the doubt."

"Seriously?" My head throbbed.

"I meant we don't have the whole story yet." He came and sat next to me, his girth making the couch groan. "I know Craig could be a pain. But he had an amazing eye for antiques. He really believed in preserving the history of South Cove. Building something future generations could enjoy."

"And he believed in tearing down sites like the mission wall that didn't fit into his plan for the town." I didn't want to get into this argument now. "Look, I appreciate your help today. If you hadn't called . . ." My throat constricted as I thought about what could have happened.

"I'm glad you're all right." He patted my hand. "For today, we'll leave it at that."

Aunt Jackie took his action as our cue to leave. "Let me drive you home. We'll do a girl's night at the house. I'll even make sausage pasta."

Leave it to my aunt to know the one thing to make me feel better after a busy evening of being held at gunpoint. I finished the beer and stood. "I think that's an excellent idea."

Thirty minutes later, I was in the backyard sitting on the stones left of the mission walls. I wondered if any of the original occupants of the mission had sat there, listening to the sounds of the evening and wondering what their future might bring. Emma lay at my feet, watching the woods for chipmunks. I couldn't be the first to use this site to meditate about things to come, changes that might occur. I thought about my friend Miss Emily, the woman who'd left me the house. Had she come out here to think, to plan, and finally, to remember her life and the men taken from her too early? I missed her.

A chill hit me and I saw a shadow. Then I looked up into the setting sun and saw Esmeralda standing there. She floated over and settled on the wall next to me, her skirts shifting and making an odd sort of music that seemed to fit my neighbor's personality.

"I stopped by to check on you, and Jackie said you were out here." Esmeralda took in the tree-lined spot. "I can see why you like it here. Very positive energy flow."

I chuckled. "Actually, I like to hang out here because it's usually quiet."

Esmeralda didn't take the bait. Obviously, snarkiness must be forgiven in a recently released hostage. "Sometimes you don't know what you need, you only think you do."

"And I'm to stay on the path." I regarded the woman sitting next to me. I wouldn't call us friends, but maybe there could be a possibility we would be more than casual acquaintances. If I stopped being rude. "Sorry, I'm on edge."

She waved her hand and the line of bangles on her arm jingled. "No worries. Look, I know people think I'm crazy, but I do have visitors from the other side. And I can't turn that part of me off."

"I'm not doubting your . . ." I paused, searching for the right word, finally settling on "gift. I have a hard time believing sometimes."

Esmeralda smiled. "You and most of the people in this town. But I can deal with nonbelievers." She leaned back and closed her eyes, drawing in a deep breath. I could swear the dwindling light from the sunset focused on her face for a moment. I was obviously feeling the effects of the second beer I'd brought out with me.

I reached down and stroked Emma's head, willing myself to enjoy the moment. Soon I'd have to head back to the house and my aunt's pasta dinner. I drank in the smell of the ocean floating on the evening breeze, cool and comforting.

"The answer is with the dog. Talk to the woman with the dog." Esmeralda's voice broke into the moment. I turned and looked at her, but she still had her eyes closed. Was this a trance?

"You okay?" I didn't move, not wanting to interrupt the signals she was receiving from wherever.

Esmeralda's eyelids fluttered, and she glanced at her watch. "I didn't realize it was so late. I've got a reading tonight." She smiled. "Got to go do my woo-woo."

I watched her stand. "So what about the dog?"

Esmeralda frowned and glanced at Emma. "She's a good dog. Very protective." She waved as she left.

I watched her leave, wondering if she'd even realized she'd spoken. And a chill ran up my spine as I considered the possibility she was the real deal. A fortune-teller—speaker with the dead—a prognosticator. That thought made me giggle, and Emma wagged her tail. "Let's go eat."

As I stood, my heel scraped against something sharp, again. I picked up my foot. This time it hadn't brought blood, but I was tired of the wall hurting me. I kneeled and dug up the dirt next to the wall. A piece of metal was stuck under a rock. I used a small, sharp rock and uncovered a dirt-encrusted item.

Back at the house, I went directly to the kitchen sink and moved Jackie's colander filled with pasta to the counter. Running water over the piece, I realized it was a sextant, one of those things ship captains used to navigate before GPS and the modern world took over their plotting. A very old sextant.

My heart raced. Jackie came over and stood by me, looking at the metal in my sink. "I think I may have found the proof to save the mission."

CHAPTER 23

When Amy showed up on the doorstep with Justin in tow, thirty minutes later, I knew she hadn't just called him to come over. I opened the door and let the two in, both tanned and smelling of sweat and the sea. "Stealing some surfing time?" I asked, smiling at the two.

Amy hugged me hard. "I can't believe we were off playing while you were being held hostage."

"Where did you hear?" And then I guessed, the story was probably all over town, *topic de jour* at Diamond Lille's even. "The diner?"

"The grocery store, actually. We ran into Sadie when we were picking up something to grill and she told us." Then Amy slapped my arm. "You could have mentioned you were held at gunpoint when you called."

"I kind of figured that was a face-to-face conversation." I smiled at Justin. "I'm glad you're here. I've got something to show you."

We walked into the kitchen, where Aunt Jackie was starting to set up the table for dinner. "You two hungry?"

"Starving." Amy went to the cupboard and grabbed plates.

I walked Justin over to the countertop where the sextant lay drying on a towel. "Is this what I think it is?"

He whistled. "I haven't seen one in such good shape outside the museum for years." He bent his head lower to look at all sides. "I'm pretty sure we'll be able to age-date it so it supports your mission wall claim."

My lips curled into a grin. "Good, because I'm tired of the thing scratching me."

Justin asked for a small box and packed the sextant carefully into the container. "I'll drive it over to the university myself tomorrow." His grin was wider than my own. "You want a receipt?"

"Is there a reason I should?" I glanced at Amy, who shook her head.

Justin hadn't seen the exchange, his focus still on the sextant. "If we're right, this could be valuable. For the historic significance alone."

Amy took his arm and led him to the table. "She's teasing you."

I raised my eyebrows as the two sat. And because I couldn't help myself, I asked, "So, how's Hank?"

Amy flushed. "I kid you not, I'm going to kill that guy if I ever see him again."

"Not if I see him first," Justin growled and squeezed Amy's hand.

Aunt Jackie set the bowl of pasta in the middle of the table next to the green salad and garlic bread. "Oh, do tell. I love gossip."

Amy filled her plate with pasta, then handed the bowl to Justin. "Remember the weekend he wanted me to drive up the coast with him?"

I nodded, filling my salad bowl and passing the salad to Jackie.

"Well, he was moving a friend. Tony. Except, T-O-N-I"—she spelled out the name—"wasn't an old buddy. She was his new live-in. And he thought we'd get along famously."

I choked on the glass of water. "He thought you'd be okay with him living with another girl?"

"Apparently, my surfing and independence led him to believe I was a free thinker." Amy shook her head.

"Yeah, like all surfers are into the free love, hippie scene of fifty years ago," Justin added.

I laughed and the action felt good, real somehow. A knock came at the kitchen door, and when I turned, Greg stood there. Jackie beat me to the door, opening it. He walked in, pulled me out of my chair, and hugged me.

"Hey, big guy," I murmured into his neck.

He shifted, then whispered back, "Don't ever scare me like that again."

I stepped away and slapped his chest with both hands. "Like I had any choice? Toby left to go chase after Ray with you. Wasn't he supposed to be my bodyguard?"

Greg grabbed a plate from the cupboard and pulled a chair up next to mine. "Don't get me started. Toby and I have been beating ourselves up for that bad decision since Josh called in the nine-one-one."

"Josh was heroic today," Jackie said as she filled Greg's plate with pasta and handed him the salad bowl.

"You sound like you like him," I teased and her face went bright pink. "You going to give him a second date?"

Her lips pursed, and then she sighed. "I've already told him he can pick me up next Saturday. We're going into town for a play."

Glancing around the table, I smiled. The group gathered seemed more like family than I'd had in a long time. A family that might be growing to include others. Although unless Josh stopped this Craig-initiated attack on the wall, I wasn't sure I was ready to have him as part of the pack I called my own.

Esmeralda's comment rang in my ear. *Talk to the dog lady.* Such a random comment, it couldn't have meant anything. But something about the case still bothered me. Fifi. I glanced at Greg.

"Did you find Ray?" I started eating as I waited for an answer.

"He's locked up over at the station. The state guys are picking him up tomorrow. They had their hands full with your friends tonight. Tim's playing guard right now." He took a bite of pasta, almost groaning in pleasure at the creamy sauce. He waved a fork at Jackie. "This is amazing."

I almost asked how he didn't know I cooked, then ignored the question. "So was he the one who tied up Fifi?"

Greg stopped shoveling the food into his mouth. He frowned. "I forgot about Fifi." He wiped his mouth and considered my question. "Why?"

I shook my head. "Nothing. Esmeralda came by with another message from beyond. I'm sure it doesn't mean anything."

Greg was already pushing back his chair. "I'll call Tim. Ray seems to be chatty, wanting to do everything he can to lessen his sentence. We found drugs at the trailer, so he knows he's doing some time. Maybe he'll answer this."

"You don't have to—" I started, but Greg put his hand on my arm, quieting my objections.

"I've learned never to dismiss Esmeralda's comments, even as random as they usually are. Sometimes she's right." He walked away, dialing his cell.

By the time he came back, Amy and Justin had finished their dinner and were dishing up chocolate-chip ice cream for the table. I loved watching them work together. Now, this was the boyfriend Amy deserved.

Greg sat down and regarded me. "You were right. Ray took Fifi out on the beach to get her out of the way for Reno and Lisa. That was his part of the whole plan. But he thought they were going to rob Craig, not kill him. At least that's what he's telling Tim."

"No wonder Fifi went crazy when she saw Ray in town. She must have remembered him taking her." I accepted the bowl of ice cream Justin handed me.

"Apparently it was more than that. Ray says the dog reacted every time he got close. Didn't like him from the first day he saw her." Greg finished his dinner, then took his plate to the sink and returned with his own bowl.

Amy sat down across from us. "Maybe she didn't like the smell of him. Ray always reeked of whatever drug he took. Alcohol, weed, crack, the guy stunk."

"Maybe she should have been a police dog. She could have sniffed out the drugs and saved us a lot of time." Aunt Jackie started rinsing dishes.

Greg stopped eating, staring at Jackie.

"What?" I asked, not sure I wanted to know.

He studied me. "Police dogs are trained to react when they smell drugs. It's not something that just happens. Someone was training Fifi."

CHAPTER 24

The big night had finally arrived. Cloaked in Mystery was about to reveal the author who was celebrating his or her launch with Coffee, Books, and More. And I still didn't know who was walking through that door.

Bill Simmons came and stood next to me near the windows. "Shouldn't you be up there?" He motioned to the front of the room, where Toby stood guarding the door to the back office.

"This is Jackie's big night. I'm letting her do the honors." I glanced over at one of the two men who'd saved me in the last week. I didn't realize I was such a damsel in distress, but I now had not one, but two knights in shiny armor. And that was before I considered my hunk of a boyfriend. And all of a sudden, I realized what I'd forgotten. "I never got back with you about the reservation. Did you cancel the author's room?"

Bill smiled. "Actually, no. I figured you had your hands full with being held hostage and all. So I'm giving your aunt the benefit of the doubt. Of course, I might be hitting you up for damages if this turns into a big scam."

"I'll pay." I was too tired to fight anymore. I hoped my aunt wasn't playing the gathered group as fools, or I'd never hear the end of it.

He put his hand on my arm. "I'm kidding. You're part of the South

Cove business community now. We have to support each other." He nodded to a woman who sat in the audience. "My wife is lonely. We'll talk at the meeting next week?"

"Sure." I couldn't say more. For the first time in the five years I'd owned my business here in South Cove, I felt like I belonged. Of course, maybe Josh Thomas opening his antique store next door moved me one step up the ladder. He was now the new kid, a role I'd played for too long. I searched the crowded room for Josh, my other knight from the last week. He sat alone near the back of the room. As annoying as he was, I wasn't going to make him go through what I had for these last years. I moved toward him, planning on sitting next to him, when a hand caught my arm.

Brenda Morgan stood next to me and grabbed me into a bear hug. I'd been getting this reaction from many people lately. I was almost used to the contact. When she released me, I smiled. "Thanks for coming tonight."

Her eyes widened. "I can't believe what happened. Are you all right?"

I led her to the back row and sat her down. "I'm fine. Shell-shocked still, but they didn't hurt me. You must be happy they've found Craig's killer."

Brenda's face flushed. "If I'd thought what I knew would have helped, I would have told Greg, really."

"I don't understand." Esmeralda's words started echoing in my head. "What didn't you tell Greg?"

Brenda glanced around the room, seeming to take in the family feel of South Cove, and I wondered if she would take the chance of moving here. "I knew Craig was transporting drugs. The feds trained me to teach Fifi to recognize drugs to help trap him. But she never picked up on anything with Craig, just Ray. And Agent Jenkins, he said that wasn't enough."

"The feds were watching Craig already?" I wondered if Greg knew how closely Brenda had been working with the law enforcement agency.

She nodded. "Of course, they wanted Craig or some guy in the gang called Sargent. But I never met anyone from the gang, not even the guy who . . ." she paused.

"Reno, the guy who tried to kill me?" I let the implication hang in the air. If Brenda had been open, Greg might have figured this out sooner. And Toby might not have left me alone. And if wishes were horses, all beggars would ride. "Look, no use dealing with what might have been. Water under the bridge, spilt milk, yada, yada. I'm glad you came today."

She smiled, then handed me an envelope. "I emptied the safety deposit box and I think you need this."

I unclasped the top of the envelope, but tucked it under my chair again when I saw Amy and Justin come in the door. "Excuse me."

I had about two seconds to greet and usher my friends into the last two seats next to Josh when the lights flickered and my aunt appeared at the podium.

She adjusted the microphone. "Thank you all for coming out for our first annual Cloaked in Mystery event. We have one prize to award before we get on with tonight's event. I said if someone guessed the author, we'd give them a set of the author's signed backlist, current release, and a night at South Cove's best bed-and-breakfast. We had only one correct guess."

I inspected the crowd that filled the room, wondering who'd figured it out.

My aunt caught my eye and grinned. "Will Sadie Michaels please come up to the front? She's our winner and will be introducing our guest."

Sadie jumped from her seat. Nick sat next to her, a big grin on his face. Apparently his heartbreak from Lisa dumping him had been eased when he found out she was hanging with the drug-dealing motorcycle club. I'd heard from Carrie at the diner he'd taken up with one of the other waitresses, a college-bound girl working the summer. Someone his mom apparently liked.

I watched as Sadie made her way up the crowded aisle. I hoped the fire marshal wouldn't start counting people as he sat in the crowded room, because we were well over the eighty he'd set as the max occupants for the shop when I applied for my city license. Instead he clapped and grinned with the rest of the crowd.

When Sadie got to the front, she turned her gaze to the door. "I want you to give a big South Cove welcome to this thriller author who got his start writing short stories as a way to pay the bills. His first novel hit the *New York Times* list for two weeks. And the rest is history. Please welcome, author of *The Silent Child*, Nathan Pike."

The room stood as the tall, bald-headed author walked into the room. Of all the people I'd considered, Nathan Pike hadn't even been on my list. The guy was a literary rock star. If Jackie planned on making this an annual event, she had big shoes to fill for next year.

As we sat and Nathan took over the podium, first charming us with his good-old-boy southern humor, then reading from his new release, I felt a hand on my shoulder. Greg stood behind me and leaned down to kiss me as I gazed up into those blue eyes. And for the second time in less than a week, I felt surrounded by family. Amy squeezed my hand, as I brushed tears away from my eyes.

This was a happy day. No tears allowed.

Three hours later, the room finally emptied out and Jackie and Nathan left to get him set up at Bill's. Toby finished stacking the folding chairs on the cart. He'd take them back tomorrow to Pastor Bill at the Methodist church. Amy, Justin, Greg, and I sat on the couches returned from the back room to in front of the fake fireplace. I was exhausted.

Toby brought over a soda and tossed me the envelope Brenda had given me earlier. "This was under a chair."

Crap, I'd almost forgotten. I tried to move the envelope closer to me with one toe. Greg laughed. "I'll get it, princess."

He reached over and grabbed the envelope, then put my bare foot into his lap and rubbed out the kinks.

I opened the envelope and dumped the contents onto my lap. It was pages from a notebook. I peered closer. I'd seen pages this size before. "Wait, this is exactly like the notebook Craig and Josh claim they found showing the true mission site."

Justin leaned closer as I put the pages and the small notebook on the coffee table that sat between the two couches. "You're right. Exact same paper. I knew something was fishy with that book."

"But it tested out." He'd told me the paper had been old.

He smiled, looking at the trial maps Craig had drawn on page after page of the notebook. "Just because the paper was from that time, doesn't mean Craig didn't do the map himself. I'm an idiot. Once the paper was tested, I never thought to time-date the ink."

"So this means?" I couldn't breathe.

"That the map he submitted to the council is probably a total fake." Justin glanced up at me. "Where did you get this?"

I thought about Brenda and her distress at my suffering. I smiled. "A friend."

Tomorrow would be soon enough to provide the commission with proof Craig had lied when he tried to torpedo the mission wall certification. And we'd be one more step closer to protecting the site.

Tonight, we were celebrating. And nothing was going to stand in the way of a mini-party with good friends. I smiled at the group. "Who wants double Dutch chocolate cheesecake?"

CHAPTER 25

Darla Taylor droned on about the ongoing Summer Festival. I sipped my coffee and half-listened while I studied the round table of business owners and representatives. We had a new member this month, and I smiled over my cup when she rolled her eyes in response to Darla's list of offenders.

"The Castle hasn't even participated in the decorating plan." Darla shook her finger at Brenda, the newly hired manager. The board of directors had been swayed by her impassioned plea to continue her husband's work at the site along with the number of shares in the corporation Brenda now owned as Craig's widow. I tended to believe her financial interest was what moved the board's hearts to hire her, not Craig's memory, but what can I say? I'm a cynic.

Brenda took a sip of her coffee before she answered Darla's complaint. "Honey, it's not like we haven't been busy around here, with the funeral and catching a murderer." When Darla had the good sense to blush, Brenda continued, "The Castle is more than willing to participate in the Summer Festival, and we'd like to do more than decorate."

Bill Simmons leaned forward in his chair. In fact, the entire table seemed on edge, wondering what Brenda was bringing to the table. Under Craig, The Castle had never even allowed South Cove flyers on the property. A slight that Bill took seriously. He tried to play it cool, though, I'd give him that. "What do you have in mind?"

"Friday Fireworks." Brenda smiled. "For the next two months, we've hired a company to set off fireworks at dusk."

"Probably on The Castle grounds," Darla huffed, feeling the mood of the table shift in Brenda's favor.

"Actually, they'll be on the city beach. Well, out in the water on a boat, but I thought we could set up a few vending booths for snacks and drinks, and maybe even a band or two that might bring in the younger generation." Brenda grinned at me. "So what do you think?"

"I'm willing to do an iced coffee stand for a few weeks." Mentally, I planned out what I'd need. Including hiring one or two local teenagers to help work the event, the idea had potential.

"The city council won't just approve something like that," Darla pushed.

I assumed her concern revolved around the customers who might be pulled away from the winery to watch the show. "You have a great view of the ocean from the winery patio. If we kept the beach alcohol-free, your customer base shouldn't be affected, right?"

Darla considered the possibility. Then Toby, who'd come in early for his Tuesday shift, spoke up from behind the bar, where he'd been making coffee. "And having the beach alcohol-free would ease the security issues that I'm sure the council will be concerned about."

And your other boss, I added silently.

The group was nodding. Brenda glanced around the table and grinned. "Great, I'll go to City Hall today and get the permits. I hear Mayor Baylor is a big fan of The Castle, so I don't expect any problems with shooting for starting at the end of the month."

Darla sank back in her chair, her righteous indignation deflated.

Bill glanced around the table. "So, if we don't have another subject, I believe we can thank our hostess and end the meeting."

Josh raised his hand. "There are just a few things."

The group at the table collectively groaned. I guess some people never changed, even if they could act heroic at times. Bill sighed and nodded to Josh. "Concerns?"

"We've never talked about the animal control issue." Josh frowned and looked over at me. "And if I'm not mistaken, Miss Gardner promised that Detective King would be at this meeting to discuss the teen loitering problem."

I closed my eyes, waiting for the group to explode. Sadie didn't disappoint me. As she went off about him and his friend who'd brought drug-dealing, murdering motorcycle gangs to our small town versus kids wanting to have a little fun, I couldn't help but smile.

Some people don't know when to shut up.

Need more South Cove?
Keep reading for an excerpt from
Jill Gardner's next adventure,
available Fall 2014

CHAPTER 1

The holidays were supposed to be a time of goodwill, celebration, and community. You couldn't tell it from the glares going around the table as Mayor Baylor talked. Earlier, the leader of our little town had the group eating out of his hand. Then all hell broke loose. Focusing on the uproar going on at the business-to-business monthly meeting, I wondered if the shop owners gathered around the mismatched tables had even seen the calendar. As South Cove's council liaison, I volunteered my shop each month for the meeting. I'm Jill Gardner, owner of Coffee, Books, and More, and president of the I-Hate-Mayor-Baylor Club. A red-faced Bill Simmons, chairman of the business council and owner of South Cove Bed-and-Breakfast, stood at the front of the table, trying to get the group to quiet down.

Aunt Jackie issued a shrill, earsplitting whistle, two-finger variety. My aunt could make me smile even in the worst situations. She'd been a rock the last year during all the craziness that had been my life. Now I didn't know what I'd do without her help with Coffee, Books, and More. Or without seeing her on a daily basis.

The room finally quieted. I'd been the city council liaison with the business community in our little coastal California tourist town for the last five years. And I'd never heard this kind of uproar over a mayor's mandate before. Maybe the Honorable Mayor Baylor was losing a bit of his power over the group.

"Look, I know it's a bad time for many of us to take on a charity project, but think of it this way, you'll have an extra pair of hands for the season." Bill pulled out what he'd thought would be his trump card.

"I don't understand what you're all so upset about. I got you free help for the busiest season of the year." Mayor Baylor glared at me, like their reaction was my fault. "These people want to work. We need to be charitable in our attitude." This time, his scowl was full-on directed at me.

I put on my sweetest smile, the one I saved for the few customers I truly didn't like. "I've already signed up the coffee shop to participate. How about the rest of you?"

"Not all of us have South Cove's finest working part-time in our shops," Darla Taylor, owner of the winery and editor of the local news for the South Cove *Examiner,* sniffed. "I heard he couldn't place these losers anywhere else, so he paid the mayor to take on these stragglers."

"That is totally unfounded speculation," Mayor Baylor blustered, his face turning a bright shade of scarlet. He turned his stare from me to Darla. "I hope I won't see anything close to that being reported in the *Examiner.*"

I turned my head so no one would see my smile widen. As one of the local media, Darla's nose for rumors was spot-on. Ted Hendricks, program director for Bakerstown's welfare-to-work program, had come to our tourist town of South Cove with an offer. Ten participants would work for eight weeks with a local business in an intern capacity. South Cove was their last chance.

The mayor's gaze shifted down the table, landing on Josh Thomas, a strong Mayor Baylor supporter. Except even I could see that His Honor wasn't winning any points with his friend today.

"Delinquents. You want me to let a delinquent run wild in my store. Talk to my customers and probably scope out my merchandise so they can steal me blind when I turn my back?" Josh owned Antiques by Thomas, the most recent business to open its doors on Main Street. Today, he pounded a chubby finger on the table.

"Of course, you'd have a problem with this. You don't even know that they are kids, or if they had trouble with the law. Just because someone is down on their luck doesn't mean they are a bad person," Sadie Michaels shot back. Sadie, owner of Pies on the Fly, was my main supplier of desserts for the coffee shop. And a strong advocate for the underdog in any fight.

We'd gone down this path before. Josh and Sadie rarely saw eye-to-eye on any discussion. For my part, I liked the way she called him on his prejudice and narrow-mindedness. Bill tried again to short-circuit the argument he saw developing. "We don't have time for a political discussion on the topic. This is a done deal. They're coming today for the initial meet-and-greet with a walk through town. Three hours on two weeknights, and six hours on Saturday. Even if you just have them stock shelves, at least they'll be learning about retail and our special niche as a tourist destination."

I jumped into the fray. "We only need three more host businesses. We've already had seven businesses volunteer. The mayor's office is even participating." My friend Amy, who did most of the clerical work for the city as well as served at the city planner, was ecstatic to have a little help, even if it was only for a few hours a week.

Aunt Jackie set a slice of cheesecake in front of Josh. They'd been dating off and on since the summer. He wanted more on; she kept saying she wanted the off. She smoothed his black suit jacket with her hand, brushing lint off the sleeve. "You could use help organizing your store. Just think of all you could get done with some young elbow grease."

Josh peered up at my aunt, and I swear I saw his heart melting, just like the big green monster in the Christmas story. "Fine, I'll take one." He sounded like he was agreeing to foster a shelter animal, rather than a person.

Darla waved her hand. "I've got plenty of work at the winery. But let's try to match me with someone who doesn't have alcohol issues." I wrote her name down. I didn't even care if she was taking on an intern for news fodder, which I suspected. Now I just had to clear the caveat with Ted Hendricks, the program manager.

I searched the faces of the group gathered around the table, drinking coffee and, except for a few who had already volunteered, not meeting my eyes. I needed one more volunteer. Ted would be there in less than thirty minutes to finalize the plans.

Sadie spoke first. "Sorry. I'd take one, but the work with the bakery is first thing in the morning. I wouldn't have anything for them to do on evenings or weekends. That's the time I devote to Nick and the church."

Sadie ran Pies on the Fly out of a remodeled garage behind her house. Calling it a bakery was a little generous.

Marie Jones, the owner of The Glass Slipper, had her head down, trying to curl up in her seat, apparently hoping I wouldn't see her. I could even see her lips moving in some sort of chant. I watched her closely, wondering if she was a fan of the Serenity Prayer, the favorite of alcoholics everywhere. Finally she glanced up, maybe feeling the weight of the entire table as they turned their attention to her.

"What?" she stammered.

"Could you take an intern?" I liked the term that Ted had used to describe his charges, not typical *work study* but not *helper,* either. And if they weren't technically interns, no one cared. As long as there wasn't trouble.

"I don't know." Marie's eyes darted from one person to the next. "I have several classes coming up this next month, and I don't have time to babysit someone."

"I bet the intern could help you with your classes. Maybe helping slower students or bringing in supplies, or even setting up the room each day." My voice sounded way too chipper, like I was a game show host, describing what was behind door number two if Marie chose to accept our offer.

"That's a great idea. People love craft projects. Maybe she'll even sit in on the classes herself." Darla smiled at Marie. "You're very generous with your time."

Marie must have known she was being played. I saw her form a response, then she just sank back into her chair, defeated. "I guess."

"Great." I glanced down at my schedule. "Ted's bringing the gang at five. I'm taking the group on a walking tour of town first, then dropping each person off at their assigned store, where you'll have about fifteen minutes to get to know each other. Then I'm hosting a small get-together here at the store. Coffee and cheesecake."

Looking up, I saw Marie's face had gone white. I started to backpedal, thinking that two meetings today must be overwhelming the woman's natural shyness. "You don't have to come, but you're more than welcome."

She took a deep breath, the tension in her body visually easing a bit. Then she mumbled, "There must be more than one Ted in the world."

"Excuse me?" I frowned, leaning forward.

She looked me straight in the eye. And lied. "I've got a class tonight."

I wasn't going to challenge her, not when I'd just won a placement for our last participant. No use looking for cracks after you've bought the house, my grans always said. Of course, that piece of advice had gotten me stuck in a loveless marriage for too many years.

"Then we're settled. The only other order of business is assigning the chair for the Holiday Festival." Darla waved her hand. The assignment was a formality; everyone knew Darla would be the chair. She'd been in charge of planning the theme and decorating for years before I even moved to South Cove.

"I've got some great ideas this year. I'm thinking a Beach Boys Christmas to play off our successful Beach Boys Summer Fun Festival." She glanced around at the people surrounding the table. "So, is everyone cool with that?"

Bill coughed and then said, "Well, you see, Mrs. Baylor wants to be involved this year."

Darla leaned back in her chair. "I don't understand. Of course she can be part of the committee. We could always use an extra pair of hands."

Bill stacked the papers on the table in front of him. He gazed at the winery owner with genuine sadness in his eyes. "That's the thing—"

Before he could finish his sentence, Mayor Baylor interrupted. "I'm sorry, Darla, Tina's got experience in this type of thing. She used to plan all her sorority parties. I think it's time we brought in a professional. South Cove needs the boost to draw in new visitors."

Darla focused a glare at the portly man. "You're telling me she's chairing the festival? Because putting up college banners around an old sorority house is professional experience?"

The mayor nodded, then glanced at his watch. "Exactly. I knew you would understand."

"Kind of like in an honorary position, right?" Darla wasn't giving in easily. I could feel the tension in the group as they watched the back-and-forth.

"No. Tina's determined to correct all the mistakes of the past, and she says the only way to do that is by completely redesigning the project. Or whatever. She'll be contacting each of you for your assignments and I hope you'll give her your full cooperation." The mayor glowered at me, again.

Taking my cue, I fumbled for words. "I'm sure Tina will do a great job with organizing this year's festival."

That got me a dirty look from Darla.

The mayor stood. "I've got a lunch engagement in the city or I'd stay to meet with Ted." He tossed an envelope toward me. "That's the contract for the session. Please make sure he gets it."

And then he strode out of the shop, the bell over the door banging in his wake.

Darla started yelling at Bill before the bell stopped chiming. "Is he freaking kidding? And you let him get away with this?"

"Calm down, Darla. Honestly, it was more than time for you to let someone else handle the burden of the committee. And we don't know, she might do a good job." Bill glanced around the room. "If there's nothing else, I need to get back to the B&B. We've got a full house this week."

"But I thought we were going to discuss animal control today. I know a bunch of feral cats have taken up in the empty apartment in my building," Josh called after him.

Bill didn't even slow down. He took off out of the shop just like the mayor had, but turned left instead of the other man's right turn.

"This meeting is a joke," Josh muttered, pushing away from the table. "Nothing I want to discuss ever gets on the agenda."

"There's a lot of stuff we have to discuss," I said, feeling guilty. I'd been putting his e-mails in a file. The round file cabinet on my floor called the trash.

He shot me a look that would have melted my face if he'd had a superpower. He nodded to Aunt Jackie and lumbered through the door.

Darla didn't even say good-bye as she left, her fingers twitching around the file she'd brought, probably filled with theme ideas. Darla loved turning the little town into a storyland. Each Christmas season, she'd brought a new look to Main Street. The first year I'd lived here, the theme had been *A Christmas Carol* and she'd even hired a band of carolers, dressed in era-appropriate costumes. I'd felt like I'd walked back in time, even though the snow was fake.

"She's upset," Sadie stated the obvious as she started collecting paper cups off the tables.

"I think it's more than upset." Aunt Jackie snorted. "The mayor better watch his back or he'll be found dead on City Hall's steps, dressed up like a holiday turkey."

"Maybe we can talk to him. Ask him to at least add Darla back on the planning committee." I moved a table back to its regular spot. "He had to have noticed how hurt she felt by being cut off."

"He won't care. Men always get what they want." Marie's small voice drew my eyes toward her where she stood near the window, watching the street. "You can't stop them once they make up their minds."

Sadie, Jackie, and I stopped cleaning. I hadn't even known Marie was still in the shop. "That's not always true. Men don't have any more power than women do. It's just that he's the mayor." I watched as Marie turned back toward me, tears filling her eyes.

"You're wrong." And with that, she fled out of the shop and into the street. I watched her get halfway across before I heard the horn.

Lynn Cahoon is a multi-published author. The Idaho native's stories focus on the depth and experience of small-town life and love. Lynn has been published in Chicken Soup anthologies, explored controversial stories for the confessional magazines, and written short stories for *Women's World* along with contemporary romantic fiction. Currently, she's living in a small historic town on the banks of the Mississippi River, where her imagination tends to wander. She lives with her husband and four fur babies.

GUIDEBOOK TO MURDER

A TOURIST TRAP MYSTERY

Dying for a visit...

LYNN CAHOON

Printed in the United States
by Baker & Taylor Publisher Services